MAYHEM IN MINIATURE

This Large Print Book carries the
Seal of Approval of N.A.V.H.

MAYHEM IN MINIATURE

MARGARET GRACE

WHEELER PUBLISHING
A part of Gale, Cengage Learning

GALE
CENGAGE Learning·

Detroit • New York • San Francisco • New Haven, Conn • Waterville, Maine • London

GALE
CENGAGE Learning

LIBRARY OF CONGRESS CATALOGING-IN-PUBLICATION DATA

Grace, Margaret, 1937–
    Mayhem in miniature / by Margaret Grace. — Large print ed.
      p. cm. — (Wheeler large print cozy mystery)
    "A miniature mystery."
    ISBN-13: 978-1-59722-899-2 (pbk. : alk. paper)
    ISBN-10: 1-59722-899-0 (pbk. : alk. paper)
    1. Retired women—Fiction. 2. Dollhouses—Fiction. 3. Large
type books. I. Title.
PS3563.I4663M39 2009
813'.54—dc22
                                    2008044394

Published in 2009 by arrangement with The Berkley Publishing Group, a member of Penguin Group (USA) Inc.

For my husband, Dick Rufer.

ACKNOWLEDGMENTS

Special thanks go to my dream critique team: Jonnie Jacobs, Rita Lakin, and Margaret Lucke.

Thanks also to my sister, Arlene Polvinen; my cousin, Jean Stokowski; and the many writers and friends who offered information, critique, and inspiration, in particular: Judy Barnett, Sara Bly, Margaret Hamilton, Anna Lipjhart, Ann Parker, Carole Price, Mary Schnur, Sue Stephenson, Karen Streich, and Mark Streich.

Thanks to Sandy Sechrest, enthusiastic mystery reader, who lent her name to a character in the story.

I'm grateful to my husband, Dick Rufer, the best there is. I can't imagine working without his 24/7 support. He's my dedicated Webmaster (www.dollhousemysteries.com), and layout specialist, as you can see by the drawing depicting the layout of Lincoln Point streets.

Finally, how lucky can I be? I'm working with a wonderful editor, Michelle Vega, and an extraordinary agent, Elaine Koster.

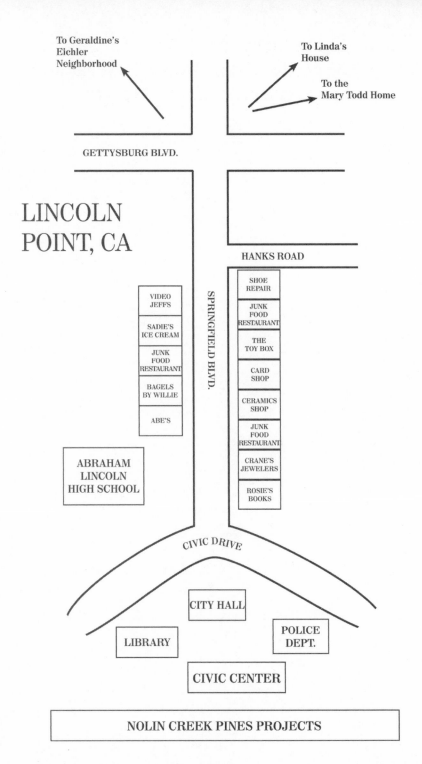

CHAPTER 1

The final test was always nerve-wracking.

The room was cozy and inviting, with a leisure chair and matching ottoman in a sweet briar rose pattern, a tall bookcase filled with the complete works of Shakespeare, photographs in white porcelain frames, a mahogany coffee table, and a hardwood floor polished to perfection. With its stately Christmas tree and holly-laden mantel, the composition might win a designer award for Victorian charm and décor, but could it hold its own against the force of gravity?

I took a breath and did the arm stretch I learned in aerobics class — the special session for the over-fifty crowd.

Then I picked up the room by the back of the chair, my fingers gripping the carved wood. Everything else came up with it, even the basket of knitting next to the chair's Queen Anne feet.

So far so good.

I tipped the room upside down and gave it a little shake, keeping a careful eye on the half-full glass of wine and the star at the top of the spruce.

I waved the room from left to right. The miniature furniture and all the accessories stayed glued to the floor, the books stayed in the bookcase, the lamp clung to the table. Only the beaded fringe on the ornate lampshade moved, sending a delicate pattern of roses and green leaves rippling through the air.

I was home free, officially done with my Victorian room box, which was ten inches long, representing ten feet (full-scale, we miniaturists called it). Tomorrow I'd take the parlor downtown to the community center — my contribution to the holiday auction. More aptly, the Mary Todd Lincoln auction, as every crafter in town competed for the most authentic Victorian-era ornamentation.

Lincoln Point, California, about forty miles south of San Francisco, took all things Lincoln seriously. Never would we lump Abraham's birthday with those of every other president of the United States. We celebrated on the day itself, February 12, no matter which day of the week it fell on.

We were equally meticulous about his wife. One of Lincoln Point's founding fathers in years gone by apparently decided that Mary Todd Lincoln's birthday, December 13, was an appropriate day for the official start of the Christmas celebrations around town, beginning with a grand ball at city hall.

Thus, not even Christmas had escaped our grasp. (And lately, we also included Hanukah, Kwanzaa, and generic winter solstices, Lincoln-izing them all.)

Linda Reed, my good friend and a much better crafter than I am, had chosen to create a model of a Victorian bedroom in half-scale (only one-half inch equals a foot of life-size space). She'd hand-sewn a mountain of tiny pillows and added embroidery picturing an elaborate skating party worthy of a Currier & Ives print.

"I'm tired of needlework," she'd told me. "Next year, I'm going to do a Victorian bathroom."

"I'll bet one dollhouse kit and a year's supply of rubber cement that you'll be doing crewel work on the towels and hand-weaving the toilet seat cover," I'd said. "Mrs. Lincoln would have liked that."

This had drawn a laugh and "You've got a point, Gerry." Linda seemed happier these days, now that her adopted teenage son, Jason, had an after-school job and was making the honor roll, and the more troublesome of her two exes was out of her life. Linda had also managed to streamline her career as a nurse. Instead of juggling part-time positions at three medical centers, she'd accepted an offer of a full-time job at the Mary Todd Home, an upscale, multilevel-care facility near her own house. I was a volunteer there myself on Friday mornings, teaching and helping residents with crafts projects.

The Mary Todd Ball was only two days away, and there was much to do in the meantime in my regular, life-size schedule. First up today was a meeting at the library with Lourdes Pino, one of my favorite GED students. She was more than ready to take the test for her high-school equivalency diploma, but she still lacked the confidence to go for it. Approaching fifty, she had a tough time with change and risk-taking. (Didn't we all.)

I had a couple more deliveries to make around town — my inability to "just say no" had earned me a spot on the decorating committee for the ball. There was also shopping and preparation for a special guest: this evening, I'd pick up my beloved ten-year-old granddaughter, Maddie, at the airport. I'd have her to myself until her parents joined us for Christmas next week.

I gave my room box a nudge on the way out the door to meet my student, poking at the table legs and the antimacassar I'd tatted for the chair back. I found it just the way I liked it — completely static.

Rrring. Rrring.

My kitchen phone. I stood in place by the front door, waiting to hear a message. I never thought I'd be one to screen calls, but I had to admit how handy it was. What had I done before answering machines, caller ID, cell phones, and call-waiting? It was a long way from the four-party line we shared in my childhood home in the Bronx.

"Geraldine, this is Dolores Muniz. I need to talk to you. Please, please be there."

Coming from my machine was the voice of the Lincoln Point City Hall. That is, of one of their high-ranking administrators, a dynamic woman with whom I'd worked on publicity and permits for the many crafts fairs and programs I helped organize. Dolores's personality leaned to the dramatic, but this seemed a little intense, even for her. I rushed to the phone.

"It's my grandmother," she said to the

15

machine, just before I picked up the receiver.

"What's wrong with Sofia?" I asked Dolores. I hoped we wouldn't be faced with losing Sofia during what should be a festive time.

I had a special bond with Dolores's grandmother. Sofia was in her mideighties, a resident at the Mary Todd Home and a regular participant in my Friday-morning crafts workshop. But more than that, she'd built me a shrine in the very dark days of my husband's long illness. Though only three inches tall, the beautiful altar with its rows of votive candles and statue of Our Lady of Guadalupe gave me great comfort. Neither Sofia nor the lovely lady in blue in the miniature scene seemed to mind that I wasn't Roman Catholic.

"Geraldine, I'm so glad you're there." I heard relief in Dolores's voice, then increased agitation. "They can't find her."

I heard the panic in Dolores's voice and wished I were there to offer relief. As it was, I had only a silly question.

"She left the home?"

"The administrator is saying she ran away, but I know she wouldn't do that. So either her memory has gotten worse, or" — Dolores's voice caught — "someone kidnapped

16

her. You know, you hear such horrible nursing-home stories these days. Who knows what could have happened to her?"

I put down my purse and tote and sat on a metal chair in my atrium. "I'm so sorry, Dolores. I assume they've called the police?"

"They did, and so did I, but the police don't care. They never do. She's just an old lady who wandered off."

The beginnings of a speech in defense of law enforcement formed in my mind as I thought of Skip, my conscientious twenty-eight-year-old nephew and one of the newest detectives in the Lincoln Point Police Department. But on the whole, I knew that Dolores was right, that a harmless, meandering octogenarian was not a high priority on the LPPD crime-fighting agenda. Perhaps we needed an old person alert, like the Amber Alert for children.

"Can you talk to Skip, Geraldine?" Not unexpected. I often got requests to intercede with Skip. Sometimes for a speeding or parking ticket, sometimes for more serious matters, like this one. It was hard to convince people that, one, I didn't have a hotline to Skip, and, two, the wishes of a retired English teacher were not what the LPPD had dedicated their lives to. "I'm going to drive around myself and look for her, but it

17

would be nice to know someone on the police force cared."

"I'll try to reach my nephew, but I can't promise anything. What I can do, if it will help, is drive for you if you want some company while you look." My own time, at least, was something I had control over. Though I questioned the usefulness of a random search of Lincoln Point's streets, I understood why Dolores would need to be doing something to find her grandmother.

I heard a loud sigh. "That would be wonderful, Geraldine. Can you pick me up at city hall?"

"Give me ten minutes."

I hung up and mentally changed gears. My call to Lourdes caught her just in time, before she left for our tutoring session at the library.

"That's okay, Mrs. Porter, I will wait here until you call me."

"Thanks for being flexible, Lourdes. Go on to the next chapter in your book, and we'll work on it later today."

Always the teacher, my late husband, Ken, would have said. *Always giving homework.* I knew he meant it as a compliment.

I gave my cozy scene one more nudge, and my atrium jade plant a quick spray. I grabbed a light jacket (Decembers are mild in this part of the world, at least for a Bronx native) and glanced at my tote full of books and materials for tutoring. Before the morning's over, I thought, Sofia will have been returned safely to her room at the Mary Todd, probably by an LPPD officer as young and handsome as Skip was (though it would be hard to find a cop with Skip's dazzling red hair).

I'd still have time for conjugations and punctuation with Lourdes.

CHAPTER 2

In the interest of efficiency, I flipped open my cell phone at the first red light and punched in the number three, for my one and only nephew. Skip teased me about coming after number one — his mother, my sister-in-law and best friend, Beverly Gowen — and number two, my son, Dr. Richard Porter, in Los Angeles.

"I know that number two is really for Maddie," Skip had said the first time he checked out my speed-dial list. "You just don't want me to realize I'm less important than a ten-year-old."

"A ten-year-old who adores you."

Skip had puffed out his chest at that. "And rightly so."

Skip's biggest threat to me was that he'd tell my friend Linda Reed she was number four. We all knew Linda could get a little testy when she thought she was being slighted.

Skip answered his phone now, with a noticeable lilt on the words of his new and exciting title.

"Lincoln Point PD, Detective Gowen."

"I like the sound of that, Number Three."

"Hey. What's new? Is the little princess in town?"

"Not yet, and you'd better not let her hear you call her that, or you'll go down a few notches on her superhero list."

"Good point. Do I hear traffic? This must be important if you're dialing and driving."

The light turned green and I moved forward, convincing myself that multitasking was safe on Springfield Boulevard, our main drag, where the speed limit was thirty miles an hour.

"A friend of mine is missing. Well, the grandmother of a friend. Actually, the grandmother is a friend, too, I guess." No response from Skip. "Someone I've worked with at city hall. Her grandmother's in my class at the Mary Todd Home. It's the grandmother who's missing. Sofia Muniz." Still no response, except a throat clearing, to let me know he was still there, I supposed. This was something Skip had gotten very good at — letting "the other guy" talk and talk, waiting until a question was asked; and even then, he was more likely to ask another question instead of answering. "Did you hear me?" I asked, more loudly than necessary.

"Did you ask a question?" I knew he heard my loud grunt, because he came back with, "Sorry, Aunt Gerry. Tell me more."

I told him as much as I knew. "Can you look into it?"

"She's how old?" he asked, in a way that sounded too close to "Why bother?"

"That's not the point." Maybe Dolores, with all her city hall connections would have commanded more of his attention than his old (to him) aunt. For that matter, why hadn't she used her government resources to track down her grandmother? I'd have to find a delicate way of asking her.

"Sorry, again," Skip said. "But I just caught a murder."

I let out a long breath. "In Lincoln Point?"

Where else? I thought belatedly. What I really wanted to know was, "Who's been killed and why in my town?" Lincoln Point had already suffered two murders this year, including that of a longtime businessman, and I didn't look forward to the new issue of a rising crime rate. Not to mention, it was a small town and I might know the victim.

"Can't say right now, and not just because

I'm out the door."

"And you can't even check to see if anyone is looking for Sofia Muniz?"

"You know, Aunt Gerry, with three . . . uh, retirement homes in town, we get calls like this almost every day."

"Not from me." I was sounding like a whiny old aunt. I'd have to examine this trend, I told myself. How could I expect Skip to drop everything and do my bidding? "Get going, Skip. Don't mind me. I'm just concerned for an old friend."

"No, no, you're right. No one is unimportant. I'll check it out, I promise. Maybe we can make a deal. You go out with Nick Marcus as I've been suggesting, and I'll —"

"Don't go there, Skip."

"Okay, but just let me know when you're ready to brave the dating world. We could double."

Clearly the police were not very busy today, even with the latest homicide, and could easily patrol the streets for a missing citizen. "Right now, I'm going to cruise Lincoln Point with Dolores and try to find Sofia Muniz."

I hung up before Skip could rattle me even more.

No way was I going on a date with Skip's mentor on the force. Or anyone, for that matter. My decision had nothing to do with Nick — I'd heard great things about him from Beverly, who worked with him on her volunteer projects. But I'd struck it rich with Ken Porter, who'd died two years ago. He was the most wonderful husband anyone could ask for. I doubted there was another man like him out in Skip's "dating world," and I didn't have the time or interest to find out.

My next call, at the Hanks Road stop sign, was to the Mary Todd Home.

"May I speak to Sofia Muniz?" I asked a female operator. Just checking.

"One moment please," and then, a long wait later, "Mrs. Muniz is not available right now."

"Has she left the residence?" Now moving past Sadie's Ice Cream Shop on my right. Too early, though I considered a chocolate shake a nutritious midmorning snack.

"I'm afraid I can't give you that information." I knew that, but took a chance on catching her off guard. "Would you like to leave a message for her?"

"No message, but I'd like to speak to Linda Reed, one of your nurses."

"She's not on break yet." *And how do you know that so quickly?* I wondered.

24

I hung up, no wiser. But, nothing ventured . . .

I pulled up to the Lincoln Point City Hall, an imposing white building at the heart of our civic center. To the right was our library, to the left the police department. I imagined Skip looking out the window of his office (except he'd left, and, besides that, he was still housed in a windowless cubicle), scratching his head, certain of the futility of what I was about to do.

Dolores was on the long, wide steps, talking to a well-dressed man who was about her age and height. Looking more closely, I saw that it was Steve Talley, a colleague of hers whom I'd met a few times. From their postures, I sensed it was not a friendly conversation. Dolores's arms were folded across her chest; Steve's hands were in his pockets. They took turns leaning into each other in an almost threatening way.

I gave a slight tap on my horn. Dolores turned away from Steve and started down the steps without a "good-bye" that I could detect. He stood there for a moment, frowning, then walked away.

"You wouldn't believe what some people will do to get ahead," Dolores said, right after, "Thanks so much for coming, Geraldine."

"A disagreement among colleagues, I take it?"

"That's putting it mildly. Once again Steve has tried to undermine me." She buckled herself and her rich-looking coat into my Ion, which seemed shabbier than ever from the contrast. "He removed my name from an interoffice distribution list, so I don't get updates on time."

I shook my head in sympathy. "How petty."

I was sure the high school faculty politics I'd endured had been tame compared to what must go on in city government.

" 'Petty' barely covers what Steve Talley is up to. But never mind him. Let's go. I need to focus on finding Sofia."

Dolores was bundled up more than the weather called for, in my opinion. She was a Southern California native, I remembered, who thought it was not an exaggeration to call fifty degrees, no wind or precipitation, "winter weather." Or maybe her long, black wool coat was simply a fashion statement. If so, it worked. Dolores was tall and thin — so was I, but I could still never pull off the elegant look, not even when I was her age, about twenty years ago. It might have been her excellent posture, which commanded the attention she needed to do her job well. It was hard to imagine a slouching city hall office manager. In the elegant department, I was also sure that in my outfit today — corduroy slacks and leather belt, cotton turtleneck, and brown tweed blazer — I looked like Dolores's poor cousin.

"We'll find her, Dolores," I said, because I felt it was my duty to offer hope, possibly to make up for my low-end car. I headed back down Springfield Boulevard in the direction of the Mary Todd. I assumed we'd start there, but I could tell Dolores had already begun her search. Even as she talked to me she peered out the window, now and then stretching her neck to look around me at the other side of the street.

"When did you find out Sofia wasn't at home?" I asked her.

"I call her every morning at seven o'clock to remind her to take her medications and do her exercises. Really just to touch base, you know. This morning her phone rang and rang, and then the desk picked up. They told me she must still be asleep. I tried for almost an hour and I know she doesn't sleep that late, so I decided to pop over and check on her. That's when they admitted to me they couldn't find her. I looked around a little, but then I had to be in my office for an important meeting, and now . . ."

Dolores paused in her rapid-fire summary to wipe her eyes and blow her nose. Her makeup still looked perfect, her shoulder-length black hair coiffed for a modern, professional image.

"Do you know when she was last seen by a member of the staff?" I asked her.

Dolores's "no" sounded more like a wail. I hoped it wasn't because my question, once I heard it myself, sounded too much like part of a missing persons interrogation. "I should never have sent her there. I should have kept her in my home. Our home."

I reached out and rubbed her shoulder. "It's normal to feel that way, Dolores, but we know that at a certain point, that's not realistic. She was ready for professional care. What are the staff at the Mary Todd doing to find Sofia?"

"Nothing that I can see. They say people leave all the time. But not my grandmother. At least I hope not. Sure, she had some memory loss. Ha, so do I. Sometimes she claims they don't give her her meds. So I check and the pharmacy at the home says, yes, they gave them to her. But those are little slips. All in all, she's" — Dolores snapped her fingers — "right there, you

28

know. Does the crossword puzzle every day. And she loves your class, Geraldine. She's making something for Ernestine, my daughter."

Dolores was rambling, veering off track, but I couldn't blame her. "Did the home send out their van, or anything like that?"

"Yeah, they said someone was out looking for her, but who knows? I keep calling back and they haven't found her." Dolores pulled her fashionable multicolored scarf, mostly red, tighter around her neck. "It's freezing out, too. What if she's out there in her nightgown?"

I could have pointed out that temperatures in the low fifties hardly constituted freezing, but I understood Dolores's worry and frustration, beyond the actual data. Also, today was overcast and, for some Californians who worshiped the sun, that alone was enough to bring on a shiver.

"Sometimes old people wander back to where they used to live," I said. "Did you check around your home?"

She nodded, and buried herself deeper into her scarf, still surveying the streets as we drove north. Sadie's Ice Cream Shop was now open and I promised myself a shake as soon as we found Sofia tucked in her Mary Todd bed with a puzzle magazine, wondering what all the fuss was about.

If I needed one, I had a good excuse to indulge, since Susan Giles, one of the crafters in our group, had left the miniature Victorian soda fountain she'd made for Sadie's window in my possession. It was my job to deliver it to Sadie's since Susan was on her way to a Christmas reunion with her family in Tennessee (*Tin*-essee, was how Susan pronounced it).

No wonder I've been craving a shake, I thought, *I've been living with tubs of ice cream, thimble-size though they were, for several days.* Susan had prepared two rows of flavors for her tiny freezer case. Whereas she'd been meticulous in modeling Victorian tables and chairs (white wrought iron), and signage (hearts, flowers, and cherubs) for the shop, she'd taken liberties with the ice cream flavors. Some were as simple as strawberry and chocolate; others more modern and elaborate, like German chocolate cake and mint-chip cookie dough with nuts. She'd also modeled one of Sadie's holiday specials: a vanilla ice cream "snowball" covered with coconut and topped with a tiny candle and a sprig of holly. A little silver scoop sat on top of the counter, and I could swear I smelled freshly baked cones every time I passed by.

Dolores had been talking while I'd been salivating over what was in reality nothing more than modeling clay (ah, the power of miniatures). I hoped I hadn't missed anything critical.

"I called the people next door to me to check. My grandmother isn't anywhere in my neighborhood," Dolores was saying. "And anyway, it's a gated community, so the guard would have seen her go in. My grandmother lived there with me until a couple of years ago when I put her in the Mary Todd." In her distraught, guilt-ridden state, Dolores was able to make "Mary Todd" sound like "San Quentin." She dabbed at her eye makeup. "It was always the three of us — me, Sofia, and Ernestine."

"I remember Ernestine in school. She's a good student." Something to brighten a needy mother's day, even if the girl wasn't among the best I'd taught at Abraham Lincoln High School. "I can't believe she's in college already. Where is she, again?" Get the mother talking about her pride and joy.

"UC Irvine. She's doing really well, a junior already. She's majoring in communications."

"You and Sofia must be very proud."

"We are. She's the first in the family to go to college, you know, but once she left, my grandmother was alone all the time. I work late a lot, and even on some weekends. I thought it would be better for her to have company, you know, be around other people, play some games, take some classes. And Mary Todd is supposed to be the best."

My friend Linda, one of its finest nurses (I was sure), would agree. And so did I, having had some experience of different care facilities myself. I was a regular on the arts and crafts circuit, working with senior residents at all three of Lincoln Point's facilities. Handling tiny pieces was beyond the physical capability of many old people, and I focused on what they could do, such as painting larger pieces, or working with fabric. A surprising number of women in the homes knitted or crocheted, telling me it was therapy for their arthritis. They loved making tiny blankets and rugs for children's dollhouses.

Sofia, I remembered, had been working on an outfit for a statue in a miniature church. She carefully explained to me how the statues of certain saints in Catholic churches wore real clothes. The Infant Jesus of Prague, she pointed out, had the most elaborate wardrobe of all.

As we passed Hanks Road, Dolores sat up in her seat. "Wait, Geraldine. Could that be

32

her? I think I saw her down there on the right. Turn around!"

I made a U-turn at Gettysburg Boulevard and turned left on Hanks. "Where exactly?" I asked, seeing no one on the street except a mailman and a multidog walker.

Dolores sank back. "I don't see her now. It was probably someone retrieving their newspaper. Wishful thinking, I guess."

She looked so despondent, I didn't correct her grammar, but instead came up with another platitude. "We're almost at the Mary Todd, Dolores, and I'll bet while we've been driving around, Sofia has been playing Scrabble with her friends."

Dolores gave me a wan smile. I knew she wanted to believe that even more than I did.

I thought about my own parents, who had died relatively young. Hard as it had been to deal with at the time, I'd long since become thankful that I'd been spared this kind of worry. I hoped my son would be spared it, too, but that was a road I was definitely not ready to go down.

A tune I couldn't place rang through my car. Dolores's cell phone. She pulled it out of her pocket (unlike me, who always had to dig in my tote) and clicked it open.

"Dolores Muniz," she said. A pause. A few "uh-huhs," then, "I'll see what I can do, but

I might not be in the rest of the morning. I'm picking up some brochures at the print-er's."

Strange. I wondered why Dolores would lie. I could understand not wanting her of-fice staff to know details of her personal life, but this seemed an occasion when she'd want all the help she could muster. And it certainly was nothing to be ashamed of.

Dolores looked over at me. She smiled weakly and shrugged her shoulders. I took the gesture as an "excuse me for lying" of sorts but not an offer to explain. I smiled back and kept driving, meaning, "Don't mind me, I'm just the driver."

CHAPTER 3

A few blocks later, the sprawling Mary Todd Home loomed in front of us.

Ken, an architect for all his working life, was always put off by the style (styles, he would say) of the home. "It's part Spanish — see the creamy stucco and the red-tiled roof? Part timbered — which could be either German or English, for heaven's sake. Part Tuscan — would you look at that balcony." He'd throw up his hands. "What were they thinking?"

"I like it," I'd say, just to tease. And he'd start again, this time pointing out the influence of Scottish Jacobean in the round turret, or the peaks of a Cape Dutch in the back.

How I missed his intelligence, his wit. Him.

Dolores hardly waited for me to set my car in park before she was unbuckled and on her way up the long driveway to the glass-paneled double door. I caught up with her at the front desk (copiously draped in a garland of holly), from which we got no satisfaction, other than, "We're doing all we can to find your grandmother," and, "Can I get you some coffee?" Finally, I persuaded the woman closest to the telephone to page Linda Reed.

"Let's look in Sofia's room while we're waiting for Linda," I said to Dolores. "It might give us a clue about where she went."

Dolores nodded absently. "Follow me," she said. Her expression told me that her mind was filled with unpleasant imaginings of her grandmother's current plight.

As we stepped into an elevator, I was greeted by two women from my crafts class, passengers from the basement, I imagined. They came forth with a duet of "Hi, Mrs. Porter."

"I bought some new paint for next Tuesday's class," Emma (or was it Lizzie?) said.

"It's Wednesday, not Tuesday," said Lizzie (or was it Emma?).

The debate went on to the second floor, where Emma and Lizzie got off, happily before I was forced to tell them they were both wrong.

Dolores and I exited the elevator on the fourth floor and headed for Sofia's quarters.

We passed lovely reading corners with a bright and attractive décor that included small bookcases and colorful lamps. The arrangements were near windows with views of nearby hills. Most of the readers were engrossed enough (or napping?) to be oblivious of Dolores and me, but a few looked up and smiled a hello, including Gertie, a particularly talented knitter, and Mr. Mooney, an excellent woodworker.

Until today, I'd seen only the main floor of the home, where the entryway and community rooms were located. Lavish as the first floor was, with enormous flower arrangements and comfortable groupings of furniture in the lobby, I had no idea the elegance and luxury carried through to the residence floors.

"You've certainly done well by your grandmother, Dolores. This looks more like a fine hotel than a senior residence." (Ken's architectural judgment notwithstanding, I said to myself.)

Signs directed us to a spa, a pharmacy, a fitness center, and a grand ballroom. I stopped to peer into a theater — a dark room with stadium seating, currently empty except for one old man asleep in the front row, obviously determined to capture a good seat. A program at the door listed the movies scheduled for the week, a mixture of classics and newer films, probably just out on DVD. We both inhaled deeply at the smell of buttery popcorn from a machine in the corner.

"I thought I was doing the right thing for Sofia," Dolores said. "The best thing was that she'd never have to move again. This is one of those 'continuing care communities,' they're called, with a care center on site."

I knew as much from Linda, who divided her time between a la carte nursing services at the home's wellness center and the more intensive care (not technically, of course) in its care-center wing.

Sofia's suite was beautifully appointed and larger than the Bronx apartment Ken and I shared when we were first married. I was sure Dolores had applied her own impeccable taste to the décor: simple lines but comfortable and inviting, in several shades of blue. A small Christmas tree with permanently attached tiny red, green, and gold balls stood on a table beside the couch. Two large, festive gift bags nearly blocked the entry to the patio.

"Two bedrooms and two bathrooms?" I asked, regretting my shocked tone.

"I didn't want her to feel cramped. And once in a while Ernestine or I come and stay here overnight. Not often enough, I realize." She ran her fingers over Sofia's dresser, lined with family photographs. A lifetime of memories. Weddings, birthdays, poolside parties, and holiday gatherings filled the light oak surface. I recognized Ernestine's formal high school yearbook photo in the collection, and one in her robes with Dolores on one side and Sofia on the other. All three Muniz women were tall and large boned. Sofia at eighty-something still had a rather stately carriage. Dolores turned to me. "Geraldine, what if she's . . . ?"

I hugged her. "You've been a good granddaughter, no matter what," I told her, basing that judgment solely on the living arrangements she'd provided for Sofia. I tried not to dwell on the various nursing home scandals I'd read about, from people stealing pensions and social security checks to euthanasia at the hands of a well-meaning (or not) orderly.

I felt uncomfortable, like a snoop in someone else's home, so I simply followed Dolores around the apartment, observing, as she opened drawers, unfolded and refolded clothes. She checked a large closet in the bedroom Sofia used, and I suspected she hoped she'd find her grandmother there, as if she were playing hide-and-seek one more time.

"You know, Sofia was never really happy in this place. In fact, she was never completely happy in my new home. I worked so hard to get us from hand-to-mouth survival in an old dump on the south side, to the beautiful home where I live now. And she'd tell me she missed the decaying old apartment."

This fit well with what I knew of Sofia. Dolores had bought her a fancy case to hold the materials for my crafts class, but Sofia carried her supplies in an old canvas tote bag. Instead of a state-of-the-art ruled cutting board that Dolores delivered to her in class one day, Sofia used a pile of cardboard as a base when she needed to score or cut. I imagined she wished she could simply discard Dolores's rich redwood lawn furniture (I guessed about this) and sit out with her friends on a government-issue porch in a rusty chaise lounge.

Dolores pushed sweaters and flowered housedresses across the closet rod. "She couldn't get used to the security at our new place. 'Like a prison, with visitors signing in,' she'd say. 'Why can't we stay where Ernestine was born?' she'd ask me." Dolores grunted. "It was in Nolin Creek Pines, Geraldine."

40

"The housing projects behind the civic center?" The one named after the site of Lincoln's log cabin birthplace, I remembered. Nolin Creek, Kentucky. Probably no other state in the country besides Kentucky and California had a Nolin Creek, thanks to us.

Dolores pulled the accordion door closed with a resigned sigh. *My grandmother is not hiding in her closet.* "That same rat hole. Funny, now I have an office at the back of city hall, so I look out my window and see those streets. It's a reminder every day of where I came from and where I never want to return."

I realized I knew very little about Dolores Muniz, except that she was a single mother with a rags-to-riches story that she usually preferred not to talk about. Not the time to quiz her, however. "Nolin Creek Pines is pretty run-down now," I said.

"It started out run-down. But Sofia never cared as long as we were together. Sometimes when she's tired or not feeling well and her memory is not great, she asks me things as if we still lived there. You know, did the landlord fix the curtain rod in the kitchen? Did I remember to buy grout for the bathtub? Do I think the roof will leak again this winter?"

I followed Dolores through a set of patio doors to a small balcony. Sofia had a view to the north, not bad this time of year when rainfall turned the hills green. Green-*ish,* Ken and I called it, remembering the rich, deep green of the Poconos in northern Pennsylvania and of the Catskills in upstate New York. I had a thought to ask a scientist (not that I could think of one among my friends) what made the difference. I wouldn't have been surprised if Maddie knew. There was a lot of fifth-grade science that was over my head.

Dolores sat down on one of the white metal chairs on the patio, apparently out of steam for the moment. I took the other chair, not knowing whether to get her talking or let her take the lead. In my mind I was constructing a miniature Nolin Creek Pines kitchen for Sofia. I could model an old-fashioned sink with a skirt around the bottom to hide the pipes. I wondered if the apartment had a radiator — something very easy to construct, with a little gray clay. If I kept it simple, I could have it done in a week, by Christmas, when she'd be back, safe, and celebrating with her family.

"Nice day, isn't it?" An old woman's voice broke into my crafty wanderings.

I knew Dolores was as disappointed as I

was to see that the greeting came from Sofia's neighbor, one balcony to the right, and not from Sofia herself. We tracked the sound to a frail-looking woman with an all-white halo of hair, her voice loud, high-pitched, and scratchy. "Very nice, indeed," I said, not to be rude. It wasn't her fault that Sofia was missing.

Then the obvious occurred to me. "We stopped by to visit Sofia. Have you seen her today?"

"I'm Sandy Sechrest," she said, seeming to stand on tip-toes. She pronounced it "seek rest," which I thought was fitting. The solid walls of the balcony hid all but her head and shoulders. She seemed to be balancing herself by the tips of her fingers (were those mittens covering them, or stretched out sweater sleeves?). "Sofia and I are friends."

While I smiled at the image of a Mutt and Jeff partnership, with the taller-than-average Sofia and the diminutive Mrs. Sechrest, Dolores jumped up. I worried that she'd frighten the tiny woman. Or attempt to vault over the space between the balconies, about ten feet, I guessed. But her cool professional training came to her rescue and she slowed down to ask in a calm tone, "Do you know where we can find her this morning, Mrs.

43

Sechrest?"

"You can call me Sandy. My friends call me Sandy."

"Thank you, Sandy. You can call me Dolores. I'm Sofia's granddaughter." Dolores took a breath. I was impressed at how well she was doing. "Is Sofia over there, visiting you?"

Mrs. Sechrest looked perplexed. "No, no. I think she went shopping." She looked to the hills beyond (focusing her eyes farther than the edge of the earth it seemed). "No, wait a minute. She was down in the garden very late last night with two men. I could see them from here. I don't sleep much so I sit out here all the time. When it's cool, I use the nice shawl my great-grandson brought back from India for me."

"You were telling us about Sofia?" I reminded her.

"Yes, Sofia. Maybe they came to take her shopping."

"Someone took Sofia shopping in the middle of the night?" Dolores asked. I could tell she was trying not to sound too exasperated.

Sandy knocked her temple with her tiny knuckle. "Not shopping. I remember now. They were taking her to jail."

"To jail?"

Mrs. Sechrest waved her arms and nearly disappeared below the wall for a moment. She came back up. "Yes, yes, that's right. One of them was the man who drives the shopping bus."

"The big yellow shopping bus?" Dolores asked her.

Mrs. Sechrest nodded vigorously. "Except this time it was a jail bus."

Dolores turned to me and whispered (unnecessarily, since Mrs. Sechrest had the very loud voice of the nearly deaf), "There's no yellow shopping bus. This woman is out of it."

"I'm so sorry, Dolores." I could see the letdown in her face, her posture, her eyes that were starting to tear up again.

"At least we have an idea of what to do now," I told her. "We can talk to some of the other residents. Someone might know what she did last night or this morning. She might have said something that will help us." That was a lot of *some*s, I realized. No wonder Dolores didn't jump at the idea.

"I can't just stay here, Geraldine. Can we drive around town again?" Dolores was full of nervous energy, fiddling with the buttons on her blouse, twisting her watch around and around on her wrist.

"This might be our best bet to find out

45

what happened last night," I said. "But if you want to leave, of course I'll take you."

Her answer was to sweep toward the door. I turned to say good-bye to Mrs. Sechrest but she'd left her balcony. Or else she'd simply dropped down to her normal, miniature height.

We were back in the entryway, ready to leave the suite, when the doorway was suddenly filled: my friend Linda Reed, looking broader than usual in her starched nursing whites (de rigueur at the Mary Todd). She was breathing heavily. I might have thought she'd climbed the four floors from the lobby, except I knew Linda could get winded just hurrying down a hallway. Still, she was a most welcome sight, beehive hairdo and all.

Help at last, I thought. Like me, Linda knew Dolores through our crafts work. Dolores was an enthusiastic supporter of our fund-raisers and did her best to move quickly on publicity, arrangements for permits, and other city hall–based details.

"Did you find my grandmother? Is she all right? Is she here?" Dolores dropped her purse and grabbed Linda's hand, as if to hold fast to our only decent source of information.

"We found her," Linda said.

Anxious looks all around. Dolores seemed to hold her breath. The phrase *dead or alive?* hung in the air. Then Dolores blurted out, "What happened? Is she all right?"

"She's getting settled in the care center." Linda pointed to the south wing of the home. We followed her index finger. Dolores drew her breath in again. "It's mostly good news."

A long exhale from Dolores. A questioning look from me, who had focused on the word "mostly." Dolores didn't seem to hear it, but then she didn't have my habit (the sometimes curse of an English teacher) of picking up on every word, every nuance. She grabbed her coat and put it on while juggling her purse and heading for the hallway. "I'm going to see her."

"Let's walk and talk." This from Linda, who had taken a team-building course last fall.

I was ready to do both.

To get to the south wing where the care center was located, Linda explained, we'd have to go down to the first floor, cross the lobby to another set of elevators, and go up three flights. I was reminded of too many airport parking garages. Which in turn reminded me of the San Jose Airport where I'd pick Maddie up this evening. I gave my watch a surreptitious glance. Though we hadn't seen Sofia yet, I felt the crisis was over and I could allow myself the pleasure of anticipating my only grandchild's visit.

Between now (eleven fifteen) and then (four o'clock) I'd have to squeeze in a makeup tutoring session with Lourdes (no Christmas recess for serious students), shop for kid food and party supplies (we always had a family gathering with Beverly and Skip on the first and last nights of Maddie's visits), and keep my schedule for delivering Mary Todd (the former First Lady, not the home) decorations around town. If anything could be dropped from today's list, that would be it, I decided. I could take Maddie with me to deliver tomorrow. The decorations would be up until New Year's Day, so there was no big hurry to have them there this afternoon.

"They found her at Nolin Creek Pines," Linda said. I shook my head. They found Sofia, not Maddie, I told myself. Linda pushed the DOWN button for the lobby.

Dolores snapped her fingers. "All that talk about the Pines neighborhood, and I didn't think of looking for her there." Her mood was cheerful, though we hadn't yet reached the part where the good news was only "mostly" and not "totally," as my twenty-eight-year-old nephew and his friends would say.

"Who found her?" I asked.

"Our van driver, Gus Boudette. It happens a lot that old people go back to where they came from. They checked her records and found that old address."

"You have that address?" Dolores sounded like one whose shady past had been uncovered.

"Since you called, we knew she wasn't at your current address, so they checked through her records for previous residences. You probably don't remember filling out those forms when we did our intake for Sofia. You had to go back fifteen years with employment and residence information."

"Are you sure the van didn't just happen to find Sofia there while they were searching the whole town?" Dolores asked, in a snappish tone, as if Linda had stolen the information. Given how sensitive Linda was, I was surprised she didn't give Dolores a caustic retort. "I have no recollection of giving you that address."

"It was three years ago, so I can see how you'd forget." This was Linda being professional. I was impressed.

"Hardly," Dolores said, still unhappy.

As we boarded the elevator, single file, I caught Dolores biting her lip. I heard a mumbled question, one that sounded like, "Will I ever really escape that neighborhood?"

We had the elevator to ourselves this time, and the whole lobby, too. I imagined the residents at morning classes, workout sessions, and spa appointments. Or maybe waiting in their rooms for their daily doses from the on-site pharmacy Linda bragged about.

We passed through the lobby, an ecumenical wonder, with menorahs, Christmas wreaths, and Kwanzaa candles interspersed. As we walked by an arrangement of flowers in front of a large hallway mirror, Dolores slowed down a bit and checked herself out. She smoothed her perfectly coifed dark hair and brushed her coat sleeve. Cleaning up after bad memories.

"So the staff was on it, looking for Sofia the whole time?" I asked Linda.

"Once Dolores called this morning, yes." Linda, puffing to keep up with us two long-legged walkers, was looking pretty pleased with herself and with her employer. "Not that Dolores believed us. We figure it's better not to involve the relatives anyway unless it's necessary, especially when we have the experience. They're always just wandering and eventually the police pick them up or Gus and his crew find them."

Linda made "them" sound like errant beads or globs of museum putty, but I knew she cared very much for the residents of the Mary Todd. She'd never been happier than lately, working in one place full time, giving her the opportunity to build a relationship with her patients.

Linda's strong point was helping the sick and infirm. At times she could be ill-tempered beyond understanding with her friends, but I'd never seen her behave or talk in anything but the most compassionate way toward her patients. And toward a patient's granddaughter today, I noted. And especially to my "patient," Ken. We'd seen her generosity during the many years of our friendship, but especially once Ken was diagnosed with leukemia. I couldn't have managed without Linda's comforting presence and very practical nursing support.

I couldn't stand it any longer. As we rounded a corner and proceeded toward the second elevator, I threw caution to the wind. "Linda, you said there was *mostly* good news about Sofia. What did you mean?"

Dolores bit her lip again. I realized she wanted to see Sofia in the flesh before hearing anything but good news. I was sorry I upset that fantasy, but Linda was well on her way to a full explanation.

"Sofia had a lot of blood on her. Her arms and legs and her clothes were all covered with blood."

Dolores picked up the pace of her stride, forging ahead of us. She bumped into Mr. Mooney and his walker, thus nearly disabling the only man in my crafts class.

"See you tomorrow," I called to him as we hurried past.

"I love the Wandering Irishman," Linda said, with a chuckle.

I knew of Mr. Mooney's reputation for walking uninvited into many corners of the home — administrators' offices, the pharmacy, and any unlocked room he came upon — possibly sleepwalking, or more likely a natural-born snoop. I'd found him searching through my crafts tote one day. "Just looking," he'd said, with a pleasant smile that made it hard to think ill of him.

"Well, of course Sofia had blood all over her," Dolores said (without a thought of or an apology to Mr. Mooney). "That whole neighborhood is full of trash and bodily fluids."

"This was more —"

"Never mind." Dolores's cell phone rang as we approached the elevators in the south wing. She ignored both Linda and her phone. "There are all kinds of ways to get scratched in that slum." Dolores pushed the UP button. She looked at me with disapproval, as if it had been my question that had spilled blood all over her grandmother.

We kept silent on our ride to the third floor.

"Thing is," Linda said as soon as we exited (had she rehearsed this in silence?), "Sofia doesn't appear injured."

"So she's fine," Dolores said, marching with her arms across her chest.

"She has some minor cuts on her arm, but nothing that would have bled so much."

"Do we have to talk about this now? Maybe she bumped up against some bum at the Pines. There are enough of them there, God knows. They're all dirty, bloody, smelly . . . I just want to see my grandmother." There was that wailing sound again.

A large sign pointed the way to the patients' rooms. Dolores widened the gap between us and strode down the hallway.

Case closed, I thought.

Then Linda tapped my shoulder. She had

53

to stand on tiptoes to whisper next to my ear. I felt the stiff strands of her heavily sprayed hair (a la the sixties, when Linda was in high school) across my cheek. "Whether Dolores believes it or not, Gerry, that blood is a problem."

"What kind of problem?"

"It's not hers."

I didn't know whether to be glad or worried.

CHAPTER 4

The care center was decidedly less plush than the quarters in the main wing of the Mary Todd. More like a hospital, its halls were pale green and white and unadorned except for an occasional bulletin board with notices and schedules. Brief glimpses into examining rooms reminded me too much of Ken's last days struggling with cancer. It amazed me that, even more than two years later, simple things like a blood pressure monitor, a stethoscope, or a hospital-style scale could spark that memory. Fortunately, jars of tongue depressors and cotton swabs now reminded me more of my crafts table at home.

Linda and I stood a respectful distance outside the door to Sofia Muniz's room. We heard her granddaughter's voice, stressed and frightened. "Nana, Nana, can you hear me?" Dolores sat on the edge of Sofia's bed. A much cleaned-up Sofia, with no sign of blood where it shouldn't be. Fast work, I thought, unless Sofia had spent the whole morning here while we were searching her rooms.

We turned to leave and nearly bumped into an attractive young man in hospital whites with a large silver hoop earring on his eyebrow. I was surprised that the Mary Todd, which required conservative dress of its staff, allowed such avant-garde ornamentation.

"Hey, Gus," Linda said. "Good job finding Sofia."

"Where was she exactly?" I asked him, not loudly enough for Dolores to hear.

"Kind of slouched near a Dumpster in her old neighborhood," Gus whispered back. "Where they always are." He brushed his straw-blond hair from his forehead, just missing getting his finger caught in his eyebrow ring, and pointed down the hall to what looked like a nurses' station. "Sorry, I've been paged. Gotta go."

"Did you catch the earring?" Linda asked. I raised my eyebrows: *How could I miss it?* "Gus is a good guy, in spite of the earring. He works part time at Video Jeff's arcade. He's the one who got Jason the job there. The jewelry fits in a little better with their image than it does here." Linda paused.

56

"Uh-oh, I hope Jason doesn't come home with a ring in his nose or something."

Linda had told me Jason had a job after school and on breaks, but I hadn't paid attention to where it was. I tried to sound interested. "What does he do there?"

"Jason? Or Gus?"

I really didn't care. I was trying to focus on the conversation between Dolores and Sofia. I couldn't hear anything. "Both," I said.

"I guess he works the retail end and helps with the machinery," Linda said. "For Jason, it's under the table since he's not sixteen yet. He cleans up mostly, and gets a big discount on DVDs and software."

For whatever reason I allowed my gaze to follow the bejeweled Gus as he took long strides down the corridor. About halfway down, he took a left, away from the desk. Just as I thought. Anything not to talk to patients' relatives.

Sofia appeared to be sleeping, a thin smile on her face. Dolores tucked the sheet under her grandmother's chin again, smoothed out the blanket one more time, and straightened the items on the tray beside the bed (this was new). Then she took a seat on the chair and settled in. She seemed to have forgotten about Linda and me.

We slipped out.

All was well. There was nothing more for me to do for the Muniz family.

I knew an hour and a half with Lourdes and a review of the rules of grammar would be enough to clear my head of the ordeal of the morning. Not my personal trauma, but intense nonetheless.

Sequence of tenses made a nice diversion. Never mind that I met my literacy students at a table in a small, airless library storeroom. Our last fund-raiser, for which my crafts group had made and piled hundreds of miniature books into a room-box library, bought us a new table at least. This one had four legs the same size — a luxury. The funds had also provided updated study guides for all standardized tests.

" 'After she graduated from high school, Katie could have went on to college,' " Lourdes read. She looked at me with the countenance of a student who knows the right answer and is about to get an A. "It should be *gone*. Katie could have *gone* to college."

"Excellent, Lourdes."

"That one was so easy, Mrs. Porter."

Lourdes and I were not that far apart in age, but before Ken died I would have passed for much younger. Two years caring for him and worrying about him took its toll, however, and now Lourdes and I looked more like the peers we were, one on the heavy side (her) and the other struggling to gain back weight lost during her husband's long illness (me).

I patted her shoulder. "Would you have thought it was easy a few weeks ago?"

Lourdes blushed. "I guess not."

Halfway through our session, we took a break to eat tuna sandwiches that Lourdes had thoughtfully prepared for us. Wheat bread, red-leaf lettuce, and lots of mayonnaise.

"Just the way I like them," I told Lourdes, who always insisted that her providing lunch or treats was only fair since I was giving her my time.

I was sometimes ashamed of my impure motives in tutoring literacy students. I was sure I got more out of the sessions than they did. What could be more satisfying than providing an opportunity to learn, watching a student move from "I'll never pass the test" to "this is too easy"?

We drank from small plastic cups we'd taken from a dispenser next to the water cooler. I'd stopped at home between the Mary Todd and the library (both time- and geography-wise) and swept a plastic bag full of my famous ginger cookies into my tote. Always thinking of dessert first.

I thought of Linda. "And still you stay skinny," she'd say every time I ordered a regular sundae with extra whipped cream at Sadie's, while she ordered the junior size with no whipped cream or nuts.

Lourdes was well on her way to achieving her goal, a common one among my older female students: a high school diploma before she turned fifty. She and her husband had worked several jobs between them to keep two children in college, also a common phenomenon in my students' families. I'd occasionally hired Lourdes's younger son, Kyle (an American name for an American boy, Lourdes had told me), to do odd jobs around my home. Lourdes carried her children's photos in her wallet, happy to tell everyone at Bagels by Willie, where she worked, about her very bright boys, two in college and one in high school.

Funny how "bright" was often paired with "opportunity," I thought.

Many conjugations, past participles, and complex sentences later, Lourdes and I left our little alcove and entered the main library, fairly empty at a little after one o'clock on a weekday. I wasn't surprised to see rain pelting the tall, narrow windows of the building. Lourdes pulled a navy blue parka over her short, stocky body and I helped her as the fake fur collar became entwined with her neat dark bun, low on her neck.

I was glad I'd picked up a raincoat as well as the cookies at my house. I was getting weather soft, I told myself as I did it. What happened to the Bronx girl who walked to school two miles in the snow?

I talked Lourdes into letting me give her a ride home, pointing out that in spite of her parka, she'd be drenched if she either walked or waited for a bus.

"No, no, no," she'd said at first, as one word.

Her eventual acquiescence was a milestone in the six months that I'd been working with her. She'd always made some excuse for me not to drive her home, and I suspected she wasn't especially proud of her neighborhood.

She lowered her eyes to zip her jacket, and to avoid mine, I thought. "It's not far. I live in Nolin Creek Pines," she said.

Well, well.

Nolin Creek Pines (there was neither a creek nor pines) was on the south side of town, behind our civic center. I always thought it ironic that the neighborhoods around government complexes were often the worst parts of town, and Lincoln Point fit that pattern.

I drove along New Salem Circle (yes, we were obsessed with references to our sixteenth president) until Lourdes pointed out one of the multilevel structures with riser-free concrete steps and orange metal hand railings.

The parking lot was dotted with embattled pickups and older model vehicles. On the street side was a row of battered newspaper vending machines and a poorly maintained bus stop shelter, within which several adults waited. Their umbrellas were open against the inevitable leaks from inadequate maintenance of the shelter.

I dropped Lourdes off in front of a building with a large blue numeral six painted on the dull gray wall. At the same time, another car pulled up and Kyle and a couple of other boys exited the backseat. Delinquent from school? Probably not, since this close to the holidays, classes were spotty. Maddie was already on vacation, for example. I noted how tall Kyle was, compared to Lourdes, and I was very pleased when he gave a quick wave in my direction.

I wondered which number building Dolores and her family had lived in. Other questions ran through my mind. Was Lourdes likely to live her whole life here? Or would her three sons become doctors or lawyers and eventually move her to the Mary Todd?

The contrast between Nolin Creek Pines and my own pristine neighborhood, with neatly trimmed Eichler homes — each with its own well-kept indoor atrium and large backyard — was striking. But one thing I was pretty sure of was that inside that decrepit building, Lourdes's apartment was spotless. From her own neat appearance, to the orderly way she kept her school files, to the pride she took in her counter work at Bagels by Willie, I could tell that she could turn any living space into a pleasant, comfortable home.

"Gracias, Señora," Lourdes had said. I doubted she realized she'd reverted to her native tongue once she was home. "Do you want a cup of coffee?" I sensed the tension in her voice, afraid I might accept.

"Thank you, Lourdes, I wish I could, but I have a lot to do this afternoon. Another time?"

"Sí, sí, another time." And she hurried off.

Time for me to get busy on the miniature projects waiting for me at home. I pictured the mostly done freestanding scene now on my crafts table, destined for the window of the Toy Box on Springfield Boulevard. I wondered if I had time to add working lamps. I'd created a playroom, its pieces glued to a ten-inch-square tile left over from my sister-in-law Beverly's kitchen remodel. The colorful "room" had an overflowing toy box (originally a small gift box, like the kind earrings might come in, covered with stickers), stuffed animals, board games, a plate of cookies (the easiest part), and an easel surrounded by art supplies (toothpicks were a great start to fashioning paintbrushes). Maybe it didn't need lighting. Kids went to bed before dark, I reasoned.

I'd reached the bus stop when my cell phone rang. For a change I was able to pull it out of my purse and catch the call before it went to voice mail.

"Geraldine, it's Dolores. I need your help."

It dawned on me that I'd left Dolores stranded at the Mary Todd. And now it was pouring. What had I been thinking? "I'm so sorry. I forgot you didn't have a car there. Shall I come and get you?"

"No, I'm already at my office. I grabbed a

cab as soon as my grandmother woke up. There was something I absolutely had to have in the FedEx pouch this afternoon." Of course Dolores would be resourceful enough to find her way back to city hall, and guilt-ridden enough to regret having left Sofia's side for the sake of her career. "It's my grandmother," Dolores said.

Déjà vu? I'd heard that same anxious voice this morning. I imagined Sofia now in a coma or dead. Or maybe Dolores, prone to overreaction, was simply frantic about something more serious than scratches on her grandmother's body.

One of my first thoughts, after *poor Sofia,* was a question: Why had Dolores chosen me to be her confidante (rescuer? supporter?) in this crisis? For the second time. This was not my dear friend, Linda Reed, calling. Or Ken's wonderful sister, Beverly. Or any of my crafter friends with whom I spent at least one night a week wallpapering tiny rooms and polishing three-inch mahogany nightstands. Though I did feel a certain gratitude toward Sofia, I doubted that was the reason. I'm not sure Dolores ever saw the Lady of Guadalupe altar Sofia gave me, since it was created and passed on to me during crafts classes.

I didn't remember any particular condolences from Dolores herself when Ken died. Dolores and I weren't even close to being let's-do-lunch or girls'-night-out buddies. I hoped she had such friends and wondered where they were in her hour of need.

Not that I wasn't sympathetic, or worried about Sofia. But why me? Maybe because my nephew was a cop? I knew what Ken would say: *Because you're easy, Gerry. You can't say no, and everybody knows it.*

"What's wrong?" I asked Dolores now. (Halfhearted, to be truthful.)

"I got a call from the police about an hour ago. My grandmother is being questioned in connection with a murder."

I must have heard wrong. "Wha— ?"

Dolores's voice cracked. "Can you meet me at the Pines, number eight, in fifteen minutes?"

I thought about my plans for a productive afternoon at the party store and my crafts table. I saw all the little items on my list waft through the air and fly out the window of my Saturn Ion like so many miniature butterflies.

At least I was already at the meeting site. Dolores must have thought I was home, allowing me fifteen minutes to get across town.

The rain had stopped. I drove my car back

into the parking lot and pulled into a slot facing the street. I picked up my latest issue of *Miniature News* from where it had slid to the floor and flipped through the pages. I knew one of my crafter friends, Karen Striker, had a how-to article in the magazine this month. She'd written a piece on constructing a jail from the days of the old West. How timely, I thought.

A few paragraphs into Karen's instructions (such as: the bars of the jail are made from the long metal sticks that sometimes come in flower arrangements) I realized I had no time for the luxury of pleasure reading. I had to tap my sources for information on Sofia's predicament and start delegating some of my afternoon chores.

My first call, to my nephew, Detective Skip Gowen, was quick but most enlightening.

"Remember that missing old woman I wanted you to check on?" I began.

"Yes, and do you remember that homicide I was working on when you called about her? Well, your friend's grandmother was walking around in the same neighborhood as the crime scene, with blood all over her. We're pretty sure it's the victim's."

"Who was murdered?" I whispered.

"You'll be hearing it soon enough so I can

tell you. It was probably no one you knew. A gardener over at the Nancy Hanks Home. His body was found in the old Nolin Creek Pines neighborhood, near Arbor Road."

I locked my car doors. I wasn't that far from Arbor Road. If I strained my neck, I could probably see the crime scene tape. "And Sofia Muniz was found also wandering here." The word was out before I knew it.

"What do you mean *here?* Where are you? Don't tell me you're already investigating."

I heard a mixture of joking and warning in my nephew's voice. I pictured his dropping down from his usual feet-on-the-desk position to full upright. Skip had reason to be concerned since I'd been building a reputation for giving unsolicited aid to the Lincoln Point PD.

"I just happen to be here. I gave my student a ride home." No need to fill in the rest of the facts — that I was now waiting for the suspect's granddaughter for who knew what purpose.

"Do you have anything else to tell me?" Skip asked.

"You're the homicide detective," I said. "Oops. Call-waiting. I'll talk to you later."

There really was a call waiting. Call number

two was incoming, from Linda, out of breath again (still?).

"Gerry, you'll never guess what's going on here."

"I heard."

"Of course you did."

"But I don't know any details. I was going to call you in the next two minutes." (This was true.)

My car was stuffy, but I was inordinately fearful of opening the windows or (worse) getting out and walking around in what must have been nice, fresh air after the rain. I hated that I was afraid in this neighborhood. After all, the alleged murder suspect that the police found wandering here was an octogenarian. I saw nothing threatening, unless you counted the garbage spilled here and there along the walls of the building and in the parking lot. I hadn't seen a single other person after dropping Lourdes off except a few respectable-looking people waiting for, and then boarding, a bus. Still, I kept a watchful eye on my surroundings.

The Nolin Creek Pines neighborhood was extensive, I reminded myself, comprised of many buildings bordered by streets of low-end shops. Some parts were better than others. The worker from the Nancy Hanks (a lower-end retirement home) had been found blocks from where I was now parked. There was no reason to think I was in any danger.

Still, I chose not to exit my car. With great difficulty, I took off my raincoat, moving forward on the seat to loosen the back from under me, then inching one sleeve at a time slowly down my arm. I did all this without losing phone contact with Linda. I could now count myself among the cell-phone literate.

"The police came and carted Sofia off around noon," Linda said. "I would have called Dolores, but I didn't find out until later. It was quite a scene in the care center, I'll tell you. Sofia didn't want to go. She kept saying, 'Don't take me to jail again, don't take me to jail again.' "

"Funny. I didn't know she was ever in jail."

"Who knows?"

I pictured Linda making a looping motion near her head, something she did often when referring to her patients who had trouble keeping contact with reality. I had to remind myself that she was very good with them, but needed to joke or vent now and then for her own sanity.

"What about the victim?" I asked. Fortunately, Skip wasn't my only source of information.

"I just heard, like, a minute ago. He works for this big company that hires the gardeners and maintenance people for all the homes in Lincoln Point. Carl something. He's worked here now and then, but mostly at the Nancy Hanks. I hated that place when I was assigned there, by the way. Very depressing. The murdered guy lived in the Nolin Creek projects. Thank goodness."

"Huh?"

"I mean thank goodness he wasn't a doctor or a nurse. Do you know what a scandal that would be? I can see the headlines: 'Elderly patient kills doctor at upscale retirement home.' " A shudder, then a pause, but no response from me, so Linda kept going. "So, are you on the case?"

"Of course not, Linda."

"Then you don't want me to see what else I can find out?"

"I didn't say that."

Still five minutes till Dolores was due. Time for another call, this one outgoing, to Beverly, Ken's sister and Skip's mother. Also, surrogate grandmother to Maddie, civilian volunteer to the Lincoln Point PD, and all-around best friend. Beverly had just one flaw, and it wasn't her fault. She'd had scarlet fever as a child and still suffered the

71

effects on her heart. It was cause for great worry for me, though Beverly played it down as much as she could.

"I figured you'd be calling," she said. "Only a cop's mother gets the scoop before you do."

I gave Beverly a rundown of my morning and afternoon. "I have no idea what Dolores wants with me," I said.

"Other than your help to clear her grandmother? You're getting a reputation, you know. Remember last summer?"

"That was different. I don't know anything about this victim. I'm staying out of this."

"Right."

Why did everyone think I was an investigator? A retired teacher, yes. A crafter, volunteer tutor, fund-raiser, yes. I'd done my master's thesis at San Jose State on Shakespeare, not Sherlock Holmes. Just because I helped the LPPD once didn't mean I was going to stick my nose in every case.

"How much do you know?" I asked Beverly.

"Ha. Actually, not much. Just that the victim was Carl Tirado and he worked for a company that supplied gardeners for all the nursing homes in the county."

"You're right. That's not much. Except

for his full name, I already knew that."

"Sorry, I'll keep you posted. I'll be manning the phones at the station later and will keep my ears open."

"You always do. Thanks."

"Are you ready for Maddie? I'll bet your crime-solving activities set you back on your schedule."

"Uh-huh. I was hoping you could pick up the ice cream cake at Sadie's shop, and tell Sadie I'll take Susan Giles's room box to her tomorrow. And also, I left my little playroom in your laundry area when I was showing it to you. Facing reality here, I'm not going to do any more with it, so can you take that to the Toy Box?"

"No problem. See you tonight. Can't wait to see Maddie. And hear how you won't have investigated."

I hung up without a word. Just a smile.

CHAPTER 5

It was nearly two o'clock when Dolores arrived. She beckoned me to her silver Mercedes. (Evidently a brief ride in my Ion was enough for her for one day.) I sat in her passenger seat, admittedly more comfortable than mine, possibly even more so than my living-room furniture. I urged her to try to calm down and tell me what she knew so far.

"I got the call from the police about twelve thirty this afternoon, just after I returned to my office." Dolores rubbed her hands together as if she were freezing. "It's not that I left my grandmother to go to a two-martini lunch, Geraldine," she explained. "I had this memo from Sacramento, with a very firm deadline. And one of my techs is out sick, and I was afraid Steve Talley would preempt me on this as usual, and on and on." Dolores threw up her hands in surrender.

I hoped I never did anything to engender this kind of guilt in my son or granddaughter. I thought of giving Richard a call and offering blanket immunity for anything that might come up in the future. "What are the police charging her with, Dolores?"

"Nothing yet, but they think she —" She pulled a tissue from a holder attached to her visor and blew her nose. "— killed that man. It's a ridiculous thought. Beyond ridiculous."

"Did you or Sofia know the victim? The gardener?"

"No. Who looks at a gardener, right? They say he worked at the Mary Todd only a few times in the nearly three years my grandmother has lived there. She's in custody now, Geraldine. I got her the best lawyer in Santa Clara County. If she's formally arrested, there'll be a bail hearing, but the lawyer's not hopeful about getting her released. He says they'll assume she's too hard to control. She's old, Geraldine. What are they talking about?"

We sat surrounded by the dumpy project buildings. I wondered which one was the Munizes' old residence.

"I worked so hard to get us out of this place, Geraldine. We barely made it out before it became too dangerous to live here.

There'd be a drug bust at least a couple of times a week, and some of our friends were afraid to visit us."

"That must have been tough, with a child especially." Maybe this was my role, Geraldine as therapist. I could do that for her.

Dolores dug in her large purse, pulled out her wallet and showed me a photograph of Sofia. A formal portrait of a strong, stately woman, with a photographer's clouds swirling in the background. A far cry from the woman I'd seen in her hospital bed earlier today.

I remembered the first time I met her, when she signed up for my Mary Todd class. The first week, she made a tiny Nativity scene out of origami figures. I was never a Catholic, but I had to admit, Christian stories were wonderful and a great source for spectacular miniature scenes.

"I want to build the Vatican," Sofia had said to me one Friday morning. "Can you help me?"

"Of course." Only other miniaturists would understand that we weren't talking about a multiyear life-size construction project requiring scaffolding and tons of cement.

Sofia's version of the Vatican was progressing nicely. She'd started with the two mushroom-shaped fountains and the obelisk that defined the square in front of St. Peter's Basilica, molding them carefully with modeling clay. We consulted a large art book she had and I helped her figure out the height of the obelisk and the distances between the fountains, in order to keep the scene on track for scale.

"Dolores took me here," she'd said, blessing herself. "I had an audience with the Holy Father."

I imagined that Dolores made every effort to fulfill all her grandmother's dreams.

Dolores had been staring at Sofia's photograph.

"What are you going to do next, Dolores?" I asked. (Translation: Why am I here with you?)

"I thought we could drive around a little. Show this photo and see if someone remembers seeing her. Maybe I'll find something the police missed. I can't just do nothing. And you're so . . . sensible, Geraldine. I could use the support."

This didn't seem the moment to tell her I was pressed for time. "Let's do it," I said.

Dolores pulled out of her spot and headed south, away from downtown, to a part of Nolin Creek Pines I'd never visited. The buildings seemed to get more decrepit, the cars more battered, the farther away we drove from the civic center. In the middle of the afternoon, the place was deserted and bleak. Dolores seemed to get older and more drawn with each building we passed. Her scarf was crooked on her neck but she made no effort to straighten it. Her makeup was smudged, and her hair, neatly turned under this morning, now fell in disarray.

As we passed Arbor Road, I caught a glimpse of yellow crime scene tape. Dolores seemed to know well in advance not to turn down that street.

"There's the bodega she used to go to," she said, turning onto Spruce. "They knew my grandmother very well. Let's go in."

Why not, I thought, feeling like Dolores and I were cop partners on a prime-time TV show. "Have you seen this woman?" we'd ask, holding out her photograph. "Let's canvass the area," one of us would say.

I made a resolution to reread a classic, perhaps *Paradise Lost,* and give up television crime dramas.

For the next half hour, Dolores and I covered the bodega, Sofia's bank, the clinic she frequented, two pharmacies, and a check-cashing place. Each time, we exited with no more information than when we entered. I knew that Dolores was hoping against hope that someone would provide her with an alibi for Sofia, or an eyewitness to another killer. Or a miracle.

I noticed that every one of the institutions except the church had metal bars on the windows and doors. And yet Sofia had felt more like a prisoner in a gated community with a security checkpoint. What a hold our pasts have on us, I thought.

As we continued canvassing in the Mercedes, Dolores talked about her grandmother and her life. *By the time the day was over,* I thought, *I'll know the Munizes backward and forward.*

She waved her hand to encompass the Nolin Creek Pines neighborhood. "Funny. I was so determined not to let my office know about Sofia's disappearance, and now this whole neighborhood knows, and soon it will be all over the newspapers that she was taken away by the police." (This was her musing between two fast-food restaurant stops, for queries, not for hamburgers, thank heavens.)

At last, I could segue to one of my basic questions. "Why didn't you tell your colleagues at city hall, when they might have been able to help you this morning?"

Dolores slammed her hands against the gray leather steering wheel. "Because I'm selfish, that's why. There's a job opening coming up on the mayor's personal staff. It would be a big promotion for me. I'd be the chief public information officer, Mayor Roberts's right-hand woman. Remember Steve Talley? He and I are the most promising candidates. All I could think of was, I didn't want anything to get in my way."

"And if they thought your grandmother was unstable and ran off they'd think less of you?" It seemed quite a leap, but I'd never understood the inner workings of the political machine.

Dolores's nod was accompanied by a sniffle. "Or that I'd be too busy to handle both a high-profile job and an ailing relative. Like a single mother, and I've already been through that phase of discrimination, thank you very much. You may think things are rosy now for women, Geraldine, but let me tell you, we're still fighting battles in the workplace. We're still debating whether a young woman should be hired if she seems to want children soon, or whether a mother can give enough attention to her job. Meanwhile, our boy Stevie Talley has three kids under twelve, and is on his third marriage, but no one ever brings that up in connection with his job. Neither one of us has a college degree, but no one brings that up about him, either."

"I'm sorry to hear that." Another wishy-washy therapist answer, but I didn't know Dolores well enough to guess what she wanted to hear.

"He drives around in his Cadillacs — he has more than one — like he owns the world. And, if you ask me, though I can't prove it, he's addicted to prescription drugs. He broke his leg skiing a couple of years ago and never got over it, if you catch my drift. His eyes are like pinpoints at certain times of the day, and also he keeps his middle desk drawer locked."

I'd never been close enough to Steve Talley to examine his pupils, and I didn't see how securing his desk was so unusual — I'd kept my teacher's desk at the high school locked just to protect my supply of chalk.

"Is that what you were arguing about this morning? I mean the job, not the pills or the Cadillacs."

"No, that particular debate was about a specific development proposal for the town. One that would have a great effect on the Nolin Creek population especially. He calls it Talley's Restoration Plan. I call it Talley's

Tally, as in votes and money."

"I didn't realize your job included matters of that nature."

"It's a small town, Geraldine. Lots of informal decision-making. One palm greasing another. Steve and I both manage offices in city hall. It's an unwritten rule that the most creative, politically aggressive office manager is the next assistant to the mayor, and then up and up the ladder.

"And you both would like to be at the top of that ladder."

"I've earned it, Geraldine. Unlike Steve, who's trying to muster community support for this plan of his by using fear tactics. He's appealing to voters who think the housing projects should be destroyed and turned into upscale condos and fancy shops and restaurants. Instead of a good cup of Mexican coffee, you'd have to buy four-dollar soy lattes. Wait until you see his model of the new neighborhood. He's going to unveil it to the public at the ball."

My ears perked up. "A model?"

"Not the kind like you make. Steve's is computer-generated."

I almost lost interest. I loved the real, physical models Ken and his staff used to create, with tiny buildings, streets, sidewalks, cars, and trees. On some scales the people would be no more than a half-inch tall. He'd never take them home, however. "I don't want you putting tiny curtains on the windows," he'd say.

Dolores had gone on to describe Steve's (inferior, in my mind) model. "Anyway, you can go to any terminal in the city hall and click on it. It rotates in 3-D, if that's what you call it. The plan is there, in living wood and paint."

"And your plan?"

"My plan, which is boring, because it's practical, is to clean up the neighborhood. Get a decent contractor in to repair the infrastructure." She used her fingers to tick off. "The plumbing, the lighting, the streets. Pick up the garbage regularly. Get more cops there at all hours. Have after-school programs to give the kids something to do besides join a gang."

I got it. "But that would cost money and all we'd have to show for it would be a safe neighborhood for poor people."

"Not so sexy as new earth-toned condos that would rent for a fortune, is it?" Dolores asked. "But no matter what's at stake, I still should never put my work ahead of my grandmother's well-being. She raised me, Geraldine. She took care of me from when I was five years old and my parents died."

83

"That must have been very hard for all of you. But you were responsible enough to take care of her when it was your turn, and you've certainly come to her aid now, doing everything you can."

It would be hard to prove Dolores heard anything I said. She continued on her own thread. "I've told myself I'm not ashamed of her, but did I ever invite her to an office party? No. Or show her around my building? No."

"That wouldn't necessarily be appropriate anyway."

Finally, I felt I'd paid my dues and earned the right to give a little advice. "Dolores, Sofia is still alive. If you think you want to do things differently there's still time."

She reached over and touched my hand. "Thank you, Geraldine, I knew you were the right person to ask for help."

Now that I thought of it, that *was* good advice, and I made a note to see how I could apply it to my own life.

When we pulled up to my Ion, Dolores leaned over and hugged me. "Thanks, Geraldine. I have an appointment with the lawyer in a few minutes. I'll let you know how it goes."

"Okay," I said. But did I want to know? Dolores had gotten support from me; Sofia had a good lawyer; my nephew was the homicide detective on the case. Surely my work with the Munizes was finally over and I could go back to enjoying the holiday season.

CHAPTER 6

It was probably the grandmother in me, but I thought Maddie lit up the whole of San Jose International Airport.

Standing as close to the gate as security would allow, I was unashamed of the handful of balloons that bounced around my head. The largest one said *Best Granddaughter.* There was nothing I could do about the teddy bears frolicking through the letters in the message; I hoped Maddie wouldn't notice immediately.

Maddie was still young enough to have to preboard on her end and deplane last in San Jose. A good thing since, as she ran toward me, her swinging backpack would have been a serious hazard in the crowd that poured out the doorway. I steeled myself for the impact and hugged her, remembering the days when I could scoop her up. I kissed the top of her red hair (which matched that of all the other Porters except me) and felt her nuzzle closer. A young woman in goth dress and enough silver jewelry to require its own tub on the security belt smiled at us, possibly remembering a similar incident in her former, pastel life.

Maddie and I had certain rituals for these arrivals. Before we went to baggage claim, we called her parents in L.A. This was less important now that Richard and Mary Lou were able to track her flight on the Internet, but we called anyway. We stepped aside, allowing what seemed like millions of other passengers to have their space. It was Thursday evening, not prime time for traveling, except that this close to Christmas, all bets were off.

Maddie took the lead, using my cell phone.

"I asked Santa for my own cell for Christmas," she told me and winked. Then, "Hello, this is Madison Porter, reporting in." A laugh. "Hi, Mom, I'm here. Yeah!" Pause. "Yup." Pause. "Yup." Pause. "Yup. Here's Grandma."

I assumed Maddie was "yupping" at warnings from her mother to be good, to eat her vegetables, to go to bed on time, and other things that weren't a grandmother's concern. Right now, she was so excited she skipped circles around me and hugged me again (causing my face to be bombarded momentarily with balloons) even as I had a few words on the phone with Mary Lou.

I handed over a bag of green and red foil-wrapped chocolate balls (another ritual, with the foil color appropriate to the season) and we headed toward Baggage Claim.

"Wait till you see what I made for the apartment, Grandma," Maddie said. Meaning the replica of the first apartment Ken and I lived in, in the Bronx. "It's sweet."

By now I knew that *sweet* had a whole different meaning for Maddie from the way I used it. I guessed she'd picked it up from Skip, who explained to me that it now means *tight* or *cool. Good thing I'm retired,* I thought. English isn't what it used to be.

"Do you want to tell me what you made, or surprise me?"

"Surprise." (Which was no surprise.)

"Shall we do crafts first thing and skip the party with Aunt Beverly and Uncle Skip?"

Maddie didn't spend a second believing I was serious. It was a huge turnabout for her that she even considered crafts worthy of her time. Before last summer she eschewed anything girl-like in favor of pastimes that required balls, sticks, and running around in protective gear.

Not that she liked pink yet, but I'd long

88

since given up buying her frilly dresses anyway. Today she was in her usual jeans with a neon green hooded sweatshirt. The big question was what I could coax her into wearing to the Mary Todd Ball over the weekend, a family affair she'd never been to.

Another big question was what I'd wear to the ball. I'd spent so much time on decorations for the town (and on my miniatures hobby, in general, truth be told) that I hadn't thought about a costume. We still had Friday and Saturday to cruise the Springfield Boulevard shops, all of which had Victorian offerings at this time of year. I'd worn crinolines to last year's ball, which Maddie wasn't around for. I wondered what kidspeak epithet Maddie would come up with if I tried to dress her in a set of white ruffled undergarments.

My Eichler home, bought with Ken many years ago, was a source of great joy for me. Typifying the California lifestyle, at the entrance of many homes of this type was a large atrium with a skylight, surrounded by a living room, kitchen–family room combination, and four bedrooms, all with predominantly glass exterior walls. I never had to check a weather report.

Maddie and I entered the atrium, to be greeted by Beverly and Skip, making as much party noise as two people could achieve. A CD of the jolliest Christmas music I own was playing, and Beverly had found noisemakers in the party store. She'd covered the Happy New Year message on a tin trinket with a label that read, "Welcome Maddie." (Maybe it wasn't too late to get Beverly interested in crafts, too.)

I wondered when Maddie would consider herself too old for this ceremony. Not this evening, certainly, as attested to by her beaming face. She hugged Beverly and Skip, then went to the large Christmas tree in the corner of the atrium. She found all the ornaments she'd made over the years — Styrofoam balls, drums of felt and sequins, gold foil stars, inedible dough Santas, macaroni angels — and all the presents with her name on them.

"Mom and Dad are bringing your presents in the car next week, but I have" — she reached into an outside pocket of her large suitcase and pulled out three tissue-wrapped items — "these!"

Ritual number four. Or was it five? We all made ornaments for each other, putting the date somewhere on its surface. Maddie was hanging the one she'd made for me (a tiny gingerbread house, in honor of my famous cookies, she said) when Skip's cell phone rang. "Hail to the Chief" was still his tune of choice, I noticed.

"Now would be a great time," we heard him say. "Come on over."

Beverly and I looked at each other and shrugged.

"I invited June to join us. I didn't think you'd mind," Skip said. Was that a twinkle in his eye, or was Santa on my mind?

A moment of silence while we processed the information. June Chinn lived in the Eichler next door to mine, the one with green trim. Beverly and I had been trying to get Skip and June together since she arrived in California from Chicago at least three years ago. And now here it was?

We all talked at once.

"I like June. She lets me talk about my soccer team," from Maddie, who knew her grandmother had no patience for stories of goals and home runs.

"When did this happen?" from Beverly.

"Nothing 'happened,' Mom," from Skip.

"How nice," I said lamely, because I'd been waiting for Skip to get a different call.

What have I become? I thought. Usually I'd be thrilled that Skip was interested in a woman I liked, such as June Chinn. But

91

here I was wishing the call had to do with the murder of the Nancy Hanks gardener. I'd been hoping to hear that the police had found something or someone to exonerate Sofia Muniz.

Were they doing anything to help this poor old woman? Was I going to have to investigate the case myself?

I laughed at the thought.

Maddie entertained us with stories of her life in L.A.; June was her most attentive listener. She'd babysat Maddie a few times, so they fell naturally into playful interaction.

"Cool ornament," June said, reaching to the branch where Maddie's ornament for Skip hung. The slightest movement caused June's short peach-colored sweater to ride up, widening the gap between it and the top of her low-slung, wide-belted jeans. Her tiny body could pull off the look, but I couldn't help thinking back to the days when even a miniature slice of displayed flesh would be a source of great embarrassment. Like having one's slip (did anyone even wear them anymore?) show beneath the hem of a skirt, as opposed to the current practice of baring all straps on purpose. Indeed, some of June's summer outfits would have passed for underwear when I was her age.

Skip's new ornament was shaped like a blue ribbon, reading *Best Uncle.* Clearly, it was the Porters' year for superlatives.

"I would have done one for you if I knew you were coming, June," Maddie said. "Best neighbor."

"Maybe we can have an ornament session this week and make special ones for each other," June said.

I looked at Skip: *she's a keeper,* my face said. His own expression said he knew what I was "saying" and agreed.

Who would have guessed that my running out of milk would help steer Skip's attention to the Sofia Muniz case?

I was setting the table for dinner when I realized the milk carton was nearly empty.

"I guess I'll have to have a soda," Maddie said, feigning resignation.

"Not on your first night," I said. "I need to at least start out following your mother's wishes."

"Let's walk down to Gettysburg Boulevard and pick up a quart," the wonderfully athletic June said to Maddie.

"It's too long a walk," said my Angeleno car-dependent granddaughter.

I threw back my shoulders, which had

been hunched over the silverware drawer. "Of course it is," I said, mentally slapping my head. "How far do you think it is from the Mary Todd Home to the apartments in Nolin Creek Pines?" I addressed my question to Beverly, who was better than a map as far as knowing the streets of Lincoln Point. Her work as a civilian volunteer for the LP Police Department took her to every part of town at one time or another. She stood on corners for seat-belt surveys and cruised around on an official moped seeking out abandoned cars. She helped out when traffic lights failed and took off at a moment's notice to any street or strip mall.

Now she had the answer before anyone could say "log cabin in Kentucky." "That would be two miles, give or take."

I turned to Skip. "Two miles. How can a ninety-year-old woman walk that distance?"

"She's eighty-seven, maybe eighty-eight, according to her file."

"Skip!"

"Sorry. We have no idea what time she started out. It's possible she walked all night, stopping many times to rest on the way. We know her granddaughter called to say good night after dinner, around seven thirty. We're just starting interviews and so far we can't find anyone who saw her after that."

I thought about mentioning Sandy Sechrest's claim that she'd seen Sofia being taken away in the middle of the night. But how much stock would Skip put in the observation of a woman probably even older than Sofia? Come to think of it, I didn't put much stock in it myself.

"What's all this about?" June asked.

I gave June a quick briefing on my morning adventure.

"Wouldn't someone have checked on the woman during the night?" June asked.

"It's not that kind of facility," I said, feeling defeated. "To be accepted into the Mary Todd, you simply have to be over fifty-five and ambulatory, not needing special medical attention. Once you're there, if — more like, when — you start to need extra care, you get it. You might be moved to their assisted-living wing, or permanently assigned to their care center, but you won't be evicted. Anyway, it's not like there are bed checks."

"Aunt Gerry, you'd be surprised how far someone can walk who is not . . . how can I say this? Not all there," Skip said.

"Dolores's grandmother is still very sharp. She does crossword puzzles and she takes my crafts class."

Skip rolled his eyes.

By now we were seated at the table in my dining room, having abandoned the milk procurement project. I noticed Maddie quietly sipping from a can of soda and gave her a surprised look. "My fruit for the day," she said, pointing to the orange label.

I knew it was wrong to reward cleverness of that kind, but I ruffled her hair in the way that (still, I hoped) made her feel good.

"Wouldn't someone see an old lady walking all that way alone?" Maddie asked between bites of Beverly's delicious rice-and-cheese casserole.

I turned to Skip. "Good question, isn't it? Why didn't anyone in that stretch of streets approach her and take her home or to the hospital, or call the police?"

Maddie grinned at the compliment. Her teeth had evened out in the time since I'd seen her so she no longer needed to cover her mouth with her fist when she laughed.

Skip sighed, as if I were ruining his date, which, in a way, I was. Beverly and June were wisely busying themselves with cutting extra bread (homemade walnut sourdough, June's contribution), pouring wine and water, and chatting about the ball to come on Saturday evening.

"Can we talk about this later, Aunt Gerry?" Skip asked.

"Excellent idea," I said. "How about nine o'clock tomorrow morning in your office?"

My nephew's "fine" was less than enthusiastic.

Maddie made up for it, however. "Yeah, we're on a case again!" she squealed.

Skip glared at me.

Uh-oh. What have I wrought?

"I'll see you in the Bronx," Maddie said as we went our separate ways to take showers and change for bed.

I'd seen her "in the Bronx" earlier, rustling around the model of our apartment, so I knew she'd already placed her "surprise" in the model. Ken had built the structure before he became ill and I'd finally been able to return to the project when Maddie became interested in working with me.

Twenty minutes later, showered and relaxed, we played Maddie's "find the new thing" game. I peered into all the rooms to figure out what piece she'd added to the furnished rooms.

"It's really small," she said, then laughed at the obviousness of her remark.

"Is it in the kitchen?"

"No."

"The dining room?" (By this time I'd seen it in the living room, but I wanted to stretch the game out.)

"No."

"The bathroom?"

"Nooooo."

"The attic?"

"N . . . there's no attic!"

"The living room?"

Silence.

"Okay, the living room!" I looked around the small living room. Our entire life-size apartment had been less than seven hundred square feet, the living room ten feet by twelve feet. The model living room, therefore, was ten inches by twelve inches.

I lifted the two-inch loveseat. "Nothing," I said to Maddie. The same with the easy chair and the table lamp (a pipe-cleaner base and the cap of a toothpaste tube for a lampshade).

I picked up the end table. "Aha," I said, examining a lovely silver (putty) picture frame, about one inch by three-quarters of an inch. An excellent representation of a frame for a standard eight-by-ten photo.

What I hadn't seen from a distance was the photograph in the frame. A stranger wouldn't know what scene Maddie had captured, but I knew. It was our wedding picture. I stared at the tiny image of Ken in a black tux and me in full bridal regalia. On one side of the happy couple was my maid of honor, nineteen-year-old Beverly; on the other side was Ken's friend and best man, Daryl Matthews. All so young. In fact, everyone in the photo was younger than Skip's age now.

Maddie could hardly contain herself.

"Dad had the old photo. I scanned it and then I had to keep shrinking and shrinking and shrinking it. I know it's not very clear, but I had to make it small enough to fit the frame. Dad helped me a little, but I'm the one who had the idea."

"It's the best idea I've ever seen."

I didn't even try to hold back the tears.

Maddie loved to sleep in her father's old bedroom, the corner room next to my primary crafts room. (The whole rest of the house was my secondary crafts room.) It might have been because I still kept Richard's old baseball motif sheets and comforter on the bed.

"Grandma, who's the old lady you're so worried about?"

I explained who Sofia was, trying at the same time to remind myself why it was I couldn't let the case go. I felt sorry for Dolores, and Sofia, after all, was one of my students. Someone who had recognized my pain at one time and had responded to it with great compassion. Maybe those were reasons enough to do what I could.

Maddie's (reading my mind?) last words before falling off to sleep: "Can't wait till tomorrow, Grandma. When we can collect some clues."

I smiled. Not that I'd actually investigate. But I did have class tomorrow at the Mary Todd, and it would hardly be my fault if talk of the murder and Sofia's pending arrest came up among her crafter friends.

Back in the living room, still wired from the intense (I was easy to excite) evening, I straightened up from the party. June (as always, a helpful guest) had done most of the dishes and Beverly had seen to her usual task of wrapping leftovers. All that remained for me to do was put away a few things and collect the trash — the tissue and assorted ribbons from the Christmas ornament exchange.

Among the papers was a crumpled envelope. I remembered seeing Maddie pull one of her ornaments out of it. Something about it looked familiar. I smoothed it out. The logo in the corner read: STANFORD MEDI-

CAL CENTER. A red shield dominated the image, with the staff of Asclepius pictured on the right side. I'd come to dread that logo, associating the world-famous center only with Ken's illness and his many months of treatments there.

The envelope was addressed to Richard. My heart skipped. What was wrong with my son? Had he been to Stanford without telling me? Not to worry me. It wasn't working. I took a breath and calmed down. Richard was a surgeon. Of course he'd have dealings with Stanford.

There was nothing to worry about.

I fell asleep dreaming up ways of asking Richard why he was communicating with that awful red logo.

CHAPTER 7

I had bad news for Maddie at breakfast on Friday morning. She took it even worse than I expected, reverting to behavior unbecoming a ten-year-old.

"How about a visit to Willie's for bagels?" I'd started out trying to put a positive spin on my plans.

"Sure," she'd said, before she realized she'd be visiting Willie's without me, while I kept my appointment at the police station. Then, "Nuh-uh. I don't think so."

"Or maybe you'd rather go to Rosie's bookstore. You know how much Mrs. Norman looks forward to your visits. She'll be happy to keep an eye on you."

"No, please, Grandma. You can't leave me. Last time you left me at Mrs. Norman's bookstore I missed everything." She kicked her skinny legs under the table. "You have to take me to Uncle Skip's office. You have to."

"You can take your books and sit in the back of the store, or Mrs. Norman might even let you help out at the register."

Maddie bit her lip and shook her head. "Nuts," she said (her favorite expletive of the last year).

I tried another tack. "It's better this way. Uncle Skip might not tell me everything if you're there, and this way I'll tell you the whole story when I pick you up."

More wailing. I hated to disappoint her on the first day of her visit. I was keeping her not only from an uncle she adored, but from fulfilling her Nancy Drew–like dreams. We were at a stalemate. I finished my second cup of coffee across the table from her, while Maddie fumed. She had her arms across her chest and as deep a frown as a child could make.

After what seemed like an hour, but was more likely two minutes, her face relaxed.

"I have an idea," she said, after spooning cold cereal (with milk, thanks to a morning run by the lovely June) into her mouth. She probably figured eating her nutritious breakfast would help in the negotiation I was sure was on the way. "I can go to the broken room."

"The what?"

"You go to Uncle Skip's office, and I can

wait in the broken room where the cops have coffee and doughnuts and a big refrigerator with sodas. And juice." The latter was added for effect.

Ah, the break room. Hmmm.

"And you would just stay in that room and not complain?"

"Uh-huh."

I thought a minute. What was she up to? "And you wouldn't try to sneak out to find us?"

She screwed up her mouth. No doubt sneaking out had been part of her plan.

"Where's the little redheaded squirt?" Skip asked.

"Right in front of me, I could say."

"Touché." Skip pointed to a security monitor high in the corner of the room. "I thought I saw her come in the building with you."

Skip had changed cubicles since I'd last visited him at his place of business. This one seemed a little larger, but the partitions were no sturdier, the colors no less dull, and the noise level no lower.

"What a good detective you are. You'll see Maddie later. She's waiting in the broken room." (I explained the malapropism.)

"So did you come to ask my intentions

with June?"

I noticed a photo of June tacked on the flannel wall behind his desk, a candid with what looked like Lake Tahoe behind her.

I was happy he still kept the old family picture of his mother, Maddie, and me posted as well. It was a sign that my recent nagging hadn't completely destroyed our relationship. He even offered me the good chair, as usual, so all was well. Skip's father died when Skip was eleven years old. He'd become a second son to Ken and me, a brother to Richard. I adored him almost as much as Maddie did.

"Things must be desperate if you're willing to talk about your love life with me."

Skip laughed. "I really don't have a lot to tell you about this case."

"Have you interviewed Sofia?"

"Coming up today. I've heard from the guys who brought her in that she claims she just got out of jail and she doesn't want to go back. I don't know what that's all about, since she certainly doesn't have a record. I think she's gone around the bend, if you know what I mean."

I chose to ignore the slight to Sofia. "I just want to know if there's anything I can do to help."

"If 'helping' means proving the old lady's

innocent, don't bother."

"Have the results come in on the blood?"

"No, but it only makes sense. We know it's not hers, so who else's could it be? She had the opportunity, and we know the weapon was a piece of rusty rebar — one of those steel rods used to reinforce concrete. There's certainly enough of that lying around the trashy parking lot, so she had easy access to it."

"Do you have the rebar?"

"Yes, it weighs about five pounds, not a stretch for a strong, tall woman like Sofia. And did I mention that we also have a motive?"

I straightened up. "A motive?"

"They had a prior relationship. The vic and the old lady."

I let out an exasperated sigh at Skip's tone and language. What happened to my sensitive, wonderful nephew? I wondered. Had making detective hardened him? Was there some wisecracking test he'd had to pass or an insulting jargon list he'd had to master to get his new shield?

"Sofia. The old lady's name is Sofia Muniz," I said. "And the vic is Carl Tirado, a once-living man. And of course there was a prior relationship. He sometimes worked as a gardener in the home where she lived.

Where there are hundreds of other residents and employees." I made a mental note to check those numbers with Linda. But surely there were *a lot* of others inside and outside of the rambling Mary Todd property. "And didn't he also live in the old neighborhood at Nolin Creek?"

My tirade seemed to have no effect, positive or negative, on my nephew. "Maybe the old guy, uh, Carl, attacked the señora in some kind of drunken stupor and she fought back and accidentally killed him. Can't say more right now," he said.

"I might as well have brought Maddie in," I grumbled.

"Unless you happen to have more ginger cookies." He reached down to my partially open tote and pulled on the bit of plastic poking out. Up came a bag of ginger cookies. "Well, well, were you holding these hostage?"

I smiled. "What are they worth to you?" I didn't think it necessary to tell him he'd have gotten them anyway. (My granddaughter's negotiating skills were rubbing off.)

"There might . . . I emphasize might . . . be something you can do when we start interviewing the Mary Todd residents, probably later today. If we need a translator. You might, you know, relate to them better."

"Meaning I'm an old lady, too?" I fluffed my hair. Maybe I should reconsider my hairdresser's suggestion to "play down" the emerging strands of gray.

Skip blushed. "No . . ." He'd already eaten one cookie and started in on another. "These are even better than usual, Aunt Gerry. You're the best —"

"I know. I'm the best baker you know. By the way, if you want to be in a casual setting with about eight old people this morning, you can come to my crafts workshop at ten thirty."

Skip's turn to straighten up. "At the Mary Todd?"

I nodded. "The one and only. We'll even give you an apron so you don't mess up your new suit."

Another blush. My "cool" nephew was self-conscious about the more professional dress required of him as a detective. His new, more mature wardrobe, which included sports jackets and ties, gave his mother and me a whole new source of gift ideas (and teasing).

I gave him an affectionate pat on the shoulder and shook the jingle bells hanging from a pushpin on his bulletin board. "Now come and say hi to your little cousin once removed."

"I'll never learn that organization chart of family relationships. I like it when she just calls me Uncle Skip."

"Whatever she calls you, she thinks you walk on water."

Maddie hardly needed another person in her queenly court in the broken room. A swarm of officers, male and female, was doting on her. She had a can of soda (at nine thirty in the morning!) in one hand and sleigh-shaped cookie in the other. There went any promise of a healthy diet at Grandma's.

At the moment Skip and I walked in Maddie was ending a presentation, between mouthfuls of junk food and drink, on Father Junipero Serra's first mission in San Diego, a project she'd tackled for her history class.

"What's it like living in Los Angeles?" a uniformed female officer asked her, as if L.A. were an exotic land, one to which she couldn't fly in just over an hour. From the way the policewoman glanced at Skip, I got the feeling she had ulterior motives in being so interested in this ten-year-old with a visitor's badge. Maddie wasn't picky about who lavished attention on her, or why, however. She pulled a photo of herself, one we'd seen last night, out of her sweatshirt pocket.

"Look what happened to me in L.A.," Maddie said. In the photo, her body was half stuffed into a giant shark, only her little derriere and long legs hanging out between the rows of enormous, pointy teeth. The officers passed the photo around.

"Whoa," another female officer said. "That looks scary."

"What's that eating you up?" Skip asked, grabbing her by the waist (he'd done this last night also, and the move was a big hit) as if he himself were a shark.

Maddie laughed uncontrollably, still the innocent little girl. I knew it couldn't last much longer and I certainly didn't want to hold her back, but it was very nice to have her this way.

"It's Jaws the Shark eating me up. It's just fake!" she told her fans. "My mom and dad took me and my friend, Devyn, to Universal Studios."

To my amazement, the officers applauded. I heard one say, "We'd better get back to work, Maddie, but come and see us again, okay?" As if there were any chance she wouldn't.

When I heard the Jaws story last night I'd been slightly horrified at the thought that

Maddie might have seen a movie about a man- (little-girl-) eating shark.

"Nuh-uh. I didn't see the movie," she'd said. "Mom says it's too gory. But lots of kids in my class saw it. And I know the whole story anyway."

Nothing I could do about that. I had to count on Mary Lou's having filled Maddie's suitcase with age-appropriate videos so Grandma wouldn't make a mistake.

Once I dragged Maddie away from her adoring fans in uniform, we set out on foot for our delivery to Sadie's Ice Cream Shop. Maddie insisted she could be trusted to carry Susan Giles's model soda fountain. I agreed, conditionally. We'd have to pack the room box into a tote with handles and she'd have to leave her backpack in the car.

"Deal," she said. Once again, I pictured a plaque on her desk in about twenty years: "Madeline Porter, Esq." or whatever female lawyers used after their names.

"Take Me Out to the Ballgame" rang through my purse as we walked down Springfield Boulevard.

"You've got to change this tune, Maddie," I said, flipping open my cell phone. "Or teach me how. I'd like one of Beethoven's

111

sonatas. Or a Dean Martin tune."

Maddie looked confused by both names, then shrugged her shoulders and smiled, hoping to fulfill my request at a time when she could make a deal, I suspected.

I clicked the button to take the call, walking and talking. My cell phone skills were increasing by the day.

"Geraldine, you'll never guess. Apparently Sofia had an excellent motive for killing Carl." This was Linda on the line, having moved, I noticed, toward the LPPD theory: Sofia was presumed guilty. "She knew him."

I started in on my "of course she knew the gardener" routine, then stopped. Something about Linda's emphasis on the word "knew" gave me second thoughts. "How well did she know him?"

"It's fascinating, Gerry. I see why you're so into detective work."

"Linda? The story?"

I pictured her in the nurses' lounge at the Mary Todd, a soda and a bag of chips in front of her. Maybe it was the crunching sound that gave it away. "It turns out Carl was the coyote who was supposed to bring Dolores's fiancé across the border to San Diego."

Coyote. Not the four-legged prairie wolf, but the dreaded mercenaries who preyed upon people who would do anything, give all they had, to enter the United States.

Maddie and I entered an empty bus shelter so I could sit for this briefing. "When was this?"

Maddie attached her iPod to her head and moved her body to some inaudible tune.

"Years ago," Linda said. (Crunch, crunch.) "Dolores was pregnant with her daughter when she and Sofia crossed. Ernesto stayed behind and was supposed to be on the next truck, or whatever, but Carl — his real name is Carlos Guzman — took Ernesto's money and it was an especially full truck, like the freight-car kind with no ventilation, and Ernesto died. I'm not sure how."

"Leaving Dolores an unmarried mother."

"Uh-huh. Apparently Sofia never forgave Carlos for making her only great-grandchild a bastard."

Did they even use that term these days? Even if the term was obsolete, I could believe that it mattered a lot to Sofia's generation and culture.

"How did all this come out?"

"An anonymous tip to the police. So, what do you think, Gerry?"

If Sofia knew the gardener, then so did Dolores. Funny that she didn't mention it. I remembered asking her that question specifically.

"Fascinating, as you said, Linda."

"There's something else, Gerry." Linda paused. I waited her out, not to confirm her pegging me as a nosy would-be detective. "It's personal. About Jason."

Uh-oh. Back to juvenile detention behavior? Linda's son Jason had spent a lot of his fifteen years in custody, on charges of petty theft, assault, and other mischief, but I thought he'd turned that around. "What about Jason?"

"He's flunking English. I was wondering if you could maybe help him?"

Whew. Much as I would like it to be, flunking English was not a crime. But happy and eager tutor though I was, I believed the best situation involved "strangers," not close friends. Or the son of a close friend. Too many opportunities for embarrassment, bad feelings if it didn't work, and general discomfort. I explained this to Linda, gently and reasonably, I thought.

"Well, isn't that just like you, Gerry. You'll help any stranger that knocks on your door, but when it comes to me or my son, you just don't have time."

"I didn't say anything about not having time, Linda. I'll take Jason to lunch or to the movies if you want. I'll even go to his basketball games." I hoped this would not be required. I didn't even like going to Maddie's games. "I just don't think tutoring someone I feel so close to would work. I can recommend any number of excellent people for him. He needs someone objective and professional, not someone who likes him too much to discipline —"

"He doesn't need discipline. He needs help writing essays. I'm sorry I asked."

With that, Linda hung up.

I knew she'd think about what I said and hopefully come around. She usually did when similar incidents had occurred. I wished I could learn to communicate with Linda more effectively. I heard Ken's voice at the back of my head, telling me that these were no-win situations with Linda, that she was always ready to be the victim.

Still, it bothered me to think I'd hurt a friend. And, to be truthful, that I may have lost a source of inside information for this case that I was not investigating. In some ways, Linda's vantage point as an employee of the Mary Todd was more valuable to me than Skip's. If I cared, that is.

It also bothered me that Dolores hadn't been completely honest with me about Sofia and Carlos. I knew about the Munizes' San Diego roots and I suppose I could have guessed that at least Sofia had been born in Mexico and transported somehow. Dolores wouldn't be able to have her job at city hall if she weren't a citizen, natural or otherwise, and Ernestine, being born here, was automatically a citizen. I wondered about Sofia's status.

I decided to let the information sit for a while and see what developed. If nothing else, Dolores's lying to me gave me a good reason to bow out of this case.

I had a granddaughter to entertain and a holiday to celebrate. I tugged at Maddie's arm (she was in an iPod trance) and we resumed our walk down the garland-laden streets.

In the twenty-four hours since I'd driven Dolores on her quest to find Sofia, nearly all the businesses along Springfield Boulevard had sprouted miniature scenes. I could identify many of them even before reading the labels. I pointed out to Maddie a miniature bookshop in the window of Rosie Norman's real-life bookstore. Its creator, Karen Striker, had represented a storefront with books displayed behind a small plastic sheet serving as a window and crates of "sale books" out front. She'd used titles of Victorian classics and strung garlands across the scene. Bits of "snow" marked the corners of the plastic "windows."

Maddie's favorite touch was the snowfall that had apparently hit Rosie's while we weren't looking. "Do you think we'll ever have a white Christmas, Grandma?"

"Probably not in L.A. or Lincoln Point, sweetheart, but maybe some year we can all go to the mountains."

"Next year, okay?"

"We'll see what your parents say."

A huff and a puff. "That's all I ever get. Mom says, 'We'll see what Dad says,' and Dad says, 'We'll see what Mom says,' and now you're saying —"

"It's tough being ten, isn't it?" I tapped her just above the waist where she was most ticklish.

She giggled herself out of her short-lived funk and we were able to move on.

Gail Musgrave, a newly elected Lincoln Point councilwoman, had managed to find time for a small scene for the card shop. She'd started with a normal-size Christmas card with a glittery spruce printed on it. She'd stiffened the card so that it could stand up on a small piece of carpet (red fabric with a felt-tip pen design). In front of the card tree Gail had piled colorfully wrapped presents of all sizes. Also a miniature bicycle and a toy train. Simple, but effective.

I hoped next year some of my seniors from the Mary Todd would have contributions for the town's decorations.

Speaking of which, "We'd better cross over to Sadie's and drop off this fountain," I told Maddie. "We have to be at the Mary Todd at ten thirty."

"Does that mean no time for ice cream?"

"That means it's too early for ice cream."

"So we can come back for lunch."

"My plan exactly."

Maddie and I weren't the only early birds to Sadie's Ice Cream Shop. Steve Talley, Dolores's nemesis, was laying out colorful flyers on the counter while Sadie's daughter-in-law and hired help, Colleen, made a shake for him. In his expensive-looking suit and overcoat, he didn't look as embarrassed as I would have, if caught ordering dessert at this time of day. I remembered old Mr. Mooney saying, "I never drink before noon, but it's always noon somewhere." I guessed it was always ice cream time somewhere, too.

"Glad I ran into you, Geraldine," Steve

said, handing me one of his flyers. I was tempted to check his eyes for pinpoint pupils but controlled my gaze. "I had these little FAQ sheets made up. Talley's Restoration Plan will be coming before the city council early in the new year, and he could use your support." He laughed, as if referring to himself in the third person was equivalent to the *New Yorker*'s cartoon of the week.

I took a flyer. "Very slick," I said, meaning both the multicolor printing job and Steve's manner. Steve had come to town only a couple of years ago, from a city somewhere between the Bronx and Lincoln Point, and had always dressed and acted much beyond his station as a city hall clerk. I found myself siding with Dolores on the matter of Talley's Restoration Plan on that basis alone, even before I knew much about the proposal. Not a very intelligent way to make choices, I realized, but that's what politicians counted on.

"Thanks, Steve," I said. "I've heard some negative comments about the plan. Does this sheet treat both pros and cons?"

"There's always going to be the naysayers out there. Right, Geraldine? But let me tell you" — he leaned into me. A secret between buddies — "this will be a feather in the cap of Lincoln Point, when we pull this off." He swept his hand toward the south. "Slums no more." He took my hand, pumped it up and down, made a tipping-the-hat gesture, and turned to leave.

"Don't forget your shake, Steve," Colleen said, winking at me.

Steve used his right hand to make a gun and shot Colleen with his index finger. He picked up his shake and was out the door.

I had a sudden burst of sympathy for Dolores Muniz and for the citizens of Lincoln Point.

"Don't you feel like taking a shower now?" Colleen asked me, rubbing her hands on her pink-and-white butcher-style apron. She was about Skip's age and a graduate student in political science. "When you have a minute, I'll be happy to give you the cons about the Talley plan."

"I'll take you up on that," I said.

"When she gets rid of me," Maddie said, putting her head in position for a hair-ruffling.

Maddie had been fussing with Susan's pint-size (literally) soda fountain. She'd wedged it between the napkin holder and the tip cup. I noticed she'd worked her magic on Colleen while I was bantering with Steve — she was now eating from a tiny tasting cup filled with strawberry ice cream.

"It's made with real fruit," Colleen said, a grin spreading over a face that was as Irish as her name.

With no cooperation from anyone in Lincoln Point, it was difficult indeed to watch over my granddaughter's diet.

On the way to the Mary Todd in the car, Maddie and I talked about how much Colleen loved the little soda fountain and what we might order for lunch after my crafts class: hot fudge sundae for Maddie, and for me the chocolate malt shake I'd been craving for a week.

I had another agenda item for this short trip with just the two of us, however. I tried to make it sound casual. "I happened to notice that envelope you used to keep one of the ornaments safe," I said to Maddie. "It was from the Stanford Medical Center. It's only a few miles from here, remember?"

"Uh-huh."

"Not that far from the shopping center we've been to."

"Uh-huh."

"What a coincidence."

"Uh-huh," she said yet again, looking through her backpack, emerging with a package of M&Ms.

"Does your dad do business with them?"

"I don't know. He gets letters from them sometimes." She gave me an embarrassed look. "I pulled that envelope out of the recycle trash in his office. It was clean, really."

"Oh, yes, I noticed how clean it was." I drummed my fingers on the steering wheel. I couldn't think of a way to probe further without alarming Maddie. I'd have to be patient and on the alert for another opportunity.

"Do you think Sadie will give you extra nuts today?" I asked her.

"Extra nuts and extra whipped cream. Yeah!"

She offered me the M&M bag. I took a couple thinking that chewing would use up some of my nervous energy.

What I wanted to ask Maddie: Does Daddy seem upset after he gets those letters from Stanford? Has he mentioned feeling ill?

I wondered if Richard had been roaming the state, going to different medical centers for tests or treatments for an unknown, life-threatening illness.

I knew he wouldn't want to worry me prematurely.

Too late.

CHAPTER 8

Maddie and I clocked into the lobby of the Mary Todd at ten thirty, according to the oversize timepiece on the wall at reception. The number of decorations seemed to have doubled in a day. Massive wrapped presents that I thought must be fake (that is, empty boxes) were spread out in front of the fireplace. Extra Christmas trees had sprouted on the end tables and bookcase shelves. A giant menorah competed with a red metal sleigh for the center of a large coffee table in an alcove. I expected Santa any minute.

Linda met us at the desk and offered Maddie an alternative to sitting with octogenarians for an hour and a half.

"I can take you to the employee lounge. There's a vending machine, and also a TV and VCR," Linda told Maddie. "And a bunch of videos for when staff members have to bring their kids to work."

I took her indulgence toward my grand-daughter to mean that she was sorry she'd hung up on me during our disagreement over tutoring Jason. This was her pattern: never apologize for poor behavior, simply make up for it another way. If only I could figure out what to do next. Tactic number one, pretend Linda had never told me her son was flunking English (then she might never bring it up again, either); or, tactic number two, bring it up and give her a list of tutors I'd recommend (in which case, she might hang up on me again or turn her back now).

I expect it was not the videos that swung Maddie toward the lounge, but rather that she foresaw another opportunity to hold court with attentive adults.

I arrived at the ground-floor classroom at ten thirty-five, more or less on time for my crafts session. A sign reminding the residents of the schedule had been duly posted on the door. I'd had no trouble last year convincing the coordinator of activities to add my favorite Mary Todd Lincoln quote to the sign: MY EVIL GENIUS, PROCRASTI-NATION, HAS WHISPERED ME TO TARRY 'TIL A MORE CONVENIENT SEASON. I didn't know the context in which Mrs. Lincoln used the sentence, but it seemed perfectly suited to inspire crafters to waste no more time getting to their projects.

I didn't think being five minutes late qualified as delinquent enough to have someone else take over the classroom, but there he was in my seat at the front of the room. Detective Eino (Skip) Gowen Jr. He must have left his office immediately and driven right past Maddie and me as we strolled up Springfield Boulevard on the way to Sadie's.

Worse, he'd already charmed the class members, as evidenced by indulgent looks from the women. Not too many cute, young, redheaded boys walked these halls, I suspected. I noticed Emma and Lizzie at the front table, having figured out which day of the week to expect a class. For my sake, I wished they wouldn't wear nearly matching housedresses, color their hair the same (ash blond) hue, wear rimless glasses from the same designer, and use identical hand gestures.

Sitting on a stool behind and to the left of Skip was a plump, fifty-something woman I didn't recognize. I squinted (producing a strange-looking smile, I was sure) as I passed her, the better to read her badge. On the lapel of her expensive-looking suit was a gold rectangle with black lettering: NADINE

HAWKES, FINANCIAL MANAGER. A tiny cameo of Mary Todd Lincoln — a widely known photo, and the home's logo — graced the corner of the rectangle.

I thought "financial manager" was a somewhat high rank to be attending this crafts class–cum–interview session. Was "escorting" a police detective a plum assignment? I'd have to ask Linda later.

Gertie, the knitter, and a few drop-ins whose names I didn't know (except for my new friend, Sandy Sechrest) had all raised their hands and were talking over each other.

"I knew her well."

"I knew her better."

"I was here when she joined us."

I presumed this was in response to a question from Skip about who knew Sofia Muniz. Even Mr. Mooney, who always pretended *not* to be paying attention (maybe in his day only girls were obedient students?), had his good ear turned in Skip's direction.

"We sat together in the theater sometimes," he said. "And I've been to her suite." I wondered if the Wandering Irishman had simply drifted into Sofia's room.

The classroom was abuzz with side comments on the visit of the young policeman. What happened to interviewing suspects

127

and witnesses separately? I wondered. I anticipated Skip's explanation — that with a group like this, where there were most likely no suspects among them, but only innocent witnesses and many contradictory views, there was a better chance of getting to the "truth" in a communal setting.

"And here's your instructor," Skip said, with a grand gesture toward his aunt, now occupying a seat at a front table. "I don't want to interfere with your class, Mrs. Porter, but it would help our investigation if I could have a few more minutes." He addressed this plea (using his most Cary Grant–like voice) to me. I was more annoyed than the occasion called for that Skip hadn't waited for me to begin his interview. I knew most students showed up at least ten or fifteen minutes early, so, I calculated, he'd already had about twenty minutes with them.

But what could I say? I didn't want to be charged with lack of cooperation with the LPPD. I gave the detective a warm smile. "Certainly, Detective Gowen," I said. "Take all the time you need." A worried look crossed his face as he saw me opening my notebook. I clicked on my pen and smiled.

"So, try to think back a few days or even a week," said Cary Grant (everyone in the room except Skip would know who Cary Grant was). "Did anyone notice Mrs. Muniz behaving any differently lately?"

Hands shot up again. Ms. Hawkes shifted her body on the stool nervously. Maybe she was worried that her residents would say something embarrassing to the management. Or maybe her chubby body was uncomfortable on the backless stool.

"She talked about her baby great-granddaughter and how awful it was she had no father." (I knew Sofia had only one great-granddaughter, Ernestine, who was no baby.)

"She missed Nolin Creek Pines more than ever." (I knew this.)

"She had a fight with the gardener." (Really?)

"Is the gardener who was killed the one she had the fight with?" Skip asked, smooth as silk.

"Yes, Carl Tirado. She had a fight with him yesterday."

"No, the fight was with her own granddaughter." (Over what?)

"No, no, the fight was with Gus Boudette, our van driver."

Ms. Hawkes frowned at that, clearly more comfortable with personal comments about Sofia, as opposed to observations related to her institution.

"She got mad at the cook. She said he made a poor excuse for a quesadilla. He spelled it wrong on the menus and used American cheese."

In the background, Ms. Hawkes grimaced, as if criticism of the Mary Todd cook was more distasteful than a murdered gardener.

The non sequiturs followed (so to speak) quickly.

"I've been here since the residence opened and nothing like this has ever happened."

"It's only been open three years."

"So we should expect a resident will commit a murder every three years?"

I stopped taking notes.

Skip thanked the group and promised to visit again soon (hardly, I thought).

Ms. Hawkes stepped down from her stool perch, straightened to her full five feet nine inches (I guessed, but about my height at any rate), and adjusted her skirt, too tight for her wide hips and thighs. Her man-style haircut, with almost no extra strands to "bounce," made her a formidable sight. "Thank you, Detective Gowen. We hope this investigation will be over soon and we can all go back to the peace and comfort we've come to expect from Mary Todd living. We know you and all the good men and women of the Lincoln Point Police Department are working very hard to put an end to this distressing situation."

"Distressing to whom?" I muttered, inaudibly I hoped. Ms. Hawkes, with her thick lips, sounded more concerned about the image of the Mary Todd than about her residents who might be upset at the situation. Or for possibly another member of the Lincoln Point community who was a murderer.

It struck home to me that the murderer might indeed be a resident or a staff member at the Nancy Hanks or even the Mary Todd. If I had to say, I'd guess I'd been picturing a lowlife who crossed into Lincoln Point from San Jose. I pictured this drifter murdering Carlos Guzman for no reason and taking advantage of a wandering senior citizen by smearing her with blood to frame her. It made sense to me. I wondered what Ms. Hawkes's theory of the case was. I thought I knew Skip's, regrettably.

Skip shuffled his feet, his little "tell" that he was eager to leave.

Ms. Hawkes opened her arms to the group. "Ladies and gentlemen" — she nodded toward Mr. Mooney — "thank you all for your cooperation this morning. Please feel free to contact my office if you have any questions whatsoever. Now we'll send the nice police officer back to work and let Mrs. Porter have her arts-and-crafts time."

By then I was so aggravated by her condescending tone to the crafters, the police department, and me, that I wanted to make a little round Play-Doh model of her and dunk it into a swimming pool (easily constructed using the kidney-shaped pans that were ubiquitous in hospitals).

I saw Skip head for the door and bumped (only slightly) into Ms. Hawkes's curvy body as I hurried to catch up with my slippery nephew. "Not so fast, Skip. Why did you start without me?" I whispered. "You used my information that they'd all be here together and then you didn't include me."

"That's what cops do," he said. If he hadn't leaned over and given me a kiss — "Love you, Auntie," he added — I might have stayed angry with him.

I looked back into the classroom. Ms. Hawkes had left. Some of the more enterprising students had become immediately engrossed in measuring, cutting, painting, or gluing. Others continued talking.

I considered how to proceed. My usual format was to present a "tip" at the beginning of each class and then wander among the tables helping each participant as best I could. I decided to forgo the tip today and work the room. I tied my heavily loaded crafts apron around my waist and approached the first table.

Of course Emma and Lizzie were working on similar projects, which were more like scrapbooking (for their grandchildren, who probably looked as much alike as they did) than miniatures. I wondered why they didn't just sign up for the straight scrapbooking class on Mondays, but maybe that was the day they did twin calisthenics. Mostly, Emma and Lizzie sat side by side arranging photos, tasseled programs, and ragged ticket stubs on typical oversize scrapbook pages. I was able to help with the occasional three-dimensional value-added item, like a piece of fabric made into a prom dress, or a scrap of leather fashioned into a suitcase for the "trips we have taken" page.

"I miss Sofia, don't you?" I said to Lizzie and Emma.

They both nodded. "Lizzie saw her that night" (aha, it must have been Emma speaking). Between focusing on a way to remember who was who (the one addressed as Lizzie had a bigger nose) and wanting to know more about Sofia's last evening before the murder, I felt a headache coming on. I persevered.

"Where did you see Sofia, Lizzie?" I asked.

"In the garden." That much I knew. "It was very late." More interesting.

"Was she talking to anyone?"

"Her granddaughter," Emma said. "They were arguing."

This is no use, I thought. Dolores hadn't seen her grandmother that night; she'd simply called her at seven thirty to say good night. I offered the women a suggestion for making tiny paper flowers into a model corsage (a la 1940s proms) and moved on to Mr. Mooney. Maybe the Wandering Irishman, Sofia's movie partner, had some juicy tidbits about her activities this past week.

Mr. Mooney had the most intricate and finely crafted project. His nearly bald head was bent over the half-scale (one-half inch equals one foot) schoolroom he was building for his great-granddaughter who taught third grade in rural Kentucky. The tiny wooden desks were stained to look old and worn. They were the old-fashioned combination school furniture, with desk and pew-type chair attached by a metal bar that sat on the floor. The "legs" holding up the desk and chair were painted to look like ornate metal supports. A potbellied stove graced the corner of the room; stencil-shaped alphabet letters were arranged across the top of a blackboard made of black construction paper. Here and there names and initials were carved into the tops of the desks. I knew the elaborate *Jane* was for his great-granddaughter. A heart surrounded a pair of initials: JM + LF. James Mooney and . . . ? I imagined a lovely young Laura or Lucy, possibly JM's wife of many years.

I often wished I could be in the room to see the delighted expressions when my crafters presented their finished products to their family members.

Linda, an excellent craftswoman herself, usually stopped by to admire Mr. Mooney's work. And to pick up some tips for her own projects. Not today, however. I hoped it was because she was busy gathering intelligence for me or checking on Maddie, and not because she wasn't ready to face me over the tutoring Jason issue.

"I'll bet Ethel Hudson is the one who knows it all," Mr. Mooney whispered to me.

I bent over to hear him better. "Excuse me?"

"Ask them about Ethel Hudson. She's probably on vacation, but she lives in a special room. She gets checks from the bank all the time. I think she's the one who can tell you anything you want to know about Sofia Muniz or anyone else."

135

"Thank you, Mr. Mooney," I said, scratching my head with a plastic scorer.

Ethel Hudson was not a name I'd ever heard, but my association with the staff and residents of Mary Todd was limited to Linda Reed and the people who took my classes. I filed the name under "miscellaneous."

At the back table, struggling with a small block of wood and a much-too-large paintbrush was Sandy Sechrest, the woman in the flat next to Sofia's. I'd never seen her in class before. In front of her was an old-style metal box of paints, like the kind I had in first grade (probably now issued to bright two-year-olds). Its little circles of primary colors were mostly caked dry. When I approached her she looked up at me and frowned. The expression could have related to the person who had given her inferior supplies, but I suspected it also had to do with her unhappy experience with me yesterday.

I decided to start out on a first-name basis.

"Can I help you with that, Sandy?" I asked. "I'm Geraldine. I was with Sofia's granddaughter, Dolores, yesterday."

"I know who you are. I'm old, but I'm not crazy."

"I'm sure you're not, Sandy. I was surprised you didn't have anything to say to the police officer who was here." (A little stretch of the truth couldn't hurt.)

"Why should I? No one believes me. You didn't believe what I told you."

"Why don't you tell me again?"

She sighed and focused on her unwieldy paintbrush.

"I promise to listen very carefully this time," I said.

Another sigh, this one her own form of condescension. "I saw them take Sofia to jail in the van. It was light brown and had bars on it."

Yesterday it was a yellow bus. Another dead end? Unfortunately, yes. I reached into my apron pocket and pulled out a thin brush and a bottle of wood paint.

"These might work better for you, Sandy. What are you making?"

Sandy stood up, not happy. She'd seen through to my disbelief. She put her wet child's paintbrush in the box and banged it shut. She was out the door in a flash, leaving behind a pitiful block of wood streaked with bloodred paint.

I was angry with myself for my insensitivity, obviously insulting a well-meaning old woman. I was no better than Financial Manager Hawkes. Sandy had come for companionship, most likely, and was willing to share her information and I'd been patronizing. I'd probably never see her in class again. I groaned at the thought that I'd given miniaturists a bad name.

Linda came by with Maddie about twenty minutes after noon, just as I finished cleaning up the room. Mary Todd seniors were a neat group, but there was always a wayward strip of glue dots or a pair of scissors or a sliver of nude wood to pick up.

"I can take my lunch break now," Linda said. "Do you want to eat here with me?"

All was well between us, I assumed, gratefully.

I felt more than heard Maddie's moan. I knew she was comparing Sadie's Ice Cream Shop on the one hand, with institutional boiled beef with carrots and mashed potatoes on the other.

"We had plans —" I started.

"Oh, not in the employee cafeteria," Linda said, guessing one reason for our reluctance. "Now that I'm full time, I get to use the main dining room twice a month, with up to four guests." She seemed to stand straighter as she threw back her shoulders. "And it's free." I had another surge of delight at Linda's newfound good fortune, which had been a long time coming. So what if she had a lapse into ill temper now and then. "It has a terrific menu and a great chef. We're even listed in the Lincoln Point tour guide."

The generously labeled "tour guide" was a four-page black-and-white booklet listing "what to do in Lincoln Point." It included the grand ball in honor of Mary Todd, should a visitor happen to be passing through on or about December 13. The listing was hardly competition for similar literature from the big cities close by, and certainly none for Steve Talley's pro-only brochure describing his grand plan for the town.

But Linda was right about the food. I'd eaten in the Mary Todd dining room as a guest of the management while they were setting up and interviewing for instructors for classes. I could attest to the fact that it was run like a fine restaurant (never mind one resident's comment on their quesadilla recipe).

"Do they still serve Sadie's ice cream for dessert?" I asked Linda, glancing at Maddie.

"Uh-huh. There's a sundae bar with ice cream and sauces from Sadie's."

That perked Maddie up a bit. "If we eat here, will you tell us the news on the case,

Mrs. Reed?" she asked. I wondered if she even knew what the phrase "the case" meant. Either way, it didn't keep her from negotiating again. She turned to me and reported, "Mrs. Reed wouldn't say anything about it to me until you were around."

I shot Linda a grateful look.

So far Maddie had gotten only my standard granddaughter talk about the Sofia Muniz case: every now and then bad people do things that aren't right and other people are hurt. Meaningless, but it was my way of trying to protect Maddie from nasty words (like "murder" and "bloody corpse") and nasty deeds (like shooting, stabbing, and slashing). And from a world that was nasty now and then, I mused.

It wasn't like Linda to use language unfit for a minor, but I wanted to set the stage anyway.

"Is this about the details of the event in that parking lot?" I asked her. Sometimes obfuscation came in handy.

"Yes, but it has to do with finances, not . . . uh, biology." Linda wasn't as good as I was at obfuscating, but she did pretty well.

"Sweet," Maddie said, with a grin at once mischievous and wise.

I tried to shut the image of her parents

out of my mind. After lunch and for the rest of the week, Maddie and I would do only fun, granddaughterly things, I told myself.

CHAPTER 9

The Mary Todd dining room had the same soft rosy hue as the building's hallways and small lounges. And the same plethora of interdenominational decorations. Looking down from the reception area of the third-floor restaurant, I admired the courtyard, with its stone fountain, manicured gardens, and groupings of outdoor tables and chairs. At this hour the dining room was crowded, but thanks to the plush carpeting and upholstered walls, the room seemed hushed.

As we passed a table of crafters on the way to our own table, Mr. Mooney and two women waved a greeting. Mrs. Sechrest turned her head away from me. I felt bad, but I could hardly blame her.

Service was excellent, and within a few minutes of ordering from a diverse menu we were treated to beautifully presented entrees. Grilled fish for Linda and me, and a hamburger (not fast food, I reasoned, when it was served with linen napkins and fine silver) for Maddie. Linda had spent a good deal of time praising the Mary Todd, its lovely surroundings, and its excellent employee benefits package.

"I can finally have Jason on my health insurance instead of depending on you-know-who."

The mystery man, I knew, was Linda's first ex-husband, a rather self-important professor with a penchant for his young coeds. In Peter's defense, however, he was neither the biological nor the adoptive father of Jason Reed, and had no real obligation to support him.

I made an attempt to send Maddie to the ice cream bar so Linda and I could talk freely about whatever news she claimed to have.

"Not again!" Maddie said. "You promised."

Rather than argue and spoil the ambience (Christmas music by the Mormon Tabernacle Choir, attentive waiters and waitresses) I moved to Plan B.

"Okay, Linda, you might as well start. You said you had information on the arrangements for living here?" I gave her a wink that I hoped she'd interpret correctly.

"Right," she said, with a nod that told me

she understood. "Well, first of all, the floor plans are all named after a Civil War battle or a general. For example, the Vicksburg is a studio apartment, about four hundred square feet, with an entrance deposit of one hundred thousand dollars, and three thousand a month in fees. The fees cover weekly housecleaning, two dining room meals a day, and utilities. Not cable though." Linda used her fingers to tick off amenities, pausing to wave to a woman with a silky red shawl and a fancy cane. "Access to the pool and fitness room and all educational programs. Like yours, Gerry. The Fort Blakely is the next size up, with a separate bedroom. You need two hundred and fifty thousand dollars to get in and then it's thirty-five hundred a month. Next is the Decatur —"

Maddie cut in. "I thought this was going to be about the case."

"It is, Maddie," I said. "I need to know all the details before I can figure out what happened to the woman who lives here."

Maddie pushed her lower lip forward. "It's like when you tell me I have to do all the boring parts of building a dollhouse, like gluing every single shingle" — here she flubbed the words and giggled — "not just the fun parts."

"Exactly." (Although I hadn't thought of that.)

"Anyway," Linda continued, "the Ulysses S. Grant is one of the largest floor plans, with two bedrooms and two bathrooms."

"May I be excused?" Maddie asked. "I'm ready for my dessert."

Linda handed her an ice cream ticket in case they were checking numbers today. "Employees get only one sundae per person," she said.

"Take your time, sweetheart, we'll just finish up this part," I said. For the first time since before she learned to walk, I felt I might have put one over on my granddaughter.

As soon as Maddie left the table, Linda, not usually given to physical displays of affection, put her hand on mine. "Gerry, I want you to know I'm sorry about, you know, getting on your case before. About Jason. I started thinking about it and I see what you mean. It's like a surgeon not operating on his own kid."

Everyone had good analogies today. And another breakthrough — this was indeed a new Linda.

"Don't think about it, Linda. In fact, I was thinking I should sort of interview Jason. I'll see what he's best at, and that way

I'll know whom to recommend. Or, who knows? Maybe we'll decide we can work together."

Linda clutched her prominent white-clad bosom. "Oh, Gerry, thanks. You're such a good friend."

"Good job on the catalog of rooms," I said. Then I had a thought. Maybe the boring descriptions inadvertently served a bigger purpose than getting rid of Maddie. "What's the most elaborate suite available, Linda?"

A confused look from Linda. "How did you know? That's what I want to tell you. Not only does Sofia Muniz live in the best suite available — two bedrooms, two bathrooms, thirteen hundred square feet — she got in under the Founders Program."

"Which is?"

She primped the sides of her many-shades-of-blond beehive. "Offered to the first fifty people who sign up when a new facility is opened. You know there's a conglomerate that owns, like, two dozen of these homes all through the state." I waited to hear what was exciting enough to merit the proud look on Linda's face. "First, I want you to know that I wasn't just being nosy, Gerry. I wanted to check on whether we had the old Nolin Creek Pines address for Sofia. Dolores was so sure she never gave it to us. Well, in the process, I discovered that Sofia should not have been in the Founders Program."

"Why not?"

"I'm not finished." Linda was back to her finger-ticking method. "They have all kinds of extra amenities and choices — carpeting, wallpaper, all that. Their escrow fees from that first entry payment are waived, and they get half of any increase in entrance fees of future residents."

"It sounds like they're shareholders."

"You know I don't understand Wall Street, Gerry, but yes, it's a pretty plum deal."

I glanced over at Maddie, who had stopped to talk to a table full of residents and young guests. Of course she'd stop, I thought, she's probably showing them her Jaws photo and making arrangements to use one of their tickets for an extra sundae. Maybe I should sic Maddie on Mrs. Sechrest, to smooth-talk her into forgiving me.

"Why do you say Sofia shouldn't have gotten the deal?"

"When people sign up, there's supposed to be a chronological list, then it's cut off right at fifty. But Sofia didn't arrive until after several others who were told they

147

missed the cutoff, like Mr. Mooney right over there, and a Mrs. Gillespie who is no longer with us."

Linda's tone indicated that Mrs. Gillespie didn't just move on to another facility.

"Maybe they dropped out, then signed up again?" I suggested.

"Nope. I was only part time then but I remember the fuss, and this one guy Mr. Lynch threatened to go to court. He demanded to see the records, with the dates. So they showed him the records, but Nadine — Ms. Hawkes. You met her today — she must have doctored the dates so it looked like Sofia signed up before a lot of other people, including Mr. Lynch."

"And you didn't say anything?"

"I didn't put it all together until I actually saw the papers today. And with my flimsy status at the time, I wouldn't have taken a chance anyway. What if I was wrong? But I don't think so."

"So Dolores may have used pull to move her mother to the front of the line? That's interesting, but do you think it matters in the long run, as far as this case is concerned?"

Linda brushed bread crumbs from her uniform. More exactly, she tugged at the top of her uniform shirt and shook the

148

crumbs off. "Dolores had a lot more than a little pull, Geraldine. She shelled out a lot of money, I mean *a lot* of money. Besides being in the first wave to sign up, it takes more than half a million up front to get into that program, plus the monthly fees are quite high for her size suite."

I looked around at the other diners. They were all nicely dressed, certainly better than we'd see at Bagels by Willie or most of the lunch places in town. The men were in cardigans or pullover sweaters, many with ties. The women wore makeup and had carefully crafted hairdos. But I didn't get the feeling I was at tea at the Waldorf on Park Avenue or dining with the Trumps at Lincoln Center. "Never mind Dolores and Sofia, how do any ordinary people afford this place?"

"They've all sold their big houses. And they're old, so their former residences were probably completely paid for. They use that as the entrance fee, and if there's not enough left over for monthly fees, then social security and pensions fill the gap. Think of it, Geraldine, if you sold your home, paid off what little must be left of your mortgage after all these years, you'd have enough money to plunk down on one of these units."

Nice as the Mary Todd was, I wasn't planning on leaving my home anytime soon. I was a very young fifty-five-plus, I told myself.

Linda's explanation made sense, however. The housing prices in California (maybe everywhere, but I knew only my region) were outrageous and most homeowners were sitting on a fortune. The idea that we would one day own a home worth more than a million dollars would have sent Ken and me into gales of laughter in our early days. But in fact a home smaller than ours in our Eichler neighborhood, with a tiny patch of yard space, recently sold for a million two. I'd come to appreciate Lincoln Point for what it offered: proximity to the industry and cultural activities of Silicon Valley, but with a small-town look and feel with a charm of its own. Apparently that cost a lot these days.

I thought back to the Muniz situation. "Dolores and Sofia didn't have a house to sell," I reminded Linda. "They moved into their first home, where Dolores still lives, from an apartment at Nolin Creek Pines. And I doubt that Sofia has a pension."

"Uh-huh," Linda said, pointing her fork at me, dripping lemon caper sauce onto her uniform. "So where did all that money

150

come from?"

It was a very good question.

It had already occurred to me fleetingly that Dolores's lifestyle was on the lavish side for a government employee, especially of a small town like Lincoln Point. She had a daughter in college also. Even at a state school, tuition wasn't trivial, and Ernestine was not a strong enough student to merit a scholarship. I'd figured Dolores was either very much in debt or one of those savvy people who could stretch a paycheck.

But now that I thought of it, the details of the financial investment Linda laid out for me took us well beyond maxed-out credit cards and into the realm of miracle worker. At the moment, however, I couldn't see how our talk of the money dealings between Dolores and the Mary Todd was anything but gossip, having no connection to Sofia's involvement (or not) in the gardener's murder.

"By the way," Linda said, "about that Nolin Creek Pines address? Dolores was right. She never gave us that information."

"Well, someone knew," I said. "Didn't the van go there directly to pick her up yesterday morning?"

Linda stared into a corner, up and to her right. Her thinking countenance. "I see what

151

you're saying, Gerry. How did Gus know where to go?"

How indeed?

Maddie was back. She'd joined another table to eat her sundaes, having given up on hearing anything interesting from Linda.

I thought I could cheer her up. "Let's go, sweetheart," I said. "We're going shopping for costumes for the ball."

"Nuts," she said.

I knew she didn't mean the kind she'd piled on her sundaes.

The string of stores that had stood along Springfield Boulevard for as long as I could remember apparently wasn't enough for the city council. In the past year the strip was expanded. Shops were added to the lot in back, producing an open mall effect, bordered by Springfield Boulevard to the west and Emancipation (no kidding) Boulevard to the east. So far, with our new city council, except for the fast-food giants, Lincoln Point had managed to keep most of the big chains at bay.

As we headed for one of the new businesses, Lori Leigh's Dress Shop, with Maddie buckled into the backseat, my intentions were to finally do something fun with her.

"Aunt Beverly is going to meet us at Lori Leigh's," I told her. "She needs a costume, too."

"Yeah. Maybe we can go to Sadie's together afterward."

"You just had two Sadie's sundaes."

"Did you see how small those dishes were? I never saw such tiny dessert dishes. They could go in our Bronx dollhouse."

After a few more rounds of critiquing Mary Todd dining, we entered Lori Leigh's shop. Like so many over-forty adults these days, Lori Leigh had been my student at Abraham Lincoln High School. We chatted a few minutes about her classmates and how business was going (very well during the holiday season) while Maddie wandered around the busy, festive store, fingering plastic icicles and tinsel.

Lori Leigh had added a special section for the ball, with both men's and women's Victorian (or close to it) clothing. When I caught up with Maddie, she was not impressed with the display. "Nuts," she said, a look of dismay on her face.

"I thought this would be fun," I said.

"You didn't tell me I had to dress up for this ball thing."

What had I been thinking? That Maddie would enjoy shopping for a Victorian outfit for the ball? Some part of my brain had clearly disengaged and gone back to the days when she was two years old and wore whatever Grandma put her in.

"What did you think a ball was like?"

"I thought it would be like our soccer banquet. Where the coach wears a tie but we all wear our jerseys."

I suppressed a smile. Maddie was not in a joking mood.

"Didn't I say 'costume ball'?"

"Costume means Halloween. I was thinking of that kind of costume. A witch or something. I guess I was confused."

Maddie's eyes darted around the store as if she had alighted in a foreign land and was looking for a way out. Which she was. "Couldn't I stay home tomorrow night? I could stay with June, or Mrs. Reed?"

"Everyone is going to be at the ball."

"Even Jason?"

Hmmm. I hadn't given that much thought. Though Linda's teenage son had begun to measure up to his responsibilities in the last few months, I couldn't quite picture him in Victorian attire. But if he was not going to the ball, I hardly thought his first choice would be babysitting (a term she hated) Maddie.

Maddie took a seat as far from the frilly

inventory as she could, at the front of the store. I cruised the racks listlessly, having lost my desire to try on cumbersome outfits.

When Beverly arrived, Maddie jumped up and began her plea anew. I stood by and watched.

"Wouldn't you rather do something else on Saturday night, Aunt Beverly?" she asked.

I was fairly sure that would be a dead end, since Beverly loved dressing up. She was always immaculately groomed, her short curly red hair in place, and she had a penchant for fancy hats. The ball was a perfect venue for her. With Maddie's negotiating skills, however, I feared for Beverly. I imagined the two of them sitting home on Saturday evening watching a hockey game with large dishes of ice cream on their laps while the rest of us ate a Victorian banquet of fish-flavored aspics and nectarine puddings.

That mental picture was shattered by my cell phone ring. I clicked it on. At the same time I poked Maddie and pointed to the phone. She laughed as "Take Me Out to the Ballgame" rang through Lori Leigh's Dress Shop.

I recognized Linda's caller ID. Though it was her dime (as we used to say) I started with my agenda and asked about Jason's plans for the weekend.

"We made a deal," she said. "He'll come to the ball if I take him driving every day for a month. He really wants his permit."

We were raising a generation of negotiators. "What's he wearing?"

"He's being very original. He's going as Abraham Lincoln. Do you think Lincoln was short and chubby as a kid?"

"I doubt it."

"I have a request," Linda said.

I glanced at Maddie and Beverly, who were engaged in intense conversation. "Sure, Linda. What is it?"

"Can I bring Jason by tonight? You know, you said you'd interview him."

So soon? I hadn't meant immediately, but I didn't dare suggest putting it off too long. "I'm looking forward to talking to him, Linda, but how about tomorrow morning instead? We'll start fresh."

"I'll take him by about ten. Thanks, Gerry!"

Linda sounded so relieved, as if she'd just been handed a ticket to Lourdes (the miracle site with healing waters, not my GED student). I was glad I'd acquiesced.

Time to face Maddie, who was sitting on the chair, her pretty little mouth all folded

156

up in tiny ridges, her skinny legs kicking wildly. Apparently Beverly had not been swayed by her charms.

Without warning, Maddie's lips formed a smile, her legs calmed down. She bounced off the chair and pointed to a mannequin above a circular rack. "That's it. There's my costume."

We left the shop a half hour later, ready for a ball. Beverly had the most elaborate hat I'd ever seen, one that would be a beacon for a large bird looking for a nest. I had settled on a red-and-green caroler's outfit, having been attracted to its shoulder-length cape and white fur-like muff.

As for Maddie — she was going to be our Little Drummer Boy.

Back home, after midafternoon snacking on cookies from my freezer, Maddie and I got to work on the Bronx apartment dollhouse. There were many more pressing things, like preparing the house for the arrival of her parents in less than a week. However, I'd never pass up a chance to do crafts instead of housework, especially when Maddie had a special request, starting with a history question.

"My dad was born in the Bronx, wasn't he?" Maddie asked me.

"Yes, at Fordham Hospital, remember? We drove around there a few years ago with Grandpa and pointed it out to you."

"Uh-huh. So you and Grandpa brought him home to the apartment we're making?"

"That's right." I placed my hand carefully in the dollhouse and rested my finger on a spot in the miniature bedroom, next to a yet-to-be-lacquered dresser. "We put his crib . . ." *Aha.* "You want to make a model of your dad's crib," I said.

Maddie smiled and nodded. "Could we?"

"That's a great idea," I said, blinking back a tear. She gave me a tight hug and the tear fell.

We sat at the workbench in my secondary crafts room (which soon needed to be an operating guest room) and searched through my scrap basket for fabric to spread on the bottom of the crib. We found several pieces of flannel with floral and other designs that were tiny and close together, suitable for a miniature crib pad.

Not good enough for Maddie, however. "Didn't you have sports things for a boy?" she asked. "I see them all the time when I have to go with my mom to get a baby gift. They're always in blue and they have, like, pink ribbons for girls."

There was that freckled nose again, screwed up, at the idea of pink. "Maybe your mom and dad put a sports-theme pad in your crib by mistake and that's why you're such a great T-ball player," I said.

"Soccer," Maddie said, missing my humor. "The little kids play T-ball."

"Sorry. Let's do another part of the crib and tomorrow we can shop for the kind of fabric you want."

"The bars. We can do the bars," Maddie said.

She pulled a box of nude wood pieces toward her and found a bag of three-inch rods with a sixteenth-inch diameter. We decided we'd need sixteen rods, eight for each side of the crib, and two solid panels for the head and foot.

"We're almost done," Maddie said.

"If we want this to look real, we'll have to paint the wood," I said.

"Oh yeah," she said, not thrilled.

I'd already discerned the kind of crafter Maddie would be: my kind, always looking for a quick and easy fix. A can of spray paint instead of a small brush and a set of bottles and tubes of acrylics. A pinked edge on a blanket instead of a neatly faced hem. I should really have Linda train Maddie, I thought. Linda didn't own spray paint and

159

would have fashioned tiny wheels for the crib instead of slapping beads on the ends of the legs.

Here was my chance to set a good example. "Your dad's crib was kind of yellowy beige," I said. "We can mix yellow and brown until we get it close to the real thing."

Maddie took a breath that amounted to rolling up her sleeves and got to work. She covered the table with newspaper and set out the rods in a long row.

"It looks like a jail," she said.

I stood and looked down on the array. "Yes, it does."

I took another look, this time as one who was practiced in seeing things not as they are, but as they might be on a different scale. *What if this design were on a life-size van? It would look like a jail.*

CHAPTER 10

My dilemma: I needed Maddie's computer expertise, but I couldn't let her know exactly what we were doing. I didn't want to give her the idea that we were seriously engaged in an investigation that was better left to the police. She'd warmed too much to the idea of being a sleuth already, and I was enormously worried that she'd go off on her own and put herself in danger. How had Nancy Drew's grandmother (did she have one?) coped?

But I needed Maddie's help to get information from the World Wide Web. I'd long ago realized that many research activities were done more efficiently online, but that didn't mean I was at home with software beyond e-mail and the occasional business letter. The same was true for Beverly and Linda, so they'd be no help to me.

Sometimes I regretted not having mastered search engines or online shopping.

But I was confident that virtual shopping would never be the pleasant experience for me that it was to some. My legs and arms were too long for me to be able to buy clothing without trying it on; and between the library and Rosie Norman's bookstore, I could order in person any book I wanted (though they probably all went online to fill my request).

Certainly it would be less fun to order miniatures online than to browse in crafts stores. Or better yet, since my particular style called for a lot of improvisation with found objects, to keep my eyes on everyday throwaway items. How would I search on-line for leftover floor tiles (to use as bases for freestanding scenes) or scraps of wide ribbon (to fold over, stuff, and turn into a pillow)? Deep down, I knew that even if there were a way to search for such "junk," I'd still rather keep my eyes on the gutters as I walked around town.

The thought of approaching Skip with my van theory swept through my mind, but I had to have more than a fleeting idea before he'd listen (if then).

No way out. I needed Maddie. I toyed with the idea of making it a game. We could pretend to play "find the bars." No, she'd see through that. Or I could pretend I wanted her to give me a computer lesson. "Can you show me how to find a Lincoln Point business with bars on its company van?" I could ask. Too obvious. I might as well just plunge in, telling her as little as possible, but not making up a story.

"What a smart observation you made about the crib, sweetheart," I started. "These rods do look like the bars of a jail."

She moved the wooden rods closer together. "Even more now, huh?"

"Even more. You're right. It reminds me of something a friend of mine said about a van that looked like a jail. Is there a way to search on the computer to see if there's such a van in Lincoln Point or a city nearby?"

Maddie's eyebrows went up to the top of her red bangs. "Is this for the case?"

My landline phone rang before I could launch into a speech about law enforcement officers versus ordinary citizens. I picked up the phone.

"Hi, Mom. I'm calling to give a status report," my daughter-in-law Mary Lou said.

My heart skipped. "Is something wrong?" I asked her, the red Stanford Medical Center design looming large in my mind.

"Not at all." Mary Lou sounded understandably confused. She called often, so there was no cause to think this was an

163

emergency or bad news of any kind. "We're just starting to pack. Well, to think about packing, and I thought I'd give you a call. See what the weather is."

"The weather's great," I said. "Not lower than about fifty degrees. No more rain for a while." I cleared my throat. "How's everyone?"

"We're both fine. Busy. Rushing everywhere. You can't imagine what this house looks like. Wrapping paper and bows all over the floor. Packages everywhere. Half of them have to be shipped to the East Coast, the other half to be stuffed in the car for Lincoln Point. It's a good thing I like Christmas!"

"How's Richard handling it all?"

"Richard is out getting the car tuned, tires checked. You know the drill. His Porter trip rituals. We're actually looking forward to the drive. Richard needs to relax." Mary Lou laughed. "I'm going to put him in the backseat with a juice box like I used to do with Maddie."

Another jolt. "Is Richard sick?"

"No, just busy as usual. Really, Mom, what makes you think anyone's sick? Is Maddie okay?"

Great, now I've gotten Mary Lou worried, I thought. "No, no, she's fine, busy working

164

on our dollhouse apartment. It's just that sometimes I'm so focused on Maddie that I forget to check on how you two are doing." Not exactly true, but I hoped Mary Lou would buy it.

"Okay. Can't wait to see you! Fa-la-la-la-la and all!"

I tried a joyous laugh. "Same here. I'll put Maddie on."

I handed the phone over and took a deep breath.

It said something that Maddie was willing to forgo another snack break to get right to the computer. As we were waiting (Maddie said "forever") for my computer to boot up and connect to the Internet, I made some notes about what I was looking for.

Businesses with bars, I wrote, smiling at the image of liquor bottles lining a long shelf in front of a wall-length mirror.

I drew a line, then started a list.

Handlebars: a bike shop? I made a check mark next to the item. Lincoln Point had a bicycle shop in the new section of the strip mall.

I looked around the room, temporarily Maddie's. She kept it neater than her father had done, I noted, with her suitcase tucked inside the closet and her clothes on hangers. It helped that she no longer traveled with a troupe of stuffed animals. I was searching for vertical shapes and found them on the windows.

Vertical Blinds. I made another check mark. I knew the owner of a window-covering store on Springfield Boulevard.

I thought of and wrote, *car and truck grilles.* I hoped this was not it; that would eliminate no one over sixteen years old.

While I was laboring with pen and paper, Maddie had managed to fill my computer monitor with bar-shaped images.

"I got one hundred twenty-five thousand hits," she said. I checked the display. Bars everywhere. "I just used the image function and Googled 'vertical bars.' "

Yet another new verb, I thought, mentally conjugating. *I Google, you Google . . .* I could hardly wait to hear a noun, *Googliza-tion,* from someone.

I peered at the screen. There were lots of vertical bars on graphs, the kind used by newsmagazines where they try to make the national budget understandable to English teachers.

The images were varied and interesting: a room-divider screen made of thin bamboo bars (good idea for a modern miniature layout) and a white sports jersey with wide purple stripes. Also the *alticorpus* fish with vertical bars on its body, and a beautiful staircase that made me wish I had a two-story home.

Maddie scrolled past charts, more fish, and a rack of fishing poles (a possibility?). I had visions of sifting through one hundred and twenty-five thousand "hits" as Maddie called them. Until, finally, on virtual page five, a new set of images made sense: vertical bar fencing.

"Stop there, please," I said to Maddie, whose itchy, practiced fingers had been clicking through the pages. These images were of metal bar fencing, picket fences, and gates constructed of vinyl rods. The van's logo could have had an image of any of them and looked like the bars of a jail.

I thought about the Lincoln Point businesses I knew. No fence company that I could think of. It had been a while since I'd been in a home improvement store. Lourdes's son, Kyle, could be called on for small chores, and Skip had graciously taken over the heavy-duty maintenance Ken had seen to, even installing a new furnace for me in the last few months. And all for a few dollars (in Kyle's case) and a steady supply of ginger cookies (for Skip).

My mind reeled at the thought of search-

167

ing in neighboring towns. Police work was harder than most of us realized.

"Look," Maddie said, tugging at my shirt. She'd been busy while I was distracted by the enormity of the task. "There's Abe's Hardware store, 4571 Springfield Boulevard, Lincoln Point, and they have an annex" — she pronounced it *anneck* — "named Field of Dream Fences." Apparently I'd walked right by Abe's and never seen it. Too focused on Sadie's Ice Cream Shop or Rosie's Books. "Let's see if they have a special van."

I nodded, not knowing if I was ready to enjoy such quick, easy results. I didn't want Maddie to be so successful at this that she wouldn't pursue one of the myriad careers I had in mind for her. A doctor (like her father), an artist (like her mother), an architect (like her grandfather), possibly even a high school English teacher. But not a cop, like her first cousin once removed. And not a computer geek, much as I appreciated their skills.

This search took longer, but eventually Maddie came up with a photo of the Abe Hardware crew at their annual picnic. Parked in the back of the picnic area was their yellowy beige van. I squinted. There were vertical bars, all right, just as we'd asked for. A thin, black metal spike came up (graphically) from each green letter of Field of Dream Fences, the effect forming a fence in itself. Written on the side of the van was GOOD FENCES MAKE GOOD NEIGHBORS. I couldn't see the whole sentence, but I caught enough to tell me that's what they'd chosen. In a throwback to my former career, I winced at the mixed themes: a play on the title of a baseball movie combined with a line from "Mending Wall," Robert Frost's famous poem.

Focusing again on the bars, I had no trouble believing that in a distressed state (I imagined her being dragged into the van) Sofia Muniz might think she was being taken to jail. The same for her sweet old friend, Sandy Sechrest, four floors up.

What to do with this information, if that's what it was?

"Did this help, Grandma? Did we crack the case?"

"That was amazing. How did you do that?" I asked Maddie, following Skip's rule of answering a question with a question. I was truly impressed with my granddaughter's work, but I also wanted to distract her from the case.

"Someone at Abe's picnic must have posted this on the Web. I'll show you."

Click, click, and we had photos of a birthday party Maddie had gone to a couple of months ago in L.A. "There's Bella," she said, pointing to a dark-haired girl about her age. "She posted the pictures so her grandmother in Florida could see them."

The photo was a candid shot of awkward ten- or eleven-year-old girls in front of a large cake. I couldn't make out the frosting theme, except to see that it was a reproduction of an animated character. A plump girl next to Maddie held two fingers over Maddie's head in a "devil's horns" shape. I was strangely comforted to know that some old tricks were still around.

"Once you post it, it's available to everyone?" I asked, awestruck.

"Uh-huh." Maddie pointed to other photographs of Bella's party, oddly not together, but scattered among other revelers at different events — for example, a bearded guy named Joe held some older Bella who looked like a pole dancer. Who knew there would be so many Bellas partying on the Internet?

I'd gotten photos of Maddie and the family attached to an e-mail from time to time, and wondered if they were also being sent to the world. Traipsing around town, busy as I was, I felt like a very young middle-aged woman — until I contemplated the changes computers brought. The walls of Richard's old bedroom seemed to open up to embrace the entire universe; on the one hand, offering opportunity and information and on the other, destroying my privacy. Maddie must have sensed my bewilderment.

"Don't worry, Grandma, I'll help you stay connected."

Lucky me.

To my delight Maddie wanted to watch a movie with dinner. That was the signal that she was tired after a busy couple of days and would probably drop off to sleep before the film was over. Fine with me, since I really needed some time to sort out all the alleged facts I'd accumulated through the day. Maddie had seen *Harriet the Spy* at least four times in my presence alone, so it would be no great loss if she missed part of it tonight.

About halfway through Harriet's snooping, Maddie nodded off. She fought it for a while, then finally let me lead her to bed.

"No shower tonight," I told her. She was at the age where this pleased her. I knew it wouldn't be long before it would take her an hour to get ready for a public appearance, even at the mall. I remembered Richard's going through those stages. For the longest time, I had to be sure he'd changed his socks every day; then, what seemed like suddenly, he started sneaking a squirt of Ken's aftershave before going to school.

Our bedtime reading was from a book on international holidays. I'd picked it up at Rosie's thinking to teach Maddie about other holidays that occurred around Christmas. Not surprising, she was way ahead of me.

"We already had a Hanukah party at school with blue and white balloons and special music. Rachel's father came and explained everything. Then we had another party for my friend Lamont. He's African American. Rachel and Lamont do Christmas, too, so I was thinking maybe me and Mom and Dad should celebrate Hanukah and Kwanzaa" — I held back from interrupting her flow with a grammar correction — "to be fair."

"And to get more presents, right?"

"Maybe just little ones," she said, with a wonderful, sleepy grin. "Why does my mom think I'm sick? On the phone she was asking me if I'm sure I'm okay."

That's because your grandmother is para-

noid. "I don't know, sweetheart. I guess she just worries when you're not around."

"Do you know the seven principles of Kwanzaa?"

I had to admit I did not, and it was too late to flip through the book to find out. Maddie enlightened me by naming two of the principles — unity and faith, which were all she could remember. "The others were more complicated, but I could look it up for you," she said.

"Not tonight, sweetheart."

I had enough to think about.

CHAPTER 11

I took a cup of chamomile tea to my reading corner in the atrium — comfortable in any weather. Tonight was clear, with the fresh, postrain smell that I loved seeping through the seams of the skylight. There'd be no white Christmas in Lincoln Point, California, but I couldn't ask for everything.

Too many isolated facts rattled around my brain. I needed to sort them out. The way that usually worked for me at times like this was to talk to myself as if I were trying to explain the plot of *Macbeth* to high school freshmen. I gazed with longing at the pile of books on my table — novels for pleasure reading — and started my one-woman lesson, talking to myself as both teacher and student.

First, Dolores is living well beyond her means, and lied or tricked her way into getting her grandmother the best deal and the

174

most expensive quarters at the Mary Todd. She also withheld her old address from the intake form. None of that is so bad, unless Dolores is moonlighting as a cat burglar to pay for her and her grandmother's lifestyle.

Not that it's any of my business. But a murder in Lincoln Point is my business, in a way, and after seeking out my help, Dolores misrepresented her connection to the victim. Also, the prime suspect is a student crafter with a special place in my heart.

It's impossible to know whether the seemingly indisputable facts about Dolores and her grandmother have anything to do with the events of Wednesday night and Thursday morning.

For which there are two theories.

The police believe that Sofia Muniz, being of questionable mind, left her rooms late Wednesday and wandered out into the night. Dressed in her nightclothes, she walked, unnoticed, almost two miles to her old neighborhood. She coincidentally ran into a current resident, Carl Tirado, aka Carlos Guzman, the coyote who took her family's life savings. Carlos was responsible for the death of the man who would have been her grandson-in-law, thus leaving her granddaughter a single mother and her great-granddaughter without a father. Sofia, a tall, large-boned woman, found a weapon of opportunity, a rusty piece of rebar, and beat the drunken Carlos to death. This activity left her covered in Carlos's blood. She then remained there until Gus Boudette, the Mary Todd van driver, found her. Although that address was not listed in Sofia's file, Gus knew exactly where to look for her. Gus didn't cover this up in any way, never claiming to have looked for her anywhere else.

Now the alternative theory — mine — glued together from scraps of observations from Mary Todd residents (put that way, I have a hard time believing it myself). Sofia might be the victim of a clever framer (not the kind who places tiny photos in miniature frames as Maddie did for me, thank you, sweetheart).

Sandy Sechrest, Sofia's next-door neighbor at the Mary Todd, saw two men in a light brown van with bars haul Sofia away late Wednesday night. (Involuntarily? I'm not sure. I should check on this. If Sandy will ever speak to me again.) The Field of Dream Fences van (do I have the best granddaughter, or what?), belonging to Abe's Hardware, has a logo that can be interpreted as the prison bars Sandy mentioned. Come to think of it, this would also explain why Sofia keeps claiming that she's already been to jail — she thought she was in jail when she was in the van with the bars.

This is good.

On that self-congratulatory note, I took a break to pull some sad-looking leaves from my jade plant and get another cup of tea, this time adding a cookie to the saucer and a sweater over my shoulders.

Back to work. There's still a lot to organize.

Gus works at the video store downtown, not Abe's Hardware in the Field of Dream Fences department. Too bad, because he's a likely suspect. I hope it's not his earring or unnaturally straw-colored, long hair that puts me off about him. I think it's the shifty-eyed way he lied about having been paged. I'll bet he just didn't want to talk to us because he was afraid he'd let something slip. Now there's a stretch.

Hmmm. If Sandy's van story is as good as it's now looking, then maybe the other residents' statements have kernels of truth also. Such as that of Emma (Lizzie? Why can't I keep them straight? I had no trouble with the Jackson twins in AP English). One of them saw Sofia in the garden late at night with Dolores, though Dolores claims only to have called, not seen, her grandmother around seven thirty p.m.

That can be another of Dolores's lies. Of course, I don't suspect Dolores of the murder. If she did it, she would never let Sofia take the blame even for a minute. One thing I'm sure of is that Dolores loves her grandmother very much and is devoted to her well-being. I wonder why Dolores hasn't called me. She's obviously found another driver. More likely, my usefulness is over since I don't have sway with my nephew and, now that the cat is out of the bag about her grandmother, there's no need to sneak around with an anonymous "friend." My goodness, do I regret that Dolores hasn't called me in a day?

Back to the residents. Mr. Mooney, the Wandering Irishman, said that someone named Ethel Hudson knows everything about what happened to Sofia Muniz. I wonder who Ethel Hudson is? Resident or staff? Mr. Mooney's deceased wife, probably! I can ask Linda, who'll be here tomorrow with Jason. She'd never just drop him off. I hope she doesn't stay while Jason and I are talking. That would be awful for Jason and counterproductive for the tutoring goal.

I guess I'm about finished. Just for completeness, though, I should add everyone else connected with this case, as far as I know it. There's the uptight Ms. Hawkes, the financial manager. Her motive could be . . . what? Nothing I can think of, unless the Mary Todd's accounts are involved. Steve Talley has a motive. He'd love to discredit Dolores, get his proposal through, and be uncontested for the promotion at city hall. Of course, why not just discredit Dolores? It seems pretty extreme to kill someone you don't know just to frame your rival's grandmother.

What about the other Mary Todd residents? There's that theory that killers show up at funerals and other places where their crimes are discussed, so I suppose I should include the crafters. Lizzie, Emma, Mr. Mooney, Sandy, Gertie . . . Nah, I don't think so.

Wait, Carl spent most of his work time at the Nancy Hanks residence. What about the people there? Right, that adds a host of staff and patients. Not much I can do about them.

Skip's job is harder than I thought.

That's about it. Terrific. There are giant holes in both theories. Too many co-incidences in the police theory and too many unfounded assumptions and unreliable witnesses in the alternative theory. And too many other people in Lincoln Point and surrounding towns whom I haven't even considered. I should quit and play with Maddie all week.

That's exactly what I'll do. Except for checking out a few things.

I was happy with my session with myself.

There were a couple of issues it would be easy to clarify, like whether Dolores was at the Mary Todd between seven thirty on Wednesday night and some time after nine thirty on Thursday morning, when she called me.

I started a list, with that as number one.

Number two was to find out who Ethel Hudson was.

Number three, to see whether Video Jeff's arcade, where Gus worked, had a van. Maybe its logo was an even better fit to what Sandy saw. I pictured an ad for a video game that featured a giant super-antihero behind bars. Or was that anti-superhero? I doubted the *Oxford English Dictionary* had a listing. Maybe there was a Mr. BarMan. I was singularly lacking in knowledge of the comics-turned-movies genre. I'd see if Maddie could use her magic Internet fingers to help with this.

Number three-B, still under Gus, was to

try to determine how he knew where to pick up Sofia that morning.

Number four was to get a timeline based on what the residents saw, if at all possible. It would be very helpful to know exactly what time their observations were made. Maybe I could get them to hook the hour to a television show, or a regular phone call from a family member, or when they took their pills, or some other part of their daily routine.

I'd done all I could without a sounding board. At nine thirty in the evening, I knew my favorite one would still be up and dressed. I called Beverly Gowen and invited her for tea.

While I waited for Beverly, I refilled the kettle, turned on the gas under it, and took out her special tea. Beverly kept a package of chai in my cabinet, which neither I nor any other guest ever drank. I cleared a chair for her, and by the way glanced through the newspapers that had covered it. I was behind in my reading of the *Lincolnite,* our local newspaper, as usual.

I wondered if the story of Carlos's murder had been covered yet. It had been only a day. I flipped through, passing up stories under headlines about a slight-injury hit-

and-run on Gettysburg Boulevard, a wine festival scheduled for early in the new year, and budget cuts for school lunches.

Buried at the bottom of the fourth page was news of the death of Carl Tirado, aka Carlos Guzman. I folded the paper lengthwise and read. After the standard date and time, the short article reported:

> Guzman's body was found in a parking lot in Nolin Creek Pines. Guzman was a fugitive from justice for decades, the police said today. A notebook found in his apartment revealed many schemes to defraud citizens in all walks of life in Lincoln Point and surrounding towns. The police think he met his death due to a drunken fall.

A drunken fall in the parking lot? Hmmm. It seemed my one-on-one lecture to myself had been for naught. Either Sofia had been cleared through some fast, efficient police work, or Dolores had used some influence to keep her grandmother's "person of interest" status quiet. If the part about the notebook was true, then dozens more suspects "in all walks of life" had now stepped into the lineup.

Frustrated, I tossed the newspaper into

the recycle stack. A byline flashed before my eyes, in the article above the Guzman piece: Christine Gallagher, a former student who went on to major in English at the University of California in Riverside. Chrissy's article reported on a proposal by Steve Talley, city hall administrator (and, though it wasn't mentioned, Dolores's competition for the next step up), to refurbish Nolin Creek Park. The article was speciously neutral, but the quotes were all from Talley, giving away Chrissy's (or the *Lincolnite*'s) position.

I wondered if "girl reporter" Chrissy Gallagher had fond recollections of the English teacher who chose her patriotic essay for the VFW award in the late nineties? Would she return the favor by sharing information on where and how the *Lincolnite* got its facts about Guzman? It seemed obvious where she got her "facts" about the Talley Restoration Plan.

Was I really thinking of tracking down a reporter? Enough. For what seemed like the tenth time in thirty-six hours, I checked myself out of the Muniz/Guzman case.

"What a day," Beverly said, stretching her long, well-toned legs in front of her. "After I left you, I went to my assignment for the force." She sipped her chai. "I love saying that. 'The force.' "

I smiled — whatever made Beverly happy made me happy. "I know."

"Even though I'm just a volunteer."

"Not 'just,' Beverly. You're too modest. The volunteers save Lincoln Point a lot of time and money."

"One hundred and twenty-four thousand dollars in the first quarter, to be exact."

"And you keep us safe by" — I put my hand over my heart — "serving and protecting."

Beverly's charming overbite smile warmed my chilly atrium. "We should probably quit before an American flag drops down from your skylight. Did I tell you they've added serving subpoenas to the list of things the volunteers can do? There are some people I'd love to serve, but we don't get to choose."

"About today?" I reminded her.

"Yes, very exciting. I was on a routine vacation house check on Knob Creek Road, and I noticed a mailman on the porch. What's wrong with this picture? I asked myself."

It took me a few seconds. "If the family's on vacation, they must have put a hold on their mail."

She saluted me with her teacup, sending a spicy aroma across the table. "Right. Not everyone does, but still, it was worth a closer look. So I check out the alleged mailman. No one I recognized, and by now I know all the postal workers. I pull over." Pause for effect. I pictured Beverly in the special car volunteers sometimes drove, white, with an amber bar light on the roof. "I call for backup, just in case, though the guy looked about fourteen. Well, he sees me and walks nonchalantly down the stairs, then breaks into a run on the sidewalk. Idiot. I'm in a car, right?"

"Did you catch him?"

Beverly gave an emphatic nod. "It was pretty funny, actually. I'm not supposed to get out of the car in a case like this, just try to trap him. So for about five minutes until a black-and-white came, I played tag with him and finally pinned him against a fence."

Whew. I'd been holding my breath, just imagining this, let alone being part of such a bust. I didn't like the idea of Beverly's taking down a criminal, no matter what his age, given her heart condition. But she looked so pleased, her fuchsia sweatshirt adding a blush of color to her cheeks. Listening to her bright voice, I couldn't spoil the moment by issuing a health warn-

185

ing. She knew what she was doing, I told myself.

"Where did he get a postal uniform?"

"Uniforms of any kind are easier to find than you think. When they took him in, they found his little mail pouch full of checkbooks, bank statements, and credit cards, all different names. He'd hit a bunch of houses where residents were on vacation. So he'd have signatures and account numbers. He even had a few little sticky notes with passwords, presumably. Setting himself up for a nice little identity theft business."

"I thought people did that through computers."

"Just because a new form of crime comes on the scene, it doesn't mean an old one goes away. Lots of crooks still operate the old-fashioned way."

"Didn't he realize a mailman might look out of place if the people were gone?"

"Who said crooks are smart? In that neighborhood everybody works, so he probably thought he was safe."

"What a day, as you said."

"That's not all. After that I get a call from Nick Marcus. He's in charge of the volunteer program." *And Skip's in charge of getting me to date him,* I said to myself. "He called me back to the station, which was unusual. He said I was needed for a special job. To train someone new. I went back, and there was a party for me! To celebrate my one thousand hours of volunteer work." Beverly dug in her purse. "I have photos. They printed them right there on this little machine attached to the camera."

I shuffled through the package of four-by-sixes. Many shots of Beverly in her volunteer outfit, black pants and a white shirt with a LPPD VOLUNTEER patch over the pocket.

"There's Nick," Beverly said, pointing to the tallest person in the group photo. "Kinda cute for an old guy, isn't he?"

"Don't start. And remember, I've met him a few times at the station. He's not as cute as he looks here."

"Cute or not, he's recommended me for head trainer for the volunteers. It comes with beaucoup perks."

"Sweet deal."

"You sound like my son. Everything is 'sweet' to him these days. I think it's June Chinn's influence. I mean, that he's crazy about her."

"I'm practicing youthspeak so I can communicate with the next generation," I told her. "And the one after that."

"So . . . it's your turn," Beverly said. "Here I am rambling on about my own stuff and you probably want to talk about the Muniz case."

"Not anymore." I pulled the *Lincolnite* out of recycling. "Did you see this?"

Beverly read the short article quickly. "Oh, yeah. I heard about that. It's a placeholder."

"Huh?"

"I'm just guessing, but I saw Dolores in the PD building yesterday, and I assume she convinced them not to issue any information until they're ready to charge her grandmother. As a diversion to keep the press at bay, they simply say it was an accident. They're still waiting for blood work before charging Sofia. It takes forever."

"How hard can it be? They have the blood from Sofia's clothes and the blood from Carlos's body."

"You'd think it would be easy, but remember how backed up our crime labs are. It's not like television where" — she snapped her fingers — "they have even DNA results in a flash, between commercials."

Uh-oh. I'd forgotten. One of Beverly's pet projects was enlightening us ordinary citizens about the pitiful state of crime labs throughout the country. Apparently, people, both innocent and guilty, sit waiting for months or years for results while untested evidence collects on shelves and degrades.

The lack of funding for staff and equipment for crime labs was a major concern of Beverly and her ilk.

I signed all the petitions to Congress to correct the situation, and donated money for the project, but I didn't want to go off on that tangent right now. I decided I wanted to brainstorm with her, after all. I read out my checklist.

"That is curious, especially about the van driver," she said. "I'll keep my ears open at the station."

That's what I hoped.

I had one more thing to run by Beverly before she left. I helped her on with her jacket. "I'm a little worried about Richard," I said.

"What for?"

I told her about the Stanford Medical Center envelope.

She waved her hands. "He's a doctor, Gerry, and that's what they have at Stanford. Doctors. I'm sure he'd tell you if there was anything wrong. You worry too much about people."

I took that to refer to both Richard and her, that I worried too much about their health.

Again, that's what I hoped.

CHAPTER 12

Maddie was in rare form on Saturday, and not a good rare. A pouty why-do-we-have-to-go-to-a-ball rare.

"You'll love it," I told her at breakfast. "Uncle Skip has all our tickets already. The police department is one of the sponsors. Imagine how disappointed he'd be if we didn't show up. And you have that great drummer boy costume."

My granddaughter held her spoon like a grinding tool and stirred her oatmeal with unnecessary force. She picked out a raisin and put it on her place mat, squishing it with her thumb as if it were a bug. Correction: she'd never squish a bug. She'd be more likely to put it in a jar and on a shelf in her room. "It's going to be boring."

"I thought you liked raisins."

"You're changing the subject. My dad does that, too. The ball is going to be boring."

"Have you ever been to a ball?"

She frowned and licked a drop of juice from her upper lip.

"No, I didn't think so. Let me tell you what fun it is. I know for a fact that the postmaster — Mr. Cooney, remember? — is going to perform with his puppets. He'll be showing Punch and Judy. And there'll be games and prizes and presents for kids throughout the evening. I wouldn't take you to a boring party."

"How long will it be?"

I laughed. "I guess you're not impressed."

Linda arrived on the dot at ten o'clock. She had already submitted her Victorian bedroom to the ball's silent auction committee, but she'd put together an extra room box in case there was an empty spot. She carried it in to show me, Jason trailing behind her.

"Christmas dinner," she said, clearly proud of her creation. And rightly so. Linda had prepared a sumptuous miniature meal for twelve. A lavish six-inch cherrywood table was set with the crafters' clay equivalent of fine china, wine-glasses, and an elaborate centerpiece of candles and holly. The tiny standing rib of beef seemed to send out a rich aroma, especially when combined with the Yorkshire pudding, oysters, and mincemeat and cranberry pies.

"It's beautiful, Linda."

"It took me many, many hours." She set it down on my atrium table and gave it an affectionate glance.

I turned to find Maddie, who I knew would like the scene, especially the tiny Santa Claus figures at each place. She and Jason were deep into conversation by the jade plant.

"I went last year," Jason was saying as I tuned in. "It's not so bad."

"Is there really stuff for kids?"

I sighed. What happened to the little girl who believed everything her grandmother told her?

"Yeah, they make up a little band, where every kid gets to play an instrument, like the fifes and whistles and this weird thing called a jaw harp."

Maddie's face softened. "I'm going as the Llittle Drummer Boy."

"Cool." Jason emptied his backpack of books. I hoped he noticed the adoring look from Maddie. I was sure he didn't get many of those looks in his life, unless it was from his mother. "Oh, yeah, and every kid gets a toy that was popular in the, you know, past. But some of them are still around. Like pickup sticks, except they called it jackstraws or something. And marbles, except they're, like, little stones."

"Can we play right there at the ball?"

"Uh-huh. There's a lot of space in the new community center, so it will be even better this year. They already contacted us older kids. We're going to have little groups and" — Jason threw his shoulders back — "we're in charge of the games."

"Maybe I could be in your group."

"Sure," Jason said. "Cool."

Linda, who had joined me in eavesdropping, poked me in the arm and gave me a big smile. "He didn't tell me he was in charge of anything. I thought he was dreading the ball. He said he'd only go if I took him for driving lessons."

"I guess he's as good a negotiator as Maddie."

I was happy that Maddie now looked forward to the ball, but even more thrilled for Jason, who had grown up with few admirers. He'd had more than his share of people who considered him a nuisance and were only too anxious to blame him for all mischievous deeds within his reach whether he committed them or not. Now some enlightened people on the Mary Todd Ball committee had the foresight and the confidence in kids like Jason to entrust them with jobs. Responsibility instead of detention. I liked it. I'd never seen Jason in this role of kindly big brother, and it warmed my heart.

I carried my Victorian living room out to Linda's car. She'd offered to deliver it to the community center for me, since I'd be busy with Jason. The tiny crystal beads on my lampshade danced on their nearly invisible strings and caught the sunlight beautifully. I allowed myself a moment of pride. All the rooms were for sale at the ball's silent auction, including the boxes displayed in the downtown windows. I hated to let this one go, and considered bidding on it, but under an assumed name.

"Jason has been doing so well lately, Gerry. I'm almost afraid to be relieved, you know? But maybe that awful phase has passed. Now if we can just get his English grade up . . ."

I caught the "we" and realized I had to make it work with Jason and me.

I hated to tear Jason away from a groupie (he and Maddie were comparing soccer stats) and was glad that Beverly did it for me. She arrived to take Maddie for an excursion to pick up her drummer boy costume at the dress shop. Lori Leigh had offered to make some alterations — it seemed the outfit in stock was not made for a skinny ten-year-old girl.

I couldn't remember the last time I'd been alone with Jason except for the occasional quick pickup from school if Linda was tied up. He was really a thoughtful boy (I considered taking his empty soda can to my recycle box thoughtful) with a lot of potential. I chided myself for not giving Linda more credit for sticking by him when he got himself into trouble.

Jason took his latest English paper out of his backpack and, with a sheepish look, handed it to me: "Themes in Steinbeck's *Of Mice and Men,*" for which he'd received a capital F, written in red and circled. Then he made himself comfortable in front of the television set and flipped channels while I read through it. I thought about what grade I would have given him. Probably the same. But I liked to think I'd have been clearer about the assignment so that an F would not have been necessary.

I could see the problem Jason's teacher had — the paper was a summary of the story rather than an analysis of themes. A typical misunderstanding on the part of high school students. My idea was to show

Jason how this paper might have gotten a better grade and explain how he could use my outline as a guide for his next paper.

"English teachers love it when you tie things together," I told him, pointing to a list of themes the teacher had provided: friendship, loneliness, control, and a string of others. "Can you connect the theme of control to the title of the novel, for example?"

It took a couple of tries, but Jason got it. "Even when you plan ahead, sometimes things go wrong," he said. "Like, how Lennie killed Curley's wife is how the man destroyed the mouse's home. They didn't mean to do it." Jason smiled. "We had to read the poem, too."

"Excellent," I said and drew an A in the margin of his notebook.

By the time we finished discussing how "the best laid schemes of mice and men" applied to Steinbeck's characters — neither Lennie, nor George, nor Curley, nor anyone else in the novel was able to fulfill his dream — Jason had the broadest smile I'd ever seen on his face. It wasn't just teachers who liked connections, but the human spirit in general.

"What do you think?" I asked him. "Does it make sense?"

He nodded. "It's cool."

High praise, I thought.

I felt I'd done my part and thought it wouldn't be too manipulative of me to try to get something out of Jason. I set out another soda and a bowl of grapes (he'd finished a plate of cookies) and sat across from him with a cup of coffee. I glanced at Jason's watch, almost large enough to see across the room if I had to. Eleven o'clock. Linda was due any minute. I had to work quickly.

"How's your part-time job going?" I asked him.

"Okay."

"What do you do at the video arcade?"

"Just stuff."

"Do you clean up?"

"Sometimes."

"You work with Gus Boudette, right?"

"Yeah."

"What does he do?"

"He works the register and fixes the machines. Sometimes he lets me help."

Jason had begun nibbling on grapes. I felt it was more to keep busy and avoid my eyes than that he was hungry or a big fruit fan. Maybe this was why he was so chubby. His reticence wasn't helping my cause. I needed free-flowing conversation to provide a good segue for me. I thought of the ladies of my Mary Todd crafts class and went for a non sequitur instead.

"Does the Video Jeff's arcade have a van?" I asked.

"Huh?"

"Do they have a minivan or some other kind of van that the store uses? Maybe to transport the machines?"

"Oh, yeah."

Aha. "What does it look like?" By now, Jason was squinting, giving me a funny look, as well he should. "I'm interested because I thought I saw one of my former students driving it and I wanted to get in touch with him."

Jason relaxed his gaze. "Oh. Well, it's kind of big and dark blue and it has this cartoon picture of a guy with a joystick sitting in front of an old-fashioned computer. It's very retro."

"Hmmm. That doesn't sound like the van I saw. I guess I made a mistake."

Linda was back shortly after eleven, hardly through the front door before asking how her son fared in the session.

"He's very smart, Linda." Always the best way to start, though this time it was true.

"We made a date for next week after school. I think he'll do much better on the next paper."

She gave me a quick hug, which was major for her, and addressed Jason. "Did you say 'thank you' to Mrs. Porter?"

"Uh-huh."

"Your bike is in the trunk, in case you want to ride it home. I have a hair and nails appointment at noon."

Jason hiked up his pants and took off, as if "hair and nails" were equivalent to "hair-shirt and spikes."

"I have some news, Gerry," Linda said, taking a seat. "After I dropped your living room off at the community center, I stopped in at the Mary Todd to pick up a bag of crafts supplies that I left in the lounge. So I had a cup of coffee with Marlene and the girls. They're all talking about the Munizes, of course. Sofia is being kept in a special room in the care center."

"The blood results aren't back yet?"

"Nope. But you can tell they're pretty sure it's going to be a match because there's a guard at the door to the room. A young cop. Dolores is furious about the security, but she ought to be glad her grandmother isn't in jail."

"How is Sofia?"

"The old lady seems to be slipping rapidly. I've seen this before. Someone seems fine, maybe a little on the edge, and then an incident like this happens — well, not murder necessarily, but one time a woman's son died, and she just let go and was never fully coherent again."

"Do you think I could speak to her?"

"You'd have to get by Dolores, which is harder than getting by the guard. She finagled some way to keep everyone away. You have to be on a list. She's afraid of reporters getting a whiff of this though it's obviously under her control at this point."

"What about Gus?"

"The van driver with the earring?"

I nodded. "Does he work on weekends?"

"He's supposed to, but he didn't come in today."

Though Linda moved on to other topics — color details of her upcoming hair and nails appointment, speculation about the food at the (life-size, not miniature) banquet, and another round of gratitude to me for taking on Jason's future as a literature scholar — my mind was at the Mary Todd.

It was time for me to visit Sofia Muniz, my crafts student and the woman I'd spent a good amount of time looking for.

CHAPTER 13

I walked with confidence to the reception desk at the Mary Todd and signed in to visit Sandy Sechrest. Half true. It was my intention to visit Sofia Muniz, also, but I didn't think it was necessary to include that small detail.

My tote was overflowing with flowers and candy for Sofia and Sandy. I decided to start with Sofia, in case Linda's assessment of her rapid decline was accurate. I took the elevator to the third floor of the care-center wing and followed the path we'd taken on Thursday, passing only an orderly with what looked like a medicine wagon — rows of paper cups with various colored pills.

I didn't know the number of the room to which Sofia had been moved, but I figured there would be only one with a guard.

Sure enough, as I rounded a corner to a part of the floor we hadn't covered the other day, I saw a young woman in an LPPD uniform.

As I approached she stood and cleared her throat.

"This is a secured area," she said, her hand slipping down to a baton hanging from her belt. Out of habit and training, or to compensate for her childlike, high-pitched voice, I assumed, and not because my new Irish knit coat sweater gave me a threatening look. I was prepared for security, and had rehearsed lines about being the aunt, practically a second mother, to LPPD Detective Skip Gowen.

Before I could embarrass myself that way, Dolores came out of the room. Not surprising that she'd be here on a Saturday.

"It's okay, Jen," she said to the officer.

"I have flowers for your grandmother," I said, reaching for one of the nosegays in my tote.

Dolores folded her arms across her chest. In casual slacks and a loose sweater, she was no less an imposing figure than in her city hall suits. I imagined Sofia with that kind of strength and comportment in her youth, even as I snuck a look at her, aged and limp, in her V-shaped hospital bed.

"I'm sure you're here for more than a flower delivery. Were you actually going to interrogate my grandmother in this state?"

Jen had moved aside, and returned to her newspaper, probably wishing she had a modicum of Dolores's commanding presence to go with the equipment on her belt.

"I want to talk to you, not only your grandmother, Dolores. After all, you did bring me into this situation, and I think I have a right to some answers." I wasn't sure how forceful this sounded given the bouquet of pink and lavender flowers in my hand, but Dolores responded with a resigned sigh.

"Let's go out here," she said, motioning me to a bench in the hallway.

"You told me you talked to your grandmother on Wednesday night, and not after that. But I have reason to believe you saw her on Thursday morning." She didn't have to know the reason was attached to the mutterings of Emma and Lizzie, two residents who couldn't keep our class schedule straight (and whom I couldn't keep straight). "*Did* you see your grandmother in the garden on the morning she disappeared?"

Dolores looked defeated. She moved her lips in a tense fashion that told me she was weighing her answer carefully. I locked onto her face and looked straight into her eyes — a technique that always worked with Richard, fully aware that I was taking advantage of her vulnerable state. She probably had not had much sleep the last couple of nights.

"Yes, I was with my grandmother, but not in the morning," she blurted out. "Well, after midnight on Wednesday, so technically, yes, it was morning."

"Why on earth didn't you tell me? Or the hospital? Anyone? It would have made some difference to know that Sofia was alive and well and in her home well into the night."

"I thought they wouldn't look for her if they thought I'd just seen her a few hours before. It's only because they thought no one had talked to her since after dinner the night before that they even considered sending that van. You know that's true, Geraldine. They would have said she's wandering the corridors visiting friends."

"Didn't you have to sign in at the desk?"

"There are ways into the garden that the general public doesn't know about."

"Why did you come at that hour?"

"I heard she was acting up. I'd already been told by the staff that they wanted me to consider moving her back to my house. I needed to calm her down."

"I heard you were arguing, not calming her down."

Dolores bit her lip. "I refuse to dignify that with an answer." *You already did,* I thought. A long sigh from Dolores, then, "Not that it's any of your business, Geraldine, but I'd take my grandmother home in a minute if I thought I could take care of her."

"I believe that, Dolores." I considered letting up on her, but instead kept at it. "You said she was allegedly acting up. How?"

"Just wanting to get away from the Mary Todd. She said there were bad people here and she needed to escape." Dolores looked up into a corner of the hallway and frowned, as if the specter of evil lurked there.

Instead we saw the orderly with the medicine wagon (my term), who had caught up with me and stopped outside Sofia's door. He checked a chart with a photo at the top. Dolores explained.

"Isn't that dumb? It's the method they came up with to distribute meds when they put new people on the shift. They're supposed to match the photos of the residents with the patients so they'll give the right medicine to the right person."

"I guess it works."

"Barely. What happens is the residents get all dressed up with special hairdos and makeup to have their photos taken, and they don't look anything like that by the time they get to this wing."

By now Dolores had gotten up and checked the name on the cup of pills. "She's in the room with the monitor," she told the orderly, who seemed grateful.

I picked up the thread of our conversation. "Do you know who these bad people are that your grandmother wanted to get away from? Or if it's just a fantasy?"

"No, I don't have any idea." Dolores had lowered her eyes, averting mine. When Richard did this, it usually took another three questions to get the truth from him.

I was convinced Dolores knew who the bad people were, but, for now, I let her off the hook.

We walked back toward Sofia's room. Dolores had apparently spent all the vulnerable time she was going to, however. As we approached the doorway and Jen the Cop, Dolores blocked the door, and took the flowers, with a "Thanks, Geraldine. I'll put these in water."

In other words, good-bye.

I headed back to the main wing with the other bouquet of flowers and two boxes of candy.

Maybe I could catch Sandy Sechrest at a similarly vulnerable moment.

Smells from the dining room followed me

as I made my way around to the residents' wing. I couldn't quite place the aroma, but I would willingly have eaten whatever was the source, since I was starving. It was after one o'clock, a long time since my bowl of cereal. I pictured Beverly and Maddie eating bagels at Willie's or tasty sandwiches at Sheridan's and wondered again why I was bothering to follow up on questions I had about the Sofia Muniz case. It was like my reaction to novels, I realized. No matter how bad the writing, I would always finish the book because I couldn't stand not knowing how things ended — what happened to every character, and why.

Now I needed to know what had happened to every character in the Mary Todd drama.

I found Sandy in a quiet corner by a window on the fourth floor. I guessed the residents liked a change of scenery from their own (mostly) small quarters. Sandy was crocheting something soft and pink.

"For a new baby?" I asked, taking a seat in the small grouping of comfortable chairs.

She looked up from her work and rolled her eyes, as if to say "who else?" I pulled out the flowers and a box of candy.

"I want to apologize to you, Sandy," I said

in my most humble voice. "I had no reason to doubt you, yet I was very disrespectful of your observations. I hope you'll take these little gifts as a gesture of my goodwill." Sandy continued her needlework in silence. "I understand that you don't want to talk to me again." I laid the flowers and candy on the coffee table. I waited another few moments, then stood to go.

"Is that See's?" Sandy asked.

I sat back down. "Is there any other kind of candy?"

Sandy gave me a slight smile and held up her work in progress. "It's for my great-granddaughter. They already know they're having a little girl. Imagine that. She'll be born April 13. They know that, too. And that will be her name. April."

Amazing what a pound of See's would do. People just opened up. I wondered if Skip knew this trick. "Congratulations to the whole family, Sandy. I'll bet there will be a great celebration and a scrapbook full of photos on that day."

Sandy looked beyond me, her eyes seeming to encompass four generations. "Yes, I have been very blessed." She paused and gave me a sheepish look. "You know, I've been thinking about what I told you that time you were on Sofia's balcony, and I realize I wasn't exactly right. No wonder you were suspicious. It wasn't a shopping bus that Sofia got into. I don't know what I was thinking. But it was a bus or a van and it did have bars on it."

"Sandy, this could be very important in helping Sofia. Could it have been a drawing of a fence that you saw?"

Sandy's eyes widened. "That's it."

On the elevator to the lobby I edited the roster of questions I'd come up with last night. It had been a very productive visit to the Mary Todd so far. I could check off *yes,* Dolores had been with her grandmother in the garden, arguing, on Thursday morning (though I didn't know the nature of the argument) and *yes* it was most likely the Field of Dream Fences van that Sofia got into later.

I still had one box of candy left. I decided to treat Ethel Hudson.

I never expected it to be so difficult to leave a package for a resident.

"Never heard of an Ethel Hudson," said the first woman I approached at reception, a tiny dark-skinned woman (OLARA, I read on her nametag) in Mary Todd whites with an elaborate cornrow hairdo and a large

209

glitter-laden Christmas tree pin on her breast pocket.

I doubted it had anything to do with suspicions of a bomb or a dose of anthrax. It had more to do with: Who was Ethel Hudson?

"Maybe she's at the Nancy Hanks?" I suggested, after spelling the name and pointing out that one of the other residents had mentioned her.

Olara shook her head, sending a small wave of rich, black braids rippling across her shoulders. "This database has residents of all our Lincoln Point homes. In fact" — she clicked around — "I can check all of northern California." More clicking, another wave of tight braids. "I'm sorry. No Ethel Hudson. She could be in a smaller facility, an independent, but she's not in our system."

I had one more idea. "Maybe she's recently deceased?"

"What is this about?" A new voice heard from. That of Ms. Nadine Hawkes, financial director (or was it manager? Was there a difference?). "Mrs. Porter, isn't it? The crafts teacher?"

For the second time, I felt I'd been demoted by her tone, though I certainly wasn't ashamed of the tag, "crafts teacher." I had half a mind to name her "records forger" in light of Linda's suspicion that she bumped Sofia Muniz to the head of the line for a special deal. "Yes, that's right. I'm looking for Ethel Hudson."

"I've been trying, Ms. Hawkes, but I can't find her in any of our northern California facilities," Olara said.

"Ms. Phillips, you should know better than to give out information about residents."

I'd had the same thought myself, but I wasn't about to question Olara. Now I worried that I'd gotten her into trouble.

"I didn't really give out information —" Olara began.

"Take your break now, please, Ms. Phillips. I'll speak to you later."

Olara gave me a helpless look and slipped away.

"I didn't mean to —" I said.

"I'll be sure Mrs. Hudson gets the package," Ms. Hawkes said.

"I'd like to see —"

Ms. Hawkes made a grab for the candy, but I pulled it back and stuck one of my business cards (quite a miracle that my rummaging fingers landed on one so quickly) under the ribbon. "In case she wants to write me a thank-you note," I said, handing it back.

I felt her stone-cold gaze and watched her strut down the hallway past the menorah, her tight haircut looking like a military helmet.

Either Ethel Hudson was in a witness protection program for the elderly, or the fleshy Ms. Hawkes wanted the See's for herself.

I still had time for one more stop. Not for lunch, alas, but to drop in at Abe's Hardware. I was tempted to stop at Sadie's but I felt a certain commitment to have ice cream only with Maddie while she was visiting. (That would be the same Maddie who probably had talked Beverly into a double sundae today.) I'd managed to find a granola bar in the bottom of my tote, and that satisfied me for the time being. I thought of the sumptuous Victorian banquet waiting for me at the ball and told myself it would be worth the wait.

Abe's Hardware, owned and operated by the Jenningses — Abe and his son, Andy — was one of the longtime family-run businesses on Springfield Boulevard.

"I got in those tiny hinges you were looking for, Mrs. Porter," Andy said.

Like most of my former students, Andy

addressed me as he did when I stood at a blackboard and he sat in the fourth row with a worn copy of *As You Like It* in front of him. Andy had been at Abraham Lincoln High when I first started teaching in the late seventies, so I put his age at about forty-five. His height had stayed the same at about five feet four. A hardware store was a wonderful place for a crafter to browse, so Andy and I had kept in touch over the years though I'd seen less of his fraternal twin, Arnie (it was a family of As).

"Thanks, I'll take the hinges and another tube of glue," I said. I fiddled with some odds and ends in a basket next to the cash register, as if I were a good bet for an impulse buy. In fact, I was stalling and rehearsing. "I actually came to ask you about your nursery and outdoor annex, Andy."

"Finally putting in a pool, Mrs. Porter?" Andy asked. He wore the same red jacket with an ace of diamonds on the pocket that I'd seen his father wear. From the way it hung so loose on his narrow, bony shoulders, I thought it might have been the same jacket, literally.

I shook my head at the pool idea. "Too much trouble. But if I ever do, you know I wouldn't go anywhere else for my supplies.

I have kind of a strange question for you, today, though," I said, leaning on the counter, closing in on his space. This exacted a similar response from him, as if he were preparing to take a quiz. "About your fencing department."

He straightened up. He knew he could pass the test. "Field of Dream Fences. My grandson came up with that name. He's a clever little kid."

"Sure is," I agreed, sight unseen, imagining another A in the family. Anthony, maybe, or Albert. I resisted asking who came up with the Robert Frost line on the van.

"Yeah, I can tell you about our fencing," Andy said, "but I thought that young nephew of yours took care of all your home maintenance."

I shuffled my feet, glad at least I knew the man. I couldn't imagine this conversation going as well with a stranger.

"I'd just like to see the van for Field of Dream Fences, if I could. I thought I saw a friend driving it the other day and want to be sure." It had worked with Jason a few short hours ago; why not with Andy?

"Funny you should ask. You know that van was stolen a couple of days ago? The police just found it way out on Thompson Avenue.

214

You know, where that old glove factory used to be? I got the call yesterday around noon."

Aha! "The van has bars, sort of, doesn't it?"

"I guess you could call them bars. They're really tall, narrow pickets."

"Of course, and what day did you say it was stolen?"

"Last I saw it was when I locked up on Wednesday. Come Thursday morning and the thing was gone. I reported it to the police, of course, but I never thought I'd see it again." Andy picked up a flyer from his counter and fanned his face with it, as if to cool down a blush. "Not that the Lincoln Point Police Department isn't just great, Mrs. Porter."

I gave him a reassuring smile: His comment on police response would be our little secret. My mind had raced ahead with the connection: the van with the bars on it had gone missing just when Sofia was seen being taken off "to jail."

A coincidence? I thought not.

I was so distracted as I left Abe's Hardware that Andy had to come running after me with the small brown bag of hinges and glue. "You don't have to worry so much about the van, Mrs. Porter. Really, it doesn't need a lot of work to get it going again. They didn't strip it or anything. And remember my brother Arnie owns the body shop now."

I patted Andy on his head, still available to me since he remained at least five inches shorter than me. "I'm relieved," I said.

My little red Saturn Ion seemed to have a mind of its own, driving south toward the police station instead of north toward home where a dressing table and a lovely Victorian caroling costume awaited me.

I called my house, where Maddie picked up the phone.

"Where are you, Grandma?" she asked (demanded).

"I'm delayed a bit," I said, passing the deserted stadium of Abraham Lincoln High School. "We still have plenty of time to get ready."

"Aunt Bev says you're probably checking on the decorations, but I think you're helping Uncle Skip."

"Uncle Skip doesn't need my help." If only I believed that, I thought, my life would be simpler. "I'll be home soon, sweetheart."

Beverly finally took the phone and assured me there was no problem with timing.

"In fact, I thought something like this might happen, so I brought all my clothes here. I'm prancing around in one-hundred-and-fifty-year-old underwear."

"You're wearing bones and lace? Aren't you uncomfortable?" I asked, not surprised at what Beverly would endure for the sake of "dress up."

"Yes, but this corset does wonders for my meager bust. Wait till you see my décolletage."

"Do you think you can get Maddie as excited about her costume?"

"We're getting there. I convinced her that drummer boys took showers very often."

"You got her to shower in the middle of the day?"

"Uh-huh. And I told her they also wore a little makeup. We're playing with a touch of lip gloss."

"I can hardly wait to see."

I needed to get Skip to look at the Field of Dream Fences van. The word *evidence* seemed to flash on and off in neon colors in front of my eyes. Alone in my car, I quizzed myself. What about chain of custody? The van had been abandoned, then taken to a body shop. How could the police be sure what evidence was picked up when? And what would they look for anyway? Sofia had been found without a drop of her own blood on her. Could she have left hairs or fibers behind? That always worked on television. I pictured a crime scene technician plucking a strand of white hair from a carpet on the floor of the van. I was used to dealing with small things. I once crocheted an antimacassar using a single-ply of embroidery thread. I could help.

As I pulled up in front of the police station, I saw Skip heading across the civic center complex to the city hall, where the ball would be held in a few hours. I drove up as close as I could to the walkway, rolled down my window, and gave my horn a slight tap.

"Calling all Lincoln Point criminals," I said when he'd seen me. "Tonight is the night the police department goes dancing."

My nephew sauntered over, doubtless aware that I had "business" with him. I could tell by the sideways look he gave me, and then by his comment. "You should be home putting on nineteenth-century lipstick, Aunt Gerry."

"Cute. I have just one question."

Skip leaned into my window and gave me a peck on the cheek. "Are you my favorite aunt? Absolutely." He stepped back and waved. "See you later."

"Skip," I said, more loudly than I wanted

to, thanks to his maneuvering. "Did you know that the Field of Dream Fences van from Abe's Hardware was stolen the same night Sofia Muniz went missing?"

He scratched his head, mussing his thick red hair. "Well, I know it was missing and located the next day. What does that have to do with the old . . . with Señora Muniz? As far as I know the van wasn't found anywhere near the crime scene."

I gave him a quick review of Sandy's comments and Sofia's insistence that she'd already been in jail. "What if someone stole that van and used it to abduct Sofia?"

"To take her to the crime scene and frame her for murder?"

"Yes."

Skip looked over his shoulder at the steady stream of people, many in uniform, exiting the police station and heading for the community center attached to city hall. Some were carrying boxes with fake pine trees sticking out of the top; others pushed and pulled clothes racks, dollies, and luggage on wheels with decorations for the ball. It was getting close to two o'clock and I could feel Skip's longing to be rid of me, but he stuck it out a bit longer.

"How does this play out in your mind, Aunt Gerry? A guy kills Guzman in the Nolin Creek Pines neighborhood, then drives to the hardware store and steals the van. He just picks that van at random, by the way. Then he rushes to the Mary Todd and kidnaps the Muniz woman and takes her to where the body is. Or did he steal the van first, get the old lady, and take her to Nolin Creek Pines before he killed Guzman? Leaving her to sit in the van while he killed Guzman, then spread the vic's blood over her? Or was it a conspiracy? One to kill Guzman, one to steal the van and kidnap Mrs. Muniz, one to —"

"Can you at least get someone to look at the van? It's in Arnie's auto shop."

"I don't want to know how you know that. I can't just order a forensics sweep of the van without a convincing reason."

"Okay, I get it. I have more work to do."

"No, you don't —"

But I'd already rolled up my window and put the car in reverse.

CHAPTER 14

Even if I didn't have all the answers, it would take more than one scrawny (Truthfully? Well built.) young cop to make me give up.

This time I didn't resist Sadie's Ice Cream Shop. I needed fuel and found it in a chocolate malt shake to go. I sat in my car and savored the sweet taste coming through the straw. I drank at least an inch without taking a breath. A few more long sips and I was ready to take off on foot for Video Jeff's arcade, two doors down from Sadie's.

Linda had said this was Gus Boudette's day to work at the Mary Todd, but he hadn't shown up. Maybe he had a better offer of time and a half at Jeff's. It didn't hurt to check. At least now I was headed north, in the direction of home.

The light ping of Video Jeff's door was in stark contrast to the ambience within. The arcade was small, noisy, and dark, except for neon running lights here and there, with many machines crowded in, side by side along the walls and back to back down the middle. It took a minute for my eyes and ears to adjust. I noticed one or two old-fashioned pinball machines and a large nonworking jukebox. The game consoles didn't look very high-tech, but rather were a throwback to the psychedelic designs of the sixties — fat, graffiti-like lettering and comic book–style clouds and bolts of lightning were scrawled on the sides of the machines — but what did I know about the evolution of pop art?

I was dismayed at how many youngsters populated the dingy operation. Outside it was a crisp, clear December day in the athletic fields and parks of Lincoln Point, and in here it was hard to tell what might be creeping or crawling around the nest of dusty wires that slithered down the walls and hugged the floor.

There were only a couple of girls among the customers, one of them holding an oversize pink plastic fake (I hoped) pistol. She was aiming at something on her screen, but her head was turned to her girlfriend at the next console. Her lips were moving, but I couldn't imagine her being heard over the thumps, pows, and explosions coming from the games, even if they hadn't both been wearing airline pilot–style headphones. Lip-reading, I thought. It would be nice to think that our kids were developing *one* useful skill while they were captive to these machines.

I stepped toward the right-hand wall, where a tall counter held a cash register. Behind it and in a glass case below it were dozens of packaged games for rent or sale — titles with *Laser* this and *Xtreme* that.

A young woman approached the register from behind the counter. She looked as if she'd answered a central casting call for the part of arcade clerk — blue-black hair and a black T-shirt featuring daggers, blood, and bone fragments.

"Hey," she said, between chews of gum (I think).

"Hey. I'm looking for Gus Boudette. Is he working today?"

"Dunno. Just got here."

"Can you check for me?"

She shrugged. "Sure."

While she was gone, I turned for a further look at how today's youth spent their free time. Boys in baggy jeans and hooded sweatshirts stood mesmerized by racing cars, flying animals, and dark-robed wizards. More boys sat in molded plastic seats wielding joysticks or steering wheels, "driving" at consoles with images of freeways on the screens. From their frowning, tense expressions, I could see how road rage might start on this spot.

"He's not here," said Goth girl, still madly chewing. I uttered a fervent wish that my granddaughter would skip this phase. "He should have been here yesterday, but we haven't seen him. Wanna leave a message or something?" Her tongue stud clicked against her teeth.

I thanked her and wondered how her mother was coping.

Back in my Ion, I extracted the large Sadie's cup from its holder and sipped the last of my shake, still cold and delicious. Another car in the lot had started up as I entered my car, but now the driver shut off the engine. I looked back and saw that it was a blue Cadillac Escalade like the one Richard drove (or I wouldn't have been able to name it). I saw that its license plate was personalized, though I couldn't read it through splatters of mud. S-something. I could have sworn the same car had been behind me in the police department parking lot.

Everybody loves Sadie's, I thought.

I called Linda.

"Jason loved his session with you, Gerry," she said. "I can't thank you enough."

I doubted Jason would have put it that way, but, I was glad to hear it, because I had a favor to ask. "I think he's going to be fine, Linda."

"Yeah. A big relief, huh? What's up? Are you ready for tonight? At the last minute I decided to make little Victorian dressmakers' models for each table to raffle off and get more money for the cause, so now I'm behind."

I understood the syndrome. I did it often — when I found myself on time or early with a deadline, I threw in an additional something that would put me in a state of panic to finish. Such as, Ken occasionally brought home clients for dinner. I'd plan a simple meal, then once I had all the dishes ready, with a half hour to spare, I'd scramble to create an extra side dish that was more complicated than all the others put together.

"I'm sure they're adorable," I told Linda now. "I'm on my way home. Beverly is with Maddie. You know, I'm still curious about how Gus knew to pick up Sofia at the old neighborhood when that address wasn't in her file. Do you happen to know where he lives?"

"You're going to his house?"

225

"I'm doing errands and I have some time, so —"

Linda gave a low, throaty laugh, a remnant from her smoking days. "Uh-huh. Sure. You happen to be in the neighborhood, huh?"

"Just curious, Linda."

"He lives near me, actually. In one of those new condos. His parents own it and he has a bunch of roommates. I hate that. Five or six kids pile into what should be for a family of three or four, and they're really loud and they make a mess and the property values go down."

I'd heard this before from Linda, how noisy her neighborhood had become lately. I didn't have a lot of time for sympathy, but I gave it a shot. "Oh, one of those groups. What a nuisance. Is Gus's place right on your street?"

"Yeah, it's the second one on the right if you come in from Douglas Street. It's light brown stucco, but it needs painting badly already. Are you really going there, Gerry?"

"I might. It depends on how much time I have. Oh, and I have another question. It's about Ethel Hudson."

"Who's that?"

"A Mary Todd resident, or maybe a staffer. One of my crafters mentioned her and I thought I'd look her up, to see if she'd like to take the class." So what if that idea dawned on me on the spot as an excuse to have Linda find Ms. Hudson. Not that I needed to keep the truth from Linda, I told myself, it was just simpler this way, what with being pressed for time today, and all.

"Doesn't sound familiar. Certainly not on the staff, unless she's very new."

"A resident then. Could you look her up for me? They weren't very cooperative at the front desk this morning."

"You were at the Mary Todd this morning?"

Busted. I had to beef up my prevarication skills. "I stopped in, yes. Can you do me that favor, Linda?" *After all I've done for you* was in my voice.

"I get it. None of my business. Okay, I'll be at work tomorrow and will look up Ethel Hudson."

"Thanks," I said, feeling like Lincoln Point's worst friend. To compensate, in my mind I doubled Linda's Christmas present — a gift certificate to our crafts store. The case of the Muniz family had cost me a lot of time, and now it was taking money, too, but it was my fault, not theirs, that I couldn't leave things alone.

I got out of my car to toss my empty Sadie's cup into a Dumpster. The blue Es-

227

calade was still there, though I couldn't tell if the driver was still in it. Maybe Ms. Hawkes was following me to be sure I didn't continue to hassle her employees.

It turned out that I did have time to detour to Gus's condo. It was getting close to three o'clock, but Linda and Gus's neighborhood was not far from my own neighborhood, on the other side of North Springfield Boulevard. It wouldn't make sense not to check it out.

I drove up Douglas Street and turned left on Hanover, Linda's street. The second unit on the right didn't look that badly in need of paint to me. Neither was there any extraordinary noise, just light traffic on this Saturday afternoon. In fact, I'd been to Linda's at different hours of the day and never heard the clamor she complained about.

I parked across from Gus's condo, facing away from Linda's house. It was a couple of blocks away, but I wouldn't have put it past her to drive down and see what I was up to. I hoped she was too busy getting Jason into his Abraham Lincoln costume and squeezing herself into a corset.

I sat in my car and scanned the street for about ten minutes, my radio tuned to an all-Christmas music station. I couldn't bring myself to climb the flight of stairs and knock on Gus Boudette's door. I was hoping for a chance encounter on the street.

Halfway through "Jingle Bells," when I was about to give up and take myself home (and go back a century and a half in attire), a young couple exited Gus's condo. They looked clean-cut (if that phrase still meant anything), in turtlenecks, khakis, and down vests, not quite matching, but definitely from the same pages of a his-and-hers outdoor clothing catalog.

I was in khakis myself, with a brand-new sweater. Not threatening, I decided, especially with hair that was turning grayer and grayer each day.

I got out of my car and walked toward the couple. "Excuse me," I said. "I noticed you came out of Gus's house. Is he at home?"

They looked at each other, as if in silent debate: *Is she okay? Shall we give up our landlord?*

"Are you, like, a relative?" the young woman asked, thrusting her hands into the slanted pockets of her mauve vest.

I considered claiming to be his grandmother or his aunt visiting from the East, but I'd been shading the truth most of the day and it was wearing on me. "Just a friend. He didn't show up at work today at the Mary Todd, so I thought I'd look in on him." It seemed I wasn't *that* tired of bending reality.

Another look, plus raised eyebrows (from her) and a shoulder shrug (from him).

"We think Gus moved out," the young man said. His vest was army green and his hands were free to gesture. At "out," he thrust his thumb to the side in a hitchhiking motion.

"Most of his stuff is gone," the woman added, "and Jerry, our other roomie, said he saw Gus carrying cartons out to his car."

"I just saw him the other day," I said, feigning the shock of a good friend who's been slighted. "When was this?"

The young woman squinted in concentration. She looked at her roommate. "Yesterday morning?" she asked him.

He nodded. "Yeah, yesterday morning. Jerry said he was coming back from a run and ran into him. I mean, not really ran into him, you know."

"Jerry asked him what was up, but Gus just said he was taking off for a vacation," the young woman said.

"Yeah, but you don't take your TiVo on vacation, you know?"

I wasn't sure what a TiVo was, but I knew

what he meant.

I thanked the wonderfully cooperative young couple and headed for my car. Gus Boudette had moved up in my mind to prime suspect.

Until the blue Escalade drove past and turned right on Douglas. If Gus, my designated killer, was out of town, who was following me?

This time I caught more of the license plate. A vanity plate, S-something-CH.

Not related to Gus's initials, and not Nadine's, either. Could the word be *stitch?* For a quilter or needlepointer? Or *swatch* for a seamstress? *Sketch* for an artist? I shuddered to think a crafter might be my stalker. I knew I was leaving out other words and wished I had a Scrabble set with me for visual aid.

I couldn't help thinking how handy it would be if I had someone on the inside at the Lincoln Point PD to run the plates.

The drive to my home was too short for all the thinking I had to do. I spoke my own thoughts out loud, but softly. Passing drivers might think I was singing along with music from my radio, which I had turned off.

■ ■ ■ ■

Who doesn't want me to find out what happened to Carlos Guzman and Sofia Muniz?

Dolores isn't happy with me right now. Although she wants my help, she wants it on her own terms. I've dredged up her lies and inconsistencies and expressed too much interest in the Muniz family history, so she might want to track what I'm doing. But Dolores drives a silver Mercedes, not a blue Cadillac Escalade.

Then there's Sofia's comment about wanting to leave the home because there was a bad person there. Carlos could be the bad person. One of the seniors, I forget who, mentioned that Sofia had fought with the gardener. That has to have been Carlos. There's no way Dolores will admit it, I know, since that would tend to incriminate her grandmother.

Nadine Hawkes was clearly upset earlier that I might see Ethel Hudson, but that can be for any number of reasons. Maybe Ms. Hudson is Nadine's mother and she likes to keep her set apart from the general population of the Mary Todd. Mr. Mooney said Ms. Hudson knows everything, but about what? She gets checks from the bank, he said, but who doesn't? Tomorrow I'll go back and visit Mr. Mooney and try to get a lead on where and how he's seen her. I wonder if he likes See's.

Who else would care how I spend my time? There's Skip, of course. It's not as if I can come right out and tell Skip I'm being stalked. I hope that's too strong a word. Just someone wanting to see what I'm up to. I wish Maddie could hack into databases for me. I'm a bad grandmother! I'll have to find a creative way to work running license plate numbers into the conversation at the ball tonight.

Ha! Look at that. Maddie saw me turn into the driveway and there she is with her hands on her hips. It won't be long before the tables will be turned again, and Mary Lou will be standing like that, ready to lecture her teenage daughter about the meaning of curfews.

"You are so-o-o-o late, Grandma."

"Sorry, sweetheart. Too many errands."

"I don't see any bags or anything."

"Couldn't get what I wanted, my little sleuth," I said, ruffling her hair.

Maddie was dressed in her red drummer boy pants, with a sports T-shirt on top. I was sure Beverly decided on a last-minute switch for the top layer to avoid a costume adorned with spills from a refrigerator raid.

"Am I in time for snacks?" I asked.

"Barely."

I reached into my tote. "Oh, I forgot. I have these," I said, waving a bag of cookies from Sadie's.

She threw her arms around me, so I knew I was forgiven. Also, from her reaction, I suspected I'd been correct that Maddie preferred Sadie's chocolate chips to my famous ginger cookies, though she'd never tell me.

Maddie skipped ahead of me to the house. I looked at my bright, completely engaged granddaughter and wondered if I dared ask her if there was a way to look up license plates on the Internet.

CHAPTER 15

Two hours later my car was full of lace, velvet, fake fur, and one little drummer boy, complete with a red-and-green drum. We headed south on Springfield Boulevard toward city hall, *rum-pa-pa-pum* blaring out of my car's tinny speakers. Maddie sat rigidly, as if the tiny bit of makeup Beverly had dusted on her face had turned her whole body stiff.

It was nice to go to an affair where I had very little to do besides show up and have a good time. I'd delivered room scenes around town and helped with the items for the silent auction for the Mary Todd ball, but those were minor activities and hardly any work, compared to times when I was in charge of fund-raisers and crafts fairs. Skip had arranged for our tickets, so even the logistics of ordering were taken care of.

The downside was that we arrived with all the other guests and jockeyed for parking rather than pulling into a prime spot hours earlier than anyone else.

I followed a line of cars into the civic center's semicircular driveway and to the left into a special lot the police department had made available for the evening. I lowered my window and turned down the volume of the Christmas music so we could chat with the people in the parking lot — the lucky ones who'd already found a spot and were now walking toward the hall.

Gail Musgrave, our newest city council member and excellent crafter (a master at the split-level ranch) leaned in on Beverly's side.

"Did you see the article in yesterday's paper about Steve Talley's newest proposal? I'll be circulating a petition against it," Gail said. The political pitch was incongruous with Gail's lovely white, square-necked gown. One of her puffy sleeves brushed against my side mirror and I dreaded seeing the smudge of dirt it most certainly deposited on the lace.

"I read the piece. On restoring the Nolin Creek Pines neighborhood, right?" I said.

"Doesn't matter what you call it. Upgrading, restoring, whatever. The point is that no one who lives there now will be able to afford to stay once Steve brings in his crew to . . . ahem . . . improve the quality of life there."

"Having just visited the area, I have to say the neighborhood could use improving, Gail."

Gail leaned in closer. "Not the kind he has in mind. What those buildings need is someone to clean them up, repair the basics — and police them." Shades of Dolores's pitch. I was glad Dolores had someone on her side. "Whatever he tells you, Steve's plan is to level the buildings. He's been itching to do that and put in upscale condos and chichi shops."

Beep beep. Gentle but firm taps on horns from the cars behind me. "We should discuss this later, Gail," I said.

"Merry Christmas, by the way," Beverly said, getting a laugh from Gail. "I guess politics never sleeps."

"Are you kidding? This is the kind of event where most of it gets done." Gail walked away fanning herself with a lovely lacy number I recognized from Lori Leigh's collection. Though the chilly evening hardly required an additional breeze, her gesture made for great theater.

Nadine Hawkes walked by on my side of the car, an old woman on her arm. I had a flash of possibility — Ethel Hudson?

"There's Nadine with her aunt Helen," Beverly said.

Too bad. I waved, but Nadine didn't make eye contact.

"Do you know an Ethel Hudson, a resident at the Mary Todd?" I asked Beverly, who knew everyone.

She shook her head. "Doesn't sound familiar. Is she in your class?"

"No. Her name came up, though."

Beverly was distracted from Ethel possibilities by the Russell family, who lived next door to her. We exchanged oohs and aahs over their costumes, collectively amounting to several bolts of silklike polyester, I guessed.

When they walked on, Beverly turned to me. "We could never have done this in the Bronx in December — visiting with our windows open. We'd have frozen."

"We didn't have a car in the Bronx," I reminded her.

"True."

"No car?" Maddie asked. She'd been quiet in the backseat, except for the occasional drumbeat in time with the music. "How did you get to school and soccer?"

"We walked to school," Beverly said.

"And there was no soccer," I said, remem-

238

bering games of stickball on Marion Avenue.

"We played with broomsticks and deflated tennis balls," Beverly said.

"Oh," said our privileged, unimpressed ten-year-old.

We spared Maddie long speeches about trudging two miles in the snow to get to school, arriving wet and freezing. What was the point? She was too young to grasp the concept. In a few decades Maddie would probably be studying genealogy and wishing she'd paid more attention to us. It was a bonus that at her age she cared so much about our long-ago apartment and her dad's crib.

Speaking of which, I wondered how Abe's Field of Dream Fences van was coming along in Arnie's repair shop. I couldn't believe Skip wouldn't have forensics check it out. I'd have to speak to that boy.

We counted at least ten Abraham Lincolns walking past us, including a couple of females. Beverly recognized a young policewoman dressed in tall hat and beard, and I saw through Rosie Norman's disguise as Honest Abe.

The now infamous (to me) Steve Talley had a leggy blonde on his arm and no fewer than five children in tow. I thought of Dolores's characterization of his family life and wondered who they all were. A blended family, perhaps. Steve seemed to have no costume other than a black bow tie, and the others were so bundled up I couldn't see how they were dressed.

More inching along, a short conversation with Lourdes and Kyle (looking more like Rhett Butler than Abraham Lincoln, with his neat facial hair), and then our turn to park, at last. I turned off the ignition and we started the laborious exit, gathering all our skirts, hats, and beaded purses. Maddie's wide pant legs got caught in her seat belt and we had a rough moment when we thought we'd have to tear them to extract her.

Maddie saw Linda and Jason walking just ahead of us. "Look at Jason! He has a beard! I'm in his group for games, you know."

"Cool," Beverly said, in a tone that didn't quite fit with her outfit — an elaborate green, off-the-shoulder gown, with cinched waist, matching long, fringed handbag, and of course, the Hat.

It was our turn to visit with drivers making their way to the back lot. The Mary Todd van — deep maroon, with no ornamentation except the name of the residence — was in line. We waved to Emma and

Lizzie and others I didn't recognize.

Maddie skipped ahead to join Linda and Jason, her floppy pants, tall hat, and waist-high drum making for an awkward gait.

About ten cars later, I saw it, parked diagonally in the same row as my car. The Escalade. The sun had set long ago, but the Escalade was under a streetlamp and its S-something-CH plate seemed to glow in the dark.

I swallowed hard. I peered closely but the letters in between were hopelessly lost to me unless I tried to scrape off the mud. Or was it paint? Was this even legal — driving around with only a partial plate?

I wished I'd hit it on the way in, just enough to take out a taillight, maybe. Then I could have announced at the ball, "Will the owner of the blue Cadillac Escalade please make him- or herself known."

Just a fantasy, but it helped me relax as I considered other options. Whoever owned the offensive (to me) vehicle had arrived not much sooner than we did, since people essentially drove single file into the spots.

I tried to remember who had walked by us. Beverly's neighbors, the Russells; Nadine Hawkes and her aunt Helen; Gail Mus-grave; Steve Talley and his family; Lourdes and her son; Linda and Jason. Of all of them, only Nadine was suspect in my mind. I ran through possible ways of staking out the car or sticking a little tracker device on it (not that I had one, but I'd seen them on television).

"Gerry? Something wrong?" Beverly asked.

I knew I'd missed some of her chatter. "Not at all."

"You have that look — like when you're making a sketch for a miniature scene. Figuring something out."

Was I that transparent? Evidently so.

In the lobby of the community center, outside the doors to the ballroom, something had attracted crowds at both ends. Taller than most people there, I was able to peer over a couple of rows of shoulders to see what the fuss was about. A display of Mary Todd–era jewelry? (Gertie had a collection.) Or Civil War guns? (Beader Mabel Quinlan's husband, Jim, had a collection.) I maneuvered into the right angle eventually and saw what the fuss was about. A computer screen.

There was the model Dolores had told me about, the Talley Restoration Plan for the Nolin Creek Pines neighborhood. The streets, houses, and shops, all in living earth-tone colors, rotated before my eyes. A constant chatter drowned out the audio, but I caught the gist of the message from the onlookers.

"Is that a lingerie shop? Wow."

"And specialty chocolates. I've been to the one in San Francisco."

"I wish my street had a park like that."

"And coffee shops!"

"A community pool."

"What a difference from what's there now, huh?"

Steve's plan to attract voters appeared to be in full swing. But I had no doubt that one of Ken's models would have been so much better.

The scene inside the ballroom was enough to push aside thoughts of rotating condo complexes and errant Escalades. Between the hardworking decorations committee and the zeal with which the citizens of Lincoln Point had thrust themselves into decking themselves out, the result was breathtaking.

I'd caught up with Maddie before we walked through the doors, eager for her reaction. "Wow," she said. Like Jason's, her highest approval ratings were usually expressed in one syllable.

A giant Christmas tree stood in one

corner, tastefully decorated with dazzling Victorian ornaments.

Each table for eight had a small antique-style lamp. Linda's last-minute four-inch dressmakers' models fit perfectly, since the corset-shaped lampshades mimicked a Victorian lady's torso — a flared top where the bosom would be, then a pinched "waist," then curved "hips," with fringe along the bottom.

Dinnerware was in Mary Todd's favorite sweet briar rose design. We all knew the china was a knockoff produced by a big discount chain, but in the dim lights, next to sparkling glasses and favors, it didn't matter. The permanent committee chair, Priscilla Davis, was in charge of keeping the place settings. She brought the plates out of storage every year, spent days running them through the industrial dishwasher in the family restaurant, and set the tables herself.

Posters depicting the life of Mary Todd Lincoln lined the sides of the room. One poster documented her 1867 trip to Scotland, and the famous quote: "Beautiful, glorious Scotland has spoilt me for every other country." Other milestones and artifacts were depicted — her "love is eternal" wedding band, her first Springfield, Illinois, home — treading carefully past the multitude of depressing moments in her life.

The one exception was the death of her husband, for which there was a diorama. In the background was a greatly enlarged photo of Abraham Lincoln with Allan Pinkerton, called by some the "original private eye," founder of an agency hired by Lincoln for his personal security. A footnote pointed out that Pinkerton's men did thwart a plot to assassinate President-elect Lincoln, and that at the time of his assassination, Lincoln's security was in the hands of U.S. Army personnel.

Perhaps this was why the Lincoln Point Police Department officers had no qualms about dressing up as Pinkerton guards for the evening. *Not our fault,* I could imagine their saying.

The assassination poster showed pictures of Lincoln's horse-drawn hearse. I looked for Mary among the mourners to make some connection between that event and her birthday ball celebration, but could see nothing. The trivia — the hearse stopped at eleven cities between Washington, DC, and Springfield, Illinois; the casket was in full view through the glass windows of the carriage — was interesting to us Lincolnophiles, however.

Maddie wanted to know if she could use

this event (the previously dreaded ball) and all the documentation for a report to her history class. I thought it was a wonderful idea and once again marveled at her resourcefulness. She removed her drummer boy hat and donned a stovepipe hat and beard from a collection of them in a basket at the door, an annual accommodation (nagging reminder?) for those who neglected to show up in a costume of their choice. Maddie wanted her picture taken as Honest Abe. A nearby *Lincolnite* photographer obliged and Maddie returned to drummer boy mode.

"If you can e-mail me a copy, I'll embed it in my report," she said to the cameraman. He seemed to know what she meant.

I joined the stream of bidders and browsers crowding the table where the items for the silent auction were displayed. The offerings were unique and special — paintings by local artists of the many wineries in surrounding towns, baskets of homemade breads and jams; sets of books by authors who lived in the area. I wasn't in the mood to bid, however. I was too distracted.

Nadine Hawkes was a couple of people in front of me, inspecting a handcrafted Mary Todd Lincoln doll. Like the First Lady (it was said), the doll had a lovely complexion, clear blue eyes, long lashes, and light brown hair with glints of bronze. She was all in white, in a typical Victorian child's outfit: linen ankle-length pants with lace trim, topped by a sundress with embroidered flowers around the hem.

I noticed how carefully Nadine handled the doll, setting it down gently on its platform before taking up the pen and writing a number on the bidding sheet in front of it.

A doll collector? Nadine didn't strike me as the type, which in my mind was someone softer and more nurturing than Nadine had shown herself to be. There were some people who related to pets or to inanimate objects like dolls better than they did to humans, however. Perhaps Nadine was one of them.

Then again, typecasting was a dangerous activity. I remembered Skip's talking about a lecture he'd heard on attempts in the nineteenth century to correlate certain physiological measurements — length and width of head, lengths of fingers and toes, vertical heights of ears, distance between the eyes, and so on — to criminal behavior.

I looked around the hall with my stalker in mind, wishing I could tell by some measurement who was so interested in my comings and goings. Even the rows of neat stitching on Joanie Russell's beautiful handmade quilt reminded me of S-something-CH, and I found myself wondering if Joanie owned an Escalade.

When Skip said he'd take care of the tickets to the ball, I thought, *how nice.* The Lincoln Point Police Department was one of the sponsors, along with its softball team rival, the fire department. I gave my nephew a healthy check and sat back and let him make the arrangements for our table. I should have been suspicious. Skip wasn't one to willingly take on logistics like this, unless he had an ulterior motive.

His intentions became clear when I found the table that sported place cards for Maddie and me. Skip had selected the party of eight. The other people at our table were Beverly, Skip, June, Linda, Jason. So far, so good. The last spot, between Linda's and mine, had a neatly lettered place card: Nick Marcus.

I wondered if Nick were within eyeshot of the table. Could I pull off a switch without being caught and labeled rude? Did I care?

Skip, dressed in his Pinkerton grays, came up behind me and whispered, "Nick doesn't know that many people. I didn't think you'd mind."

I whispered back, partly covering my face with my white caroler's muff. "He's lived in town all his life. He's ready to retire from the police force and he doesn't know many people? That doesn't say much for his social skills."

"C'mon. It's not like I'm making you prince and princess of the ball. I figured you could handle a little friendly conversation." He gave me a playful punch. "Get in the party spirit, Auntie."

I paused and breathed in the aromas of roast beef and gravy (real this time, not Linda's miniatures), cranberries, and buttery biscuits that filled the hall. An eclectic mix of Civil War songs and holiday music wafted through the rafters. A plethora of Queen Victorias and Scarlett O'Haras swooshed by me, along with men in knickerbocker suits and others in the straw hats, striped vests, and canes of barbershop quartets. Golf attire abounded throughout the room, as did décolletage. A few couples already graced the dance floor.

Skip was right. I needed to work up some spirit.

"Hi, Nick," I said, as he approached the table in his Abraham Lincoln costume (more suitable on his lanky body than on Jason). "Would you like to dance?"

CHAPTER 16

If I had to follow Skip's rules for seating, I was going to get something out of the evening, I decided. During dinner, he sat across the table from me, between June and his mother.

"Tell us, Detective Gowen, did Carlos Guzman really have a notebook with names and numbers, as the *Lincolnite* reported?" I asked, with all the sweetness of maraschino velvet, one of the many "authentic" treats that graced the long dessert table. "I'm assuming the numbers were dollar amounts? Or maybe telephone numbers?"

Skip grunted and forked a piece of roast beef into his mouth.

"We know he was a coyote," said Linda, not one to miss an opportunity for inside information, or for gossiping in general.

"Did you say coyote?" June asked.

"I guess there aren't any in Chicago," Beverly said. "They're the lowlifes who take advantage of poor people who want to get across the border from Mexico. Most of the time they take the money but they couldn't care less about the safety and well-being of their so-called passengers."

I wouldn't have started this conversation unless Jason and Maddie had already asked to be excused to go to the game room. There was never a good time or place to expose children to the harsh realities of the world, but a charity ball was definitely off limits. I'd introduced the topic tonight simply to make my nephew pay for trying to manipulate my social life.

"So, if this coyote kept a notebook, it might have names of people he brought here illegally, and maybe he wanted to get more money from them," June said.

I liked her style.

Skip gave her an annoyed look, and, for all I knew, a warning kick under the table. "Don't you read the newspaper? Carlos Guzman died from a drunken fall."

I looked at Nick to gauge his reaction. None. He had chosen that moment to take a pill and a long gulp of water, the Adam's apple on his long, thin neck moving as he swallowed.

"From that conversation we had at your aunt's house on Thursday evening, I figured that news release was a cover-up," June said. "Until you get the evidence you need to charge someone, right? Isn't that how you do it?"

I wished I could get up and hug June. She gave Skip a look I admired. It was a perfect combination of loving girlfriend and independent spirit.

"Are you the cop in this family now?" Skip asked. Teasing, but not without a touch of aggravation.

"June's right about the notebook," I said. "That gives you a long list of possible suspects."

"Including Dolores and Sofia Muniz," Skip said and went back to his dinner.

That silenced me for now.

In an age-old ritual, Beverly and I checked under the stall doors before starting our conversation in the ladies' room. All clear, which was a first in my experience with public events.

"I had no idea Skip was going to seat us with Nick Marcus, Gerry. Honestly."

"Why doesn't he nag you or try to set you up?" I asked Beverly. I inspected my lipstick, which I wore about three times a year, whether the situation called for it or not.

"I'm his mother. I can still send him to

his room without his Walkman."

"I think they're called iPods now."

Beverly combed her red curls with her fingers. Even though her locks had been squashed under an enormous hat for most of the evening, they had survived beautifully. "So, Gerry, are you telling me you have no interest in dating Nick?"

"That's what I'm telling you."

"I feel it's my duty to tell you what a nice guy he is. I work with him a lot and he's very thoughtful and easygoing."

"I'm happy to hear that."

"I saw you two dancing out there before dinner. Skip says it was you who asked him."

"I lost my head for a minute. Really, it will never happen again."

Beverly, who wore makeup as a matter of course, took my face in her left hand and with her right, did something to my lips, using a stylus like the one I used to push glue around on small pieces of wood. "His wife died a long time ago, maybe five or six years. I mean it's not like he's divorced and you have to worry what's wrong with him."

"Thanks for telling me."

"Also, he's very generous. You know what most guys do, when you go around collecting contributions for a birthday or a retirement cake?"

I nodded, knowing where Beverly was going with this. "Rob Levinson in history used to jingle the change in his pockets and eventually cough up a few coins."

"Right, and Detective McConnell will even throw pennies into the mix. Well, Nick is not like that. He pulls out his billfold and gives up a five and asks, 'Is this enough? Let me know if you need more.' "

"Admirable."

"Still no interest?"

I couldn't imagine why Beverly was being so persistent. "No. Double no."

She primped her hair one more time. "Okay, then."

"Okay then, what?" I looked at her grin and got it. "You? Beverly? You're into Nick?"

She lowered the shoulders a tad on her deep green gown and gave me a flirty smile. "Only if you're sure."

"Go for it," I said. I felt a burst of excitement for Beverly and a heavy burden lift from my shoulders.

It wasn't until I saw Chrissy Gallagher, one of my best former students, that I remembered her article on Steve Talley's slum-to-upscale condo proposal in the *Lincolnite*. Chrissy was in her mid to late twenties, if I calculated correctly. She was tall and slender

255

enough to pull off the sophisticated version of Victorian style — her black dress had a white tuxedo front, a V-shaped cinched waist, a neatly fitted torso, and three rows of ruffles that fanned out at the bottom.

I wished she'd been wearing the little-girl, puffy-sleeves style, with pink ribbons everywhere, since I planned to evoke the former teacher/student relationship we'd had. I'd mentally prepared a true-false quiz on the "Guzman died from a drunken fall" story. I wanted an essay from her on how the police could be keeping Sofia's confinement from the press unless the fourth estate was cooperating. Was the *Lincolnite* withholding the facts from the reading public? If *I* knew Sofia was under guard at the Mary Todd, I was sure a reporter could have found out.

Chrissy was standing by the twelve-foot Christmas tree, posing for a photo. I recognized the photographer as a man from the professional studio downtown, though I couldn't put a name to him. The last time I saw him, years ago, Maddie was sitting on Santa's lap wearing a red hat and squirming, as she still sometimes did.

Conveniently, it was time for me to mingle and make my way around the room. Linda had gone off to monitor Jason, who was monitoring Maddie, who was probably monitoring her peers. Beverly and Nick were dancing, as were June (a lovely Scarlett O'Hara this evening) and Skip (the useless Pinkerton detective).

I waited to the side and timed my arrival at the fragrant (sprayed on?) tree to coincide with the end of Chrissy's photo shoot. The photographer, introduced as Mike, offered to take my official Mary Todd Ball photo, which would be available at the end of the evening for only ten dollars, 15 percent of which would be donated to the police and fire departments. I declined.

Chrissy and I exchanged enthusiastic compliments on our respective outfits, and then I made my move.

"You seem to be doing really well at the paper, Chrissy. I always knew you'd have your name in a byline. You have a great future ahead of you." I splayed my hands, palms down. "Woodward and Bernstein, move over!"

A big laugh from Chrissy. "Oh, thanks, Mrs. Porter. It's a sweet job. I'm hoping to do more investigative pieces, you know." I felt a surge of excitement. *We could be partners!* crossed my mind. "So far, they're just putting me on stories like why the public library can't stay open later on school nights, and how the fire hydrants need paint and stuff."

Uh-oh. Now it looked like I didn't have much to work with, but it would have to do.

"I'm sure they're grooming you for bigger issues. I saw your report on the Talley proposal." In fact the story was perfunctory, not investigative, but I was counting on the positive effects of flattery. "And also the one on that man who was found dead at Nolin Creek Pines." Here, I tsk-tsked.

"I didn't do that piece" — I knew that — "but, yeah, isn't it awful? I guess he was drunk and hit his head on something."

I scratched my head. Poor confused Mrs. Porter. "I've been wondering though. If it was just an accident, why do you think an elderly woman who lives at the Mary Todd residence was taken in for questioning?" More tsking. "And now she's under guard in a separate wing of the home." I raised the pitch of my voice at the end of the sentence. Just a question from a curious reader of the *Lincolnite*.

Chrissy's eyes widened. She threw her shoulders back and licked her lips. I heard a small gasp. I could tell she smelled "scoop."

The unintended consequences of what I'd instigated dawned on me. Chrissy had had no idea that there had been a murder and that Sofia Muniz was a suspect. I'd planned this little maneuver deliberately, but it was intended for my benefit, to call Chrissy's bluff, to scope out whether the *Lincolnite* staff knew more about Carlos Guzman's death than it printed. I certainly hadn't meant to play Chrissy's Deep Throat.

I felt a wave of uneasiness. What had I done? Exposed Sofia if indeed no one outside a small circle knew about her plight?

I doubted it was a secret; or at least I wanted to believe everyone already knew. I recalled the details of how I found out about Sofia's semi-confinement. It had been Linda who told me, which most likely meant that the whole staff and all the residents of the Mary Todd knew. Surely that let me off the hook as the leak.

I had an image of Skip, in his Pinkerton uniform, charging at me with a long pistol. Or, even more terrifying, Dolores coming at me with her withering gaze and the power of her office in city hall.

Chrissy had an expectant look. I wouldn't have been surprised if she pulled a notebook from her bosom, except that her cleavage was unavailable to her. Unlike Beverly's gown, which I now realized was designed to enchant Honest Abe, aka Nick Marcus, Chrissy's was buttoned to the neck, where a stiff collar circled her throat.

"So, the police have ruled it a murder, and someone's been charged?" Chrissy prodded.

"No, no. Not yet. We're still waiting for some test results."

We? Now I was sounding like an LPPD spokesperson. I could feel my makeup undergoing meltdown, taking on the texture of runny carpenter's glue, as I started to perspire.

"Can we go somewhere quiet?" Chrissy asked.

It was hard to talk anywhere in the crowded ballroom, and we were in an especially busy corner. Dozens of children, let loose from game time, ran around the Christmas tree looking for a present with a number that matched one on a ticket they'd plucked from a large bowl. They were all younger than Maddie, and I assumed the children were being dispatched by age. I pictured my impatient little drummer boy holding a ticket and dancing around the game room, waiting to be sent to find her present.

"Mrs. Porter?" Chrissy tapped me with a black lace fan I hadn't noticed before. "Did you say there was a suspect? Under guard?"

Now or never. I took a breath. "Sort of."

Archie Carey, the aging lead singer with

the band was belting out, "And Her Golden Hair Was Hanging Down Her Back," a lively Civil War–era tune that had everyone dancing. I was happy for the couples, but why did Skip and June have to jig by at that moment?

Unlucky for Chrissy.

Skip stopped midhop and dragged his lovely Scarlett O'Hara through the ring of squealing children.

"Hi, Chrissy. You look charming," Skip said. He introduced her to June and made a comment about the magnificent floral arrangement the newspaper staff had contributed to an elaborate centerpiece on the side table for coffee and tea. A slow buildup, then, "Doing some off-hours investigative reporting?" Skip asked. He rotated his head from Chrissy to me, and back to Chrissy.

Chrissy was smarter than I thought. "Afraid not. I'm covering the ball. We're planning a big photo spread this year."

"You don't say."

"Uh-huh," Chrissy continued, addressing Skip as if she were just so happy to explain things to him. "We've got two photographers here, and Mike from Springfield Photos is helping us." She glanced my way. "Your aunt and I were discussing how newspapers and newsmagazines have so many graphics these days." She clicked her tongue. "The number of inches of text is way down. People are getting lazy. They just want to see pictures."

"Is that right?" Skip asked, rocking back and forth on his heels.

"Gotta go," Chrissy said, looking at her decidedly non-Victorian watch. "People to see, things to write. You know."

Chrissy said good-bye to me with her thumb and pinky, in a "we'll talk on the phone" gesture.

"You take care," Skip said.

"And you serve and protect," Chrissy said.

Both were smiling. The subtext was thicker than the poached pears on the dessert table.

I spent the rest of the evening trying to avoid Skip and Dolores. The latter, who came in late, was dressed as Queen Victoria in a long off-white veil, mantilla style. She took a place next to me at my table, where now only June and I were sitting. I'd seen her work the room, stopping at each group, as if she were running for office. I was nervous at first, but I could tell immediately by her attitude toward me that she hadn't seen me with Chrissy Gallagher, girl reporter.

Dolores nodded at June, then leaned into

me. "You probably think I shouldn't be here, Geraldine."

"Not at all. I —"

"Believe me, it would be worse if I didn't come. It would be like declaring that my grandmother is guilty."

In the loud room it was possible — though rude, I thought — for Dolores to address me without anyone else hearing. I made an attempt to include June, but Dolores had her own agenda as usual.

I gave in to it, also as usual. "How's your grandmother doing?" I asked.

A big sigh. "She's in and out of awareness. She keeps saying she doesn't want to go back to jail. And I swear, Geraldine, she has never been in jail."

June stood up to leave the table. I gave her a smile and a shrug that said it was not my fault, but of course it was. Ken would have reminded me what a wimp I was, giving away power, too concerned about being liked. With his voice as inspiration, I decided not to tell Dolores about my discovery of the Field of Dream Fences van, aka jail. It was my turn to direct the conversation.

"I'm sure your grandmother's just confused. About being in jail, that is," I said. "I don't think for a minute that my friend Sofia is a killer, Dolores, but I must say the police have some legitimate questions."

Dolores's head jerked under the ill-fitting pillbox-shaped crown from which her lacy veil flowed. "Such as?"

My, my. It was easier than I thought to take control and get her attention.

I was fully aware that my status as a police detective's aunt was on her mind. I had to restrict my line of vision to a spot just past Dolores's right ear. I couldn't look her in the eye while essentially posing as a spokesperson for the LPPD, and I couldn't afford glancing around the ballroom lest I inadvertently catch Skip's eye. I knew he'd be looking for an opportunity to quiz me about my conversation with a reporter.

I reminded myself how much my nephew owed me for changing his diapers those many years ago.

I cleared my throat and addressed Dolores. In an authoritative way, I hoped. "Well, for one thing, they're wondering how she can afford the superb accommodations at the Mary Todd."

"What does that mean? They can't think she's a thief or anything."

"From what I understand, there was a bit of special treatment when she signed up."

I was all too conscious of how this could backfire. Dolores might call my bluff and go to the police to explain, which would blow my cover, since the LPPD had no idea what I'd learned from Linda. I thought of several other remarks she might make, including, "I don't believe you," and, "It's none of your business," after which she would walk away in a huff, ending the discussion.

What I didn't expect was that Queen Victoria, noted for her stubbornness and sharp temper, would cry.

I felt a pang of guilt, then listened to Ken's voice. *Be strong. This is all for the greater good: solving the murder of Carlos Guzman and keeping Sofia Muniz out of prison.* "Is there something you want to tell me, Dolores?" I asked.

She dabbed at her face with a lace hanky and adjusted the teal-green banner that lay across her chest. It was draped diagonally, in a way that was reminiscent of a beauty pageant contestant.

"Can we talk some other time, Geraldine? Maybe tomorrow morning?"

I kept my countenance stern. "That would be fine, Dolores. Where do you suggest?"

"We might as well meet at the Mary Todd. I spend almost all my time there when I don't absolutely have to be at work. There's a little parlor on the third floor of the care-center wing." She sniffed and got control of her breath. "Ten o'clock?"

"Ten would be fine." Still stern. Then I spoiled the effect by giving Dolores a warm hug.

Around eight thirty, Beverly found me at the silent auction table placing a too-high bid on a half-scale miniature Victorian pram, in brown wicker with a pink floral umbrella-shaped canopy. It would make a lovely present for Linda, who was constructing a Victorian nursery for a friend's baby shower.

"Nick offered to drive me home later," Beverly said. Her face had a glow I hadn't seen on it in a long time.

Beverly and Nick had been together all evening, alternating between huddles at the table and dancing the slower numbers.

"Is that a blush?" I asked.

She tapped me gently with her fan and twirled away.

Two hours and many announcements and music sets later, guests started claiming their contemporary outer garments from the coat-check room. The ballroom population dwindled and I thought it might be time to go home. I found Maddie asleep in a corner of the children's room, clutching a large soccer ball, her prize from the Civic Club, which had donated all the presents under the tree. I hadn't supervised her food choices since forcing her to try the asparagus and eggs on toast. I was sure she'd hit the dessert table more than once and now had a sugar low.

I was too tired to go back to the auction table to see who had the high bid on my Victorian parlor. The last time I checked Steve Talley was alternating with one of the Russells, each adding the requisite five dollars to the other's bid. I'd been surprised to see Steve's name on the list, and figured he planned to use the scene as a goodwill present to his wife or a bribe to his children to be quiet. Also on the nasty side of second-guessing, I wondered if he was high on prescription drugs as Dolores claimed and didn't know what he was doing.

But I realized I was unduly influenced by Dolores — it could very well be that Steve Talley was a bighearted public servant and wanted to support our community charities. Politics aside, maybe he wasn't such a bad guy after all.

We were beyond the days when I could pick up my granddaughter and carry her to wherever I wanted. Besides Maddie, I had to tote the large box (mostly protective bubble wrap) that held my wicker pram, Maddie's soccer ball, and a number of bags with serving items and linens I'd lent the ball committee. The long, cumbersome dress of my velvet caroler's outfit restricted my motion and added to the difficulty, so I enlisted Skip and June to help me.

"Anything to avoid another jig," Skip said, glancing sideways at June.

Maddie rode out of the building on her uncle's back, her arms draped around his neck while he supported her legs. Fortunately for Skip, she woke up enough to walk, leaning against him, the long trek to my car. June and I trudged behind them with the rest of the bundles.

The few people who were with us in the parking lot were quiet, partied out, as we were. An array of unkempt Abraham Lincoln beards and battered hats littered the asphalt.

June and I were within three cars of my Ion, when I heard Skip's firm voice. "Hold it," he said. He sent Maddie back to us. "Everyone wait there."

A ripple of fear went through me. I knew by his tone and his posture that he was in cop mode. I felt Maddie's tense body against me. The three of us stood stark still until we heard Skip's voice again. "All clear."

All clear of what?

Then I noticed what had given Skip a reason to be on guard. My tires had been slashed. Both front and back, giving the car a crippled, defeated look.

I spun my head around, suddenly remembering the Escalade. I saw it drive by in the row next to us. The window was rolled down, and as the car passed under a streetlight, I saw the driver.

It was Abraham Lincoln.

CHAPTER 17

June nonchalantly suggested that she drive Maddie to her house. "I have a guest room that's hardly ever used," she said to Maddie. "And don't tell Grandma, but there's a TV in the room that you can fall asleep to."

Maddie looked at me, worry in her eyes and on her face.

"It's going to be all right, sweetheart," I said, mustering every ounce of strength I could. "It's just some kids who should know better."

She turned back to June. "Will you stay in the room until I fall asleep?"

"That's what I had in mind," June said, with a bright smile designed to put everyone at ease. I couldn't help picturing her as my niece-in-law.

Skip scooped up Maddie. "Nothing to worry about, Princess. Oops, I mean drummer boy. You go home with June and we'll clean up this little mess, okay?"

I was glad he thought it was a *little* mess, not the huge mess I considered it.

No ordinary auto club service for the family of a police detective. No sooner had June and Maddie and all the ball paraphernalia taken off than the LPPD tow truck rounded the corner from Civic Drive.

I'd shrugged off Skip's idea that I have June take me home also. "It's my car," I'd said. "I want to stay with it."

"Good," Skip said. " 'Cause we need to talk."

I thought as much.

My mind went back to Abraham Lincoln driving the Escalade. It could have been any one of dozens of people. There had been a glut of Abes at the ball — not only males, like Jason Reed and Nick Marcus, but females like Rosie Norman and even Maddie for a moment. The basket of extra stovepipe hats and beards at the door was available to just about every citizen of Lincoln Point.

The truck pulled up to my sorry Ion and two men alighted. "Sorry to take so long, Detective," said the burlier of the men. It had been all of ten minutes. Too bad unconnected citizens couldn't get this service. "We were clear across town."

271

"No problem," Skip said. "We'll be back there if you need us." He pointed to a small landscaped section of the parking lot.

We half sat on a stone plant tub with a narrow rim. This late at night, Lincoln Point was almost cold enough to imagine the sound of sleigh bells. When I shivered slightly Skip put his substantial Pinkerton cape over my shoulders. Gallant, or softening me for a grilling? He folded his arms across his chest. "What's up, Aunt Gerry?"

A grilling it was. "What do you mean?"

"I mean what have you done to deserve this?"

Seeing the slashed tires had unnerved me. What if this *were* some kind of threat or warning to me? What if Maddie had been in the car when whoever it was decided to trash it? I couldn't dwell on that. I glanced toward my car. The men worked with great efficiency, as if this were not the first time they'd been called to a four-slashed-tire scene, a sign to me that this kind of thing happened regularly.

"Are you blaming me because some hooligan picked my car to vandalize?"

"What were you and Chrissy Gallagher talking about?"

"As she told you, we were chatting about the decline of literacy in our society. News-

272

papers and magazines are filled with photos and very little text. You'd be amazed at the long, wordy stories in newsmagazines years ago. I had occasion to look up an old issue of *Time* and —"

"So this is all a huge fluke? You're snooping around town looking for a murderer, and just by chance your car is targeted by a couple of kids who skipped the ball?"

"What do you mean snooping around?"

"I have someone on you."

I gave him a wide-eyed look. "Does that mean what I think it means? You're having me followed?"

"Uh-huh."

"By a police car?"

"A cop, yes. But not in a police car, of course." Skip smiled, the first I'd seen since before the ball, I realized. "We're not the Keystone Cops."

I had a fleeting image of the Escalade, driven by one of Lincoln Point's finest, tonight in an Honest Abe costume for further cover. "Where was he while my tires were being lacerated? Inside watching me dance?"

"He must have figured you were safe with all us Pinkertons around."

At least I wasn't being stalked. I thought it strange that an unmarked LPPD car would have a vanity plate, but maybe they were using private cars these days, or using the personalized plates as a distraction. It worked for me. A warm ripple ran through me and I felt a release of tension.

Then annoyance kicked in.

"Why are you following me?"

"I took you up on the van angle and went to talk to Abe at the hardware store. You know, Field of Dream Fences, with the bars and all."

"So you do listen to me. I'm amazed."

"Abe tells me, 'What a coincidence. Your aunt was just in here asking about the van, too.' " How nice to live in a small town. "I put out an informal BOLO."

I frowned. BOLO, BOLO . . . it was on the tip of my tongue.

"Be on the lookout," Skip said. "For two reasons. One, you might be in trouble, and two, you might be pursuing something else we should know about."

"I'm flattered."

"Don't be. You were seen at Video Jeff's. I must admit we were baffled there. Until we figured out that Gus Boudette, the Mary Todd van driver worked there, and so on and so on."

"Does all this mean that you're warming to my idea that Sofia Muniz was framed?"

"It's possible, yes."

"What about the van? Did you find anything in it?"

"Our forensics guys looked it over. There was nothing obvious, but we sent it to San Jose where they have a much better setup."

"Are you releasing Sofia?"

Skip sighed heavily. "Can't do it yet, Aunt Gerry. The blood results are back and it was definitely Carlos Guzman's all over the lady's clothes."

"But —"

Skip showed me his palms. "That's enough. I've already told you too much. Just stay out of it, okay?"

"You admit my idea to follow up on the bars and the van was a good one, don't you?"

"Maybe. Just maybe. It depends what we get from San Jose."

"One more thing. Did you know that Gus Boudette has probably skipped town? I talked to a couple of his roommates."

"I know. We were on you there, too. We're looking for him."

"Isn't it possible that it was Gus who framed Sofia and has now just fled?"

Skip shook his head, still covered by his Pinkerton cap. "Do you have a motive handy? We don't."

"How long have you been looking into it? If you didn't even think of it until after you saw me in his neighborhood, that's what" — I looked up at the big clock on the city hall tower — "seven or eight hours, during most of which you were dancing. And one more thing —"

"You've already said that."

"Then, two more, okay? Gus Boudette went straight to Nolin Creek Pines to find Sofia. He told us that. But, you know what? Nowhere in Sofia's files does it have that address."

"It's somewhere."

I shook my head. "Dolores worked very hard to keep her past address off the record. Whoever knew where to look, it was because they took her there."

Skip grunted, in a tone that said "interesting."

I waited him out this time.

"Okay," he said, after a moment. "I will definitely put that in the mix."

"Huh?"

"I'll give it some thought, add it to the list of things to check. You know, investigate."

I laughed, more from nervousness than amusement. "Thanks."

Skip pointed in the direction of my car and the workers, who were finishing up with

276

my wheels. The smaller of the two men carried my four battered tires to the truck and threw them into the large bed. "See that? It's not funny."

"I know. I want you to find out who did this. Isn't there some kind of database for this? A file on previous tire slashers? Or were you thinking of pinning this on Sofia Muniz also?"

"Only if she managed to get past her guard."

"That's another thing. What can you possibly hope to accomplish by essentially imprisoning an old woman who hardly knows what day it is?"

"It's for her own good." It didn't seem that long ago that his mother and I had said that to him. I didn't see how it applied to Sofia. "Believe me, I'm hoping you're right, that some kids with too much time on their hands picked your little red car to party with."

"At least you're not blaming Jason Reed this time." A reference to the many times Jason was accused of any and all mischief within a certain radius of his home and school.

"That was a low blow."

"I suppose."

"Look, we have to cover all bases and take

into account that this tire disaster might be related to the Guzman case. So I want you to pretend it's almost Christmas, and you have to get a tree —"

"Christmas is almost two weeks away, and I have a tree, remember?"

"Then make up the bed for my cousin Richard, and do Auntie things, okay?"

"I suppose."

"Make me some ginger cookies."

"Okay."

"And by the way, no one says *hooligan* anymore."

"Well, no one refers to the Keystone Cops, either."

Skip followed me home in a department car. I half expected to look back and see S-something-CH on the license plate. I made a note to ask him what the significance of the word was, whatever its middle letters. It occurred to me there might not even be letters in between, like a heart. S-someone loves CH.

There were no surprises along the way to my Eichler neighborhood on the north side of town, but Skip walked in with me and checked my house, room by room. I was required to stand in the entryway while he did this.

I looked wistfully at the house next door where my granddaughter was sleeping, I hoped. June's lights were out except for a few glowing night lamps. I was confident that one of them was in Maddie's temporary bedroom. I thought of remarking to Skip what a wonderful person June Chinn was, but didn't want to make too big a deal of the relationship. She wouldn't be the first of Skip's girlfriends whom we all loved and had to do without eventually.

Skip gave me a hug at the door. "I love you, you know," he said.

I knew that, and that he had only my best welfare at heart. I was glad we parted friends.

I had a message on my answering machine from Chrissy Gallagher. She must have called me immediately upon arriving home, even before extracting herself from her high-collared, cinch-belt Victorian gown.

"So nice to see you tonight, Geraldine. I'd love to chat with you again. How does tomorrow sound? Give me a jingle at . . ."

Gone was "Mrs. Porter," I noticed. We were now partners in journalism.

I was too tired to decide what to do about Chrissy. I didn't want her to go off on her own willy-nilly, printing what I'd said at the ball, but neither did I feel right meeting her and sharing even more information. It was getting harder and harder to keep straight what I knew from my own snooping (I was sure a better word would come to me after a night's sleep) and what I learned from Skip. While he didn't exactly swear me to secrecy, I intended to act as though he did.

Also, I had a meeting with Dolores at ten in the morning at the Mary Todd. I could hardly remember why we were getting together, except that it had to do with how she could afford to keep her grandmother in such luxury. It didn't seem to matter at the moment.

There was Maddie to think of. I'd have to find the words to downplay tonight's tire incident. I'd promised her that we'd spend Sunday putting the finishing touches on the Christmas decorations in the house and yard, and shopping for gifts for her parents.

I peeled off my caroler's outfit and ran through the possibilities for someone to take care of Maddie in the morning while I met Dolores. June wouldn't be working, but I didn't want to impose on her. I'd probably already cut into her weekend time with Skip.

Neither did I want to call on Beverly. She'd been doing too much lately and I wanted her around for a very long time. I also wanted her to have enough energy for her burgeoning dating life.

My best bet was Linda, who'd be working tomorrow at the very site of my meeting with Dolores. I'd offer Maddie the employee lounge again, this time with her own videos, and we'd have a Sadie's treat for lunch.

With all I had ahead of me — wrapping presents, cleaning out the guest room for Richard and Mary Lou, planning the menu for Christmas dinner, getting the last of my cards in the mail — I crawled into bed wondering if Ethel Hudson had been at the ball. My last thought before falling asleep was to remember to ask Nadine if she had delivered the See's candy.

CHAPTER 18

I had only a few minutes of quiet with my coffee before Maddie bounded into the house on Sunday morning, before eight o'clock, her new soccer ball under her arm. June trailed her, carrying the bundles I'd thrust on her so I could wait with Skip for my car to come back from life support.

"June has cable and DIRECTV and DSL," Maddie said, in an accusatory tone.

"Maybe you should just move in with June," I said, planting a kiss on her uncombed red curls. Apparently June didn't demand much grooming, either. Not the first time it crossed my mind that June might make a better grandmother.

June, dressed for her morning run, smiled at us. "We had a good time, but don't let her fool you. All she talked about last night was her grandmother. How Grandma reads to her, how Grandma fixes her pillow, how

Grandma teaches her crafts, and on and on."

"Wait till she hears what Grandma has in mind for today," I said.

"Uh-oh," Maddie said, tapping her soccer ball with her foot so it rolled across the atrium. I knew she was giving it a hard mental kick.

"Don't worry. Our route includes Sadie's," I told her. "It can't be all bad."

"Again?" Maddie said, as I gave her the itinerary.

A second breakfast of cookies and milk had done only a little for her spirits.

"How about a little dollhouse work?" I suggested. "We don't have to leave until quarter to ten."

"We need a couple of pillows," Maddie said. "I was thinking of putting two on the loveseat, and a small one in the crib."

"Let's go." I led the way to her room, where I kept my fabric.

Minutes later we were rummaging in a three-tiered storage cart, looking for scraps with the right designs. Maddie put aside a pale yellow, narrow stripe for the crib (excellent choice). She picked up a bold floral for the loveseat. The flowers were much too big for a tiny pillow, but I didn't

283

say a word. I watched her hold up the piece and turn it around at various angles. She held her thumb and index finger about an inch apart, roughly the size of the pillow-to-be, and moved them over the fabric. Then she discarded the design in favor of a smaller print.

"I saw you do that when we were looking for material for the bedspread," she said, grinning.

She may not have known exactly why I hugged her so hard.

How could I drag this child to my boring excursions when she gives me so much pleasure? I berated myself. Today was definitely the last time.

We took the materials out to the atrium, so pleasant in the morning light.

"We need stuffing," Maddie said after we'd cut the fabric and hand-stitched (that word, a possible for S-something-CH, rang in my ears) three sides to make a pouch. Maybe the wife or girlfriend of my cop chaperone was a miniaturist.

"The stuffing is already here," I said.

"I don't see it."

"What do you see?"

"Not the cotton batting. That's in the other room."

"No, not the cotton batting."

Her eyes darted around the atrium. She had that intense look that I'd seen on her grandfather when he was focusing on one thing and one thing only.

"I don't see any stuffing."

"Shall I tell you where it is?"

"Give me a hint."

"Okay. We need a very small amount. If we use the regular polyester stuffing or cotton batting, such a tiny gob will be very stiff. The pillow will not flop nicely. We need something —"

"Loose! Like tiny rocks!" she said, pointing to the gravel in the bed around the atrium.

I hadn't thought of pebbles. "That would work, or . . ."

She held up her hand and gave me a satisfied smile. She reached over and picked up the saltshaker I kept on the table.

We high-fived, then set to work. We filled the pouch with salt, stitched the last side, and inspected it. I placed it on the table, took my finger and moved some grains around, making a head mark.

"Wow. Cool."

I figured I'd redeemed myself a bit.

After our pillow session, Maddie was a

much less reluctant passenger in the Ion (with its four new tires), holding on to her tote of videos and a package of ginger cookies from my freezer. If the employee lounge at the Mary Todd was to become my daycare center, the least I could do was contribute to the snacks.

"Just an hour at most. Then we'll go shopping wherever you want. How's that?" I asked.

I caught her expression in my rearview mirror. "Resigned" came to mind.

"Fine," she said.

No "wow" or "cool." But no "nuts," either. I was grateful for the "fine."

I handed Maddie off to Linda, feeling like I was sentencing her to a prison term. She headed for the lounge, her shoelaces hanging down the sides of her sneakers, while Linda and I were still talking. It bothered me that she knew just which way to turn.

Linda and I spoke simultaneously.

"Did you find out anything about Ethel Hudson?" from me.

"When can I bring Jason by again?" from her.

There was the same overlap in our answers.

"Not yet. I just got here a few minutes

ago, and I have to do my rounds first."

"Has he done the homework I gave him yesterday?"

The strains of "I Saw Mommy Kissing Santa Claus" lightened the moment. As did a troupe of children dressed like Santa's elves marching loudly through the lobby, bound for one of the recreation rooms. Morning entertainment, evidently.

"You first," Linda said. "What is it you want to know exactly?"

"I'd like to know if she exists," I said. Linda's quizzical look pointed out to me how odd that sounded. "I'm looking into something for Dolores."

"Okay, I get it. I'll see what I can find out. Where are you meeting Dolores?"

"She says there's a small parlor on the third floor of the care center."

"Uh-huh. I'll take you there, and we can talk on the way."

About Jason, I presumed, but I had one more clarification. "Can you also find the names of Mr. Mooney's relatives? Maybe Ethel Hudson is one of them."

"I'll see what I can do. I have to time it when certain people are on break."

I didn't want to know more than that.

The elevator music was less upbeat than

the music piped through the lobby. We heard the kinds of bland arrangements that made even "Jingle Bell Rock" sound like a waltz.

"Has Jason done anything with the outline I gave him?" I asked Linda.

"He worked at the video place yesterday afternoon and we were out late last night, like everybody else, Gerry."

I understood her tone of annoyance and defensiveness. Of course, Jason would have had very little time to work on an essay. I'd done so much, and so much had happened to me in the last twenty-four hours since my session with him that I'd lost track of time. "Sorry, I forgot how busy he is," I said. "Let's wait until he has a chance to work on what we talked about yesterday, then we'll schedule another day."

That seemed to satisfy her.

As soon as we exited the elevator I saw Dolores pacing the floor in front of the little parlor. It was two minutes after ten o'clock.

I questioned the choice of the Abraham Lincoln quote on the wall of the visiting area in the care center: "Die when I may, I want it said of me by those who knew me best, that I always plucked a thistle and planted a flower where I thought a flower would grow." The sentiment gave the small, windowless room the feel of a mortuary parlor. I imagined a minister saying of a dear departed, "He always planted a flower . . ." and so on.

Not wanting Dolores to have the upper hand because of her power outfits, I'd dressed better than I normally would on a casual Sunday morning, in brown slacks and a new beige sweater set (I was glad they were back in fashion). I needn't have bothered. Dolores was in what I might call Nolin Creek Pines clothes — jeans and a hooded plain gray sweatshirt that, though clean, looked no better than what I might wear gardening. Only her knee-length black boots looked nice and highly polished.

"How's Sofia?" I asked. I was beginning to feel that Sofia Muniz, like Ethel Hudson, was a figment of my imagination. I'd had only a brief glimpse of Sofia in her hospital bed, and even then, I hadn't seen the woman's face. For all I could attest to, Dolores had kidnapped her grandmother, tucked her in a safe place in her gated community, and was only pretending that Sofia was in confinement at the Mary Todd.

Dolores had continued her pacing in the parlor, while I sat on an uncomfortable chair with a fake leather look and feel.

"I honestly don't know how my grand-mother is. She comes in and out of reality. When she asks, I pretend that the cops outside the door are for her safety and security. Which I suppose they are, because whoever really did kill Carlos might come after her."

I hadn't thought of that. I wondered if that's what the LPPD had in mind from the beginning. I found it interesting that even with a nephew on the force, I wasn't inclined to give the police the benefit of the doubt for decisions I didn't agree with. It was quite possible, I realized, that that was what Skip had meant by Sofia's "own good" in keeping a guard on her.

"Did you see the bimbo Steve had with him last night?" Dolores asked. "Where does he shop for these women?"

"I saw that he had quite a few children with him."

"I know. Can you believe it? He's not even embarrassed to traipse around town like that, with his and hers kids."

"Are you saying that wasn't his wife with him?"

The next sound was something like "phtt." She sat down, which was a relief since her nervous pacing made me jittery. "Trixie?" Dolores shivered, as if the image of Steve and his friend were accompanied by a chill wind that swept through the room. "That's not really her name, but it might as well be. Her name is Ronnie, which is just as bad. She's Steve's new secretary. He gets itchy when his wife is out of town. Just like he gets itchy when he wants something for himself, like more money or a promotion."

All very interesting, but not why I was sitting in the Mary Todd's most unattractive room instead of out shopping with my sweet granddaughter.

"You had something to tell me, Dolores," I said, hands in my lap, businesslike.

I heard a sigh that came from her boot-encased toes. "You said the police wanted to know how I can afford this." I did not correct her as to who was the curious party in those matters. Dolores swept her arm to encompass the room, which, ironically, looked like accommodations the poor immigrant Sofia could have afforded herself. "The truth is I had help. From someone who owed me. Someone who could never repay me for what he did to my family, no matter how much money he gave me."

She looked at me. I saw anger, defiance, sorrow.

"Carlos Guzman," I said.

A slow nod. "He was a millionaire, Geral-

291

dine. He kept it hidden because he was a fugitive. He took on a new identity and worked as if he were just a poor gardener, but he had lots of money from years and years of exploiting people."

"Was Carlos the bad person Sofia wanted to get away from?"

"Yes. I recognized Carlos more than three years ago when I was starting to look for a place for my grandmother. The good homes, like this, were so expensive, and the others . . . well, I couldn't leave her in a place that wouldn't be much better than Nolin Creek Pines."

"I'm guessing that Sofia knew as soon as she saw Carlos that you were blackmailing him."

"That's not how I thought of it, but yes. She put two and two together and wanted no part of it. Carlos didn't usually work at the Mary Todd. That was part of our agreement. He had something on his boss — he never stopped exploiting people — so he could pretty much choose his terms of employment. But he showed up here one day recently as a fill-in and Sofia saw him."

"So, they were right," I said.

"Pardon?"

I hadn't realized I'd spoken my thought out loud.

Yet another unheeded remark from one of my crafters had proved to be true. I couldn't remember who it was, but I knew one of the Mary Todd residents had remarked about seeing Sofia arguing with the gardener. I hoped I could get across to them how helpful they'd been with the investigation. We just hadn't believed them soon enough.

"Nothing," I said. "I was thinking of something else. Go on."

"That's about it. Once Sofia knew how it was we could afford our new lifestyle, she argued with me every time I came. Blood money, she called it."

"Is Carlos responsible for your new home as well as Sofia's suite?"

Dolores had resumed pacing. "Mostly."

I wondered why no one had questioned Dolores's upward mobility, but I supposed if she planned it right, it might have looked as though her successful career made it all possible.

"And it was Carlos who paid off someone to get Sofia in on the Founders Program even though she wasn't among the first fifty people to sign up?"

Dolores stopped in her tracks. She looked at my lap as though she might see a crystal ball there. "Yes," she said, with hesitation.

"And that someone would be . . . ?" Pushing my luck.

"I'd better not say."

"The financial manager, Nadine Hawkes?"

"Really, Geraldine —"

Don't lose her now, I told myself. "I understand. I'm sure you know how all this looks now that Carlos has been murdered."

"I'm the last one to want him dead, Geraldine. He was an evil man, but I had no reason to kill him." I didn't remind her that Sofia had reason, even more than we thought. "Not only has my financial well dried up, but I'm scared to death that my name is in that notebook he supposedly kept."

"Will your grandmother be able to stay here now?" *If she doesn't get sent to prison,* I added silently.

Dolores sat down again. "Don't think I haven't gone back to the drawing board since I got the news. Ernestine has only one more year of college, and she'll have to get a job, but all her friends have jobs so that's not a problem. I'm in much better shape salary-wise now than I was three years ago, so we should be okay. The big things were the down payments for my home, and for Sofia." She caught her breath. "You don't think they can do anything about that, do you? Can the police make me give it all back? Who would I give it back to anyway? He has no family."

I noticed that "Can they send me to prison for blackmail?" never came up. I realized that in her mind, Dolores had done nothing wrong except go against her grandmother's wishes. She'd simply tried to get what she felt was her due. Like damages awarded at a civil trial — this was the life she would have had if Carlos had not let her fiancé, the father of her child, die.

"I have no idea about those things, Dolores, but you know you have to go to the police with this information."

She nodded and sighed audibly, a loud exhale. "I know. And I'm glad, believe it or not. It has been a very, very tense life for me, and now it will all be out in the open and there'll be no more secrets." She looked at her watch. "I have to get back to my grandmother now."

I stood and walked with her to the door.

It occurred to me again how uncanny it was that so many of the residents' ramblings had turned out to be correct. I might as well try one more.

"By the way," I said to Dolores, as we were about to part. "Have you ever met Ethel Hudson?"

"Here at the Mary Todd?"

"Yes. You've been coming almost three years and I thought you might have run into her."

"I don't think so. But then, I don't know all the residents. How long has she been here?"

I was too embarrassed to say I had no idea, that she might just be an old man's fantasy woman. "She was on the staff." Dolores seemed surprised at this. "But now that I think of it, she may have left before Sofia arrived."

In the corridor, two staff members pushed identical medical wagons from the Mary Todd's fully stocked pharmacy (a bulleted item in their brochure). The wagons, plus the sight of a male patient struggling through a slow constitutional, hugging the walls as he moved, his IV drip trailing, reminded me of my husband's last days.

I hurried from the hospital wing — I wanted to run from it — and tried to fill my mind with other memories, of a stronger, more vital Ken Porter. Tonight would be a good time to take out my old photo albums and show Maddie pictures of her grandfather at Christmas parties past. Dressed as Santa when she was a toddler, climbing the ladder to put the star on top of the tree, giving me joke presents that made him laugh more than me.

By the time I heard Bing Crosby crooning "White Christmas" in the elevator, I couldn't tell if my tears were happy or sad.

CHAPTER 19

My fond hope was that when Dolores went to the police she would not blow my cover. I imagined her beginning with, "Geraldine Porter told me you had some questions about how I could afford my lifestyle."

I decided to take preemptive action. I called Skip and was routed to his voice mail.

"Dolores Muniz will be coming in to talk to you soon, about her and her grandmother's connection to Carlos Guzman. I hope you'll be understanding." I was about to sign off and thought I'd lighten the mood. "By the way, what does the expression mean on the license plate of the car you have following me? SWATCH? SNITCH?" I laughed. "See you soon."

I'd promised Maddie not more than an hour before we'd begin our fun time. It was now ten thirty. Plenty of time to pay a visit to Mr. Mooney and his Ethel Hudson.

■ ■ ■

A call from Beverly on the way to the lobby made me smile. I'd been eager to hear how her evening with Nick had gone, but didn't want to call too early, in case she was still having a good time with him.

"He's so nice, Gerry. A perfect gentleman."

"Too much a gentleman? Or . . ." A trailing thought.

"I'm blushing. He walked me to my door, a kiss good night, and blah blah blah."

It was the blah blah blah that was most interesting, of course, and she quickly explained. "It's very embarrassing at this age to know that everyone is wondering. Did they or didn't they? So I'll just tell you, he didn't stay over." A long breath.

I perched on a settee in a hallway off the lobby. "I can't help thinking how Skip has been pushing for Nick and me to get together, and all along Nick had his eye on you. You two could have been going steady by now."

"You're funny. No, I don't think so at all. I think it was just serendipitous last night."

"What's next?"

A beep. "A call from him. Talk to you later

with more details."

"Not too many, please."

I found Mr. Mooney in the lobby. A lucky break for me since the woman at the reception desk seemed to be a veteran staffer, as opposed to the young Olara with whom I'd dealt yesterday. I hoped Olara and her fascinating cornrows hadn't been fired because she tried to assist me in my search for Ethel Hudson.

"I'm waiting for my great-granddaughter," Mr. Mooney said. She'll be here at twelve thirty to take me to my cousin's place down in Santa Clara." The highlight of his day, or month, I figured, and that's why he was nearly two hours early.

Mr. Mooney sat on a sofa, his walker nearby, his few strands of hair glistening, as if he'd applied glitter glue to keep them in place on his head. His long thin legs were stretched out under a coffee table that held a large box.

"Is that your Kentucky schoolroom?" I asked him, pointing to a carton, which read DONOVAN MEDICAL SUPPLIES. I wondered if he'd gotten it during an unsolicited sojourn to the pharmacy.

"Yup. My great-granddaughter is coming in from Winchester today." Mr. Mooney

300

wiped his forehead with a large hanky. The room was comfortably cool, but perhaps not to someone on a variety of medications as I knew he was. "Did I say thank you for helping me with the project?" he asked me.

I'd actually done little for the talented Mr. Mooney, providing advice on varnish and glue while he did the difficult tasks of sanding and sculpting. "You certainly did thank me, and you showed me the photograph she sent you. Her name's Jane, right?"

"Yup."

"She's going to love the little scene, especially when she sees her name carved in that desk. Does she know it's there?"

"Nope."

With the bias of a person who had spent her life on one coast or another, I was ready to proclaim Kentucky the land of yups and nopes.

My cell phone rang as I was considering the idea of imposing on Maddie to wait till Jane arrived so I could witness the exchange. I took a seat in the grouping next to the one with Mr. Mooney's sofa and clicked my phone on.

"Something funny is going on with Ethel Hudson," Linda said.

"Can you be more specific?"

I heard a beep that I recognized as call-waiting, but not for me.

"I'd better take that," Linda said. "I'm using my Home phone. I mean my work Home phone. You know what I mean."

I guessed she meant her Mary Todd Home work phone. Just when it was getting interesting. It was my day to be a victim of call-waiting.

I walked back to Mr. Mooney and sat across from him. "I was thinking about what you said the other day. About Ethel Hudson?"

"Yup."

"I heard she wasn't feeling well and I'd like to visit. Do you know which room she's in?"

I saw a twinkle in Mr. Mooney's eyes and a grin forming at the edges of his bluish lips. "Probably she's with old Dominik Ostrowsky." He slapped his knee as if he'd told the best joke of his life.

Now what? Another person to track down, or another blip in Mr. Mooney's brain?

"Is Dominik Ostrowsky a friend of yours?" I asked, tripping over the last name.

Mr. Mooney was still laughing, partly coughing, his eyes tearing up. "You might say we're twins."

"You have a twin brother?" With a different last name at that. Even a different ethnic background. Hopeless.

Mr. Mooney stopped laughing as quickly as he'd started. His countenance turned grim; his body stiffened. He pulled his legs in close so that the heels of his highly polished boots hit the bottom edge of the sofa.

"Uh-oh. I shouldn't have said anything. I wasn't supposed to tell anyone. The only reason I found out about them is that I got lost one day and ended up in Miss Hawkes's office and I knocked something off the desk and there were all these checks . . ."

I felt a shift in Mr. Mooney's attention. I turned, expecting to find Ms. Hawkes, true to her name, hovering in the vicinity, but I saw just a quick shadow. We seemed to be alone in this part of the lobby.

"Have you seen Ethel Hudson or Dominik Ostrowsky lately?"

"Nope."

The old man's reaction was strange, part annoyance at me, part concern. Part my imagination, I thought. If it weren't for Linda's teasing bit of information, I'd bet Ethel Hudson was Mr. Mooney's own deceased wife and Dominik Ostrowsky a name out of the blue. I wondered if there were anything more to be gleaned from the deteriorating mind of Mr. Mooney.

I tried a little soft-toned coaxing. "You told me how Ethel Hudson was such a special person. Well, I certainly wouldn't tell anyone about her, Mr. Mooney. I'm just a little worried about her."

"Miss Hawkes said never mind about her. Miss Hawkes says she never receives visitors. And Dominik Ostrowsky was just my own little joke. I'm supposed to mind my own business, and that's what I'm going to do."

With that, Mr. Mooney worked his lower jaw so that it seemed to overlap his upper jaw and touch his long beak of a nose. He lowered his head and pretended (I'm fairly sure) to nod off.

I called Linda and got her Home (Mary Todd) voice mail.

Nothing left to do but collect my granddaughter and enjoy the afternoon.

"I wish I had a cell phone," Maddie said. "I would have called you to see where you were."

"Were you bored?" A vigorous nod in response. "I know I'm a little late. I'm sorry, sweetheart. I haven't been a very good grandmother, have I?"

"There's still time to make it up to me."

There was that adorable grin. I shuddered

to think how she might use it later in life.

We were quite successful at Lori Leigh's Dress Shop.

Lori Leigh helped Maddie pick out a scarf and a wallet for Mary Lou, and an antique-looking pocket watch (left over from the merchandise she'd stocked for the ball) for Richard. These were to supplement the gift she'd made for her parents. I'd seen the scrapbook she put together, a class project at her school. Evidently Maddie's teacher was a craftsperson. The book was worthy of a production by Emma or Lizzie, with family photographs, drawings by the little artist herself, specially written captions, and puffy stickers to decorate the pages. I knew Mary Lou and Richard would cherish it long after the scarf, wallet, and watch had worn out.

I put in a quick call to Skip, leaving a voice-mail message. I was very curious about whether Dolores had been to see him yet ("turned herself in" seemed too strong), but otherwise I gave my full attention to Christmas shopping. I was definitely on the mend.

My cell phone rang often during our lunch at Bagels by Willie. My A+ GED student, Lourdes, brought our order during Beverly's call. Her son, Kyle, wearing a trainee badge, put glasses of water at our places. Lourdes smiled at Maddie. "Very busy lady, your grandmother."

Maddie rolled her eyes and nodded.

"You're at Willie's? I'm on my way," Beverly said.

"Great. Shall I order plain cream cheese on a cinnamon bagel for you?"

"Light on the cream cheese. I need to lose a few pounds."

Of all my friends, Beverly was in the best shape, neither overweight like Linda, nor underweight like me. "Uh-oh. Did Nick tell you that?"

"Of course not."

"Good. I'm going to ask for extra cream cheese."

I clicked the phone off just in time to take Linda's call.

"I'm on my own phone now, on my lunch break," Linda said. "The Mary Todd phone might be wiretapped anyway. I came out to the garden so I can talk freely."

A bit dramatic, but she had my attention.

"I was very lucky, Gerry, and very smart. I timed my little trip to the records room to coincide with the new girl's shift and got a lot of info. She let me sit at her monitor while she got a soda."

I hoped the new girl's name wasn't Olara, banished to records, about to receive her second violation.

My fingers traced the Christmas wreath on the napkin Lourdes had provided. "Good for you, Linda. What's the scoop?"

"Oh, before I forget. Jason promised to work on whatever it was you told him to do, so he should be ready for another session tomorrow, okay?"

"Tomorrow's fine."

I was sure in her mind, Linda had just made a deal — information in exchange for attention to her son, which she could have gotten from me anyway. But that was Linda being Linda, as Beverly, Ken, and I always said.

"Your Ethel Hudson is on some lists, but not others. We have no medical records for her, for example."

"What if she's just never been sick?"

"Doesn't matter. We should have a file on everyone from the day they come in, from the primary care physicians."

"That makes sense. Maybe the file is misplaced?"

Across from me, Maddie gestured madly. She pointed in the direction of Sadie's Ice Cream Shop, two doors up, and made table-to-mouth eating motions with her right hand. Her eyes asked permission.

Sadie's and Willie's had a reciprocal agreement that Maddie knew about — a bagel customer could take Sadie's ice cream in to Willie's for dessert, or vice versa. I nodded permission, pointing to my own chest: I want some, too.

I handed over a ten-dollar bill. Maddie put on her jean jacket and went off.

Linda was still talking. With my new multitasking skills I didn't miss a word.

"She has a CG designation, which means she's here on a charity grant."

"Some charity supports residents at the Mary Todd?"

"Uh-huh." I heard the crunch of Linda's daily serving of potato chips, and the sound of a lawn mower in the distance. "Some county-wide group — it's called the Senior to Senior Foundation — supports up to three residents at a time. When one dies, they take on another. I think they also fund housing at the other Lincoln Point homes. I knew about this but never paid much attention. It's like a scholarship."

"From the name, it sounds like some old rich people are giving money to old poor people."

"That's about it."

"How does one get such a grant?"

"Every now and then I see an announcement in the paper or on a flyer around here, telling you there's an opening and you can apply. I'm not sure what the prerequisites are, other than you can't afford the Mary Todd on your own."

Something Dolores could have looked into instead of blackmailing Carlos Guzman. I understood, however, that would be completely out of character for her. She'd never make her situation public that way. How ironic that now it was as public as it could be.

"Tell me how that charity grant works. Do they send money to cover the expenses for the residents?"

"I can't tell. It looks like they deposit it into the resident's regular account. Maybe the home draws monthly expenses or the bank sends a check. I'm assuming money is coming here to pay Ethel Hudson's bills, but I have no way of knowing that. That would be Hawkes's department."

Hmmm. "Linda, do you know the names of the other two charity residents at the Mary Todd?"

"You'd be proud of me, Gerry. I wrote out the names on the list. There are three residents, compliments of the foundation. Looks like they're going for diversity. We have your Ethel Hudson, Juanita Ramirez, and Dominik Ostrowsky."

A chill went through me. I pulled my jacket over my shoulders. I looked over at Lourdes and Kyle, taking care of a small line of customers. I needed the reassurance that there were real people in my world, and not just names. "Have you ever met these residents?"

"Nuh-uh. I've never seen any of them."

"Is that unusual — that there would be residents you'd never come across?"

"I'll say. Between my days here as a part-timer and now, I've covered every part of this home and met everyone at least briefly. I can't figure it out. Maybe they're embarrassed or the Mary Todd is embarrassed to have them in the general population. Like prison, you know?"

I didn't quite get the analogy. "Is there anyplace else you can look?"

"I checked a couple of other lists, besides medical, like the meal tickets and laundry. Sometimes the names are there, sometimes not. Isn't it strange, Gerry?"

"Yup."

I sent a nonverbal, long-distance apology to Mr. Mooney.

CHAPTER 20

I was glad Beverly hadn't arrived and Maddie was taking her time returning to Willie's. I needed a minute to sort out the information from Linda's call. I asked Kyle for another cup of coffee and sat at my table doodling away, pen to napkin. I made a flowchart of where money was coming from and where it was going. From the foundation to the residents' bank accounts to the Mary Todd? By check from the bank? To the residents themselves and then to the Mary Todd?

Where on the way could the money be intercepted? I tapped my pen.

I'd just about decided that was what was happening. Someone — my first choice was Nadine Hawkes — was skimming money from the foundation and/or the Mary Todd Home. Not that I had an innate mistrust of accountants. I usually tried to resist that kind of categorization in any profession. I'd personally known several people in the field who were very honest and likeable, Ken's financial manager among them. I also hoped the general public would be as kind in their overall evaluation of high school English teachers. But money manager Nadine was another story. There was a reason she was keeping the public (me) away from Ethel Hudson. I thought of trying to deliver See's candies to Juanita and Dominik.

I wished I knew what Mr. Mooney had seen in Nadine's office and why she was so intent on his not telling anyone. She could be very intimidating and had clearly strong-armed or threatened Mr. Mooney in some way. I was convinced he saw Nadine, or thought he saw her, in the lobby while he was talking to me.

I tried to remember Mr. Mooney's exact words. Had he found checks to Ethel Hudson? From Ethel Hudson? And what did he mean that Dominik Ostrowsky was his twin? I needed to talk to him again. It was almost one o'clock, however, and Mr. Mooney was probably on his way to Santa Clara with Jane for a well-deserved family reunion.

Just as well. I couldn't ask Maddie (who was bounding in to Willie's right now) to succumb to another trip to the Mary Todd so soon.

I'd have to sneak away another time.

"How's it going, Grandma? Did you and Mrs. Reed solve the case?"

I looked around. Fortunately, there was no one near enough to hear her. The Sunday traffic at Willie's had been mostly for take-out — dozens of bagels at a time left the store in brown bags, each with a grainy photo of Abraham Lincoln's son, William Wallace Lincoln, who died just after turning twelve years old.

Maddie's question reminded me of my tire-slasher. I wondered if Skip was right, that someone didn't like my snooping around, as he called it.

"Aunt Beverly's going to join us in a few minutes," I said, knowing that would easily distract Maddie from "the case."

"Cool."

"What did you bring me from Sadie's?" I asked.

She reached into a pink-and-white paper bag and brought forth a tall malt shake for me and a hot fudge sundae for her. Then she showed me her empty pockets.

"There was just ten cents left so I left it as a tip."

What had made me think the ten-dollar bill would cover it all? A throwback to the days when a single would have done it? I

313

pulled two one-dollar bills from my wallet. "Would you mind running back and giving these to Sadie? I promise not to start dessert without you."

But I might make a phone call, I said to myself.

"It was Colleen, not Sadie, but I'll do it." My literal granddaughter ran off again.

Giving me time for a quick call to Linda. I'd be off the phone before Maddie returned.

Linda picked up, still on her lunch break, I gathered, from the chewy "Hello" I heard.

"Linda, could you do me a favor and see if by any chance Mr. Mooney is in the lobby? He was supposed to be picked up at twelve thirty, but you know with traffic and all, his great-granddaughter might be late."

"Where was she coming from?"

"Kentucky."

"Thanks, Gerry. You always make me laugh."

"Someone has to do it. I'm not sure where Jane is staying locally."

"I'll check the lobby and call you back."

I placed the phone on the table, in front of me, looking alternately at the tiny cell phone screen and at Willie's "snow"-covered door. Was it only Californians who insisted on a white Christmas, no matter what? I wondered if the windows in Florida were spray-painted white also at this time of year. From all the Christmas cards I'd seen and the legends I'd heard, the original Nativity was in a desert not unlike Southern California.

The door proved to be more interesting than my phone. Steve Talley walked in, alone. No Bambi on his arm, and no flock of children. He was wearing the very unattractive clothing of a serious bicyclist — skintight black shorts, long-sleeved red T-shirt with a tiny logo I couldn't make out. He carried a helmet that looked like the brain it was intended to protect. He gave me a sweeping wave and headed for my table.

"Geraldine, imagine running into you. My favorite craftswoman." He pointed to the third chair at the table, the one I'd dragged over for Beverly. "May I?"

"Certainly." I knew Steve wasn't the kind of guy to linger. He'd make his point and move on. "I was surprised to see your name on the bidders' list for my room box."

"High bid, too. It's a Christmas present for my youngest, Caitlin. She fell in love with it. Luckily, she wasn't paying any attention to the bidding so I'll be able to give it to her from Santa."

This was a new, very pleasant side of Steve Talley. I wished Dolores could see it.

The mention of a small child sent my attention to Maddie's sundae, now starting to melt. I reached over and put the plastic cover back on the cup, wondering if that would help keep it colder or make it melt faster. I wished I'd paid more attention in grade-school science. Even then, my idea of science was as another road to a crafts project: one year I built a miniature volcano that took many hours and spent only ten or twenty minutes on the science part, copying a "scientific" paragraph about it from the encyclopedia.

"Does Caitlin do crafts herself?" I asked Steve.

"A little. She's only five, so she's not too dexterous. She strings large beads onto leather strips to make jewelry and knits with those big needles. That kind of stuff."

"That's a good start."

"Say, I'm sure you heard about the murder over in the old neighborhood."

Not much of a segue. Steve must be in a hurry. "I heard. It's very upsetting, isn't it?"

"No kidding. I hope this will help people understand why my proposal is so important. That part of town is a disgrace and a breeding ground for all kinds of criminal

316

activity. Where else are you going to find pieces of rusty rebar lying around, unless you're at a construction site? It's a slum and we need to clean it up, Geraldine."

I looked over at Lourdes, neat and professional, ringing up a sale, and at Kyle, wiping down a table in the far corner, happily neither of them near enough to hear Steve trash their neighborhood. I wondered how the Pinos felt about the Talley Restoration Plan, if perhaps they'd seen the computer model in city hall. If they even knew about it — often those most affected were the last to know. How would I feel if I knew my bedroom was destined to be a fancy ethnic restaurant I couldn't afford, for example?

I felt obliged to speak up. "Cleaning it up doesn't have to mean tearing it down and putting up high-rent condos that the current residents can't afford." I seemed to be channeling Dolores and councilwoman Gail Musgrave, but I did agree with them on this point.

"I'll have to give you one of my brochures, Geraldine. Say, speaking of crime and murder and all, how's that investigation going?"

"Excuse me?"

"I was just wondering, with your nephew being a cop and all, I thought you might have the inside story. The papers are pretty quiet about it."

"I'm afraid I don't know any more than you do. Do you have some special interest in the outcome?"

"No, no. But it is my town, you know, and I do want to say again — this situation is just what the Talley plan is meant to correct."

Having made his point — twice — Steve slapped his hand on the table and got up. "Well, I'll be off. I gotta take breakfast back for the troops. I just wanted to say hi."

Sure you did.

Maddie smacked her lips at every spoonful of chocolate chip ice cream, while Beverly scraped the extra cream cheese from her bagel and poured much less cream than usual into her coffee. She also cut back to only one packet of sugar.

This was serious. "You said you wanted some advice, Beverly?"

She looked at Maddie, seeming to question the timing. "Why not? I'm having a hard time deciding what to wear on a" — she looked at Maddie — "a date."

Maddie grinned. "It's okay, Aunt Beverly. Devyn's father left and her mother is dating and she's always modeling for us to see

318

which dress she should wear when she goes out. We get to vote and all."

"What's this world coming to?" Beverly asked. "Don't kids just play games anymore?" She gave Maddie a gentle poke in the arm and took a nibble from her bagel. "I've been through every outfit in my closet and found a reason to reject each one. Too short. Too long. Too bright. Too dull. Too loose across . . . you know."

"Devyn's mother has the opposite problem," Maddie said. "She says she's too busty." She ran her hands across her own flat chest, causing an eruption of laughter from her grandmother and aunt.

"Where are you going on this date?" I asked, when we'd calmed down.

"Don't laugh."

"I'll try not to."

"To a retirement dinner."

I kept my laugh in check. "You're going to his retirement dinner as his date?"

"Not his. Someone else's. John Bodden's. John actually retired a few months ago, but he was on vacation, so we're just having it now."

"Wouldn't you be going to that anyway?"

"Uh-huh, but not as Nick's *date*."

"What does that mean, exactly?"

"He'll pick me up and we'll go to the

restaurant, and we'll sit together and dance, and he'll drive me home."

We both looked at Maddie, who had lost interest. She was chasing a cherry around her paper cup. I knew she was itching to pick it up with her fingers.

"Okay, then. It's a date," I said. "Now, what to wear? Nothing fancy, right?"

"Right. But no microfiber. That's only for travel."

"What about that paisley pants suit with the flared tunic top?"

"It's very 'look at me.' "

"The beige sleeveless with the embroidered jacket?"

"Too 'old lady.' "

After several more rounds, Maddie had the answer.

"Let's go back to Lori Leigh's and buy you something."

Beverly seemed as shocked as I was that Maddie had suggested a visit to a dress shop.

"Really?" Beverly asked her.

Maddie scraped the last of the sticky hot fudge sauce from her bowl. "It's across the parking lot from the Toy Box."

That cleared things up.

I stepped to the register to pay the bill for

our bagels and drinks.

"No, no, Mrs. Porter. It's all taken care of."

"Who — ?"

Lourdes had a big smile on her face. She pointed to her son, who had finished restocking Willie's large refrigerator. "Kyle paid from his share of the tips."

Kyle's smile was equally wide, and accompanied by a wave as he lumbered toward us in his too-tight Willie's jacket. "Thanks for helping my mom, Mrs. Porter."

"He's proud of me like I am of him," Lourdes said.

"That's very thoughtful, Kyle, but you don't have to do this."

Kyle, nearly as tall as me, and considerably broader, met my gaze. "Yes, I do, Mrs. Porter."

Sometimes it was easy to hold on to my great faith in the youth of today.

"Take Me Out to the Ballgame."

My cell phone tune rang through Lori Leigh's shop. Annoying as the song was, it served the purpose of bringing a smile to Beverly's face. She was treating the details of her date with Nick far too seriously to suit me.

Skip was on the line. (Was there a "line"

for cell phones?)

"You called?"

"Did Dolores talk to you?" I asked.

"Yup."

"Anything you care to tell me about it?"

"Nope."

"Have you been to Kentucky lately?" I asked, though Skip's clipped tones were nothing like Mr. Mooney's long, drawn-out syllables.

"Huh?"

"Never mind. What's going to happen to Dolores?"

"It's not up to us. Dolores knows city hall as well as we do. She's probably already talked to the DA."

I covered the speaker of my phone and whispered to Beverly, who had exited the dressing room wearing a knee-length little black dress. "Too formal," I said. Then, pointing to my phone, "It's your son."

She shook her head, meaning, I took it, that she didn't want her son to know she was putting this much effort into a date.

"You're welcome, by the way," I said to Skip.

I heard his deep laugh. "Okay, you're right. I do have you to thank for uncovering that little scheme Dolores cooked up. I'm sure you realize it only strengthens the case against Sofia Muniz."

Any comment would only be repeating myself, so I let it go. "Any news on Gus Boudette, the van driver?"

"He's still MIA."

"Doesn't that tell you something?"

"We're keeping that option open."

"Whatever that means. I have another lead for you. There's something going on with the finances at the Mary Todd."

"Against my better judgment, I'm listening."

I gave Skip a brief rundown on Ethel Hudson, Juanita Ramirez, and Dominik Ostrowsky.

"If I promise to check this out, will you keep your distance?"

"I'll try."

"Weren't you even a little scared last night when you saw your car sitting on its axles?"

"A little. Let me know what you find at the Mary Todd, okay?"

"New subject. Have you talked to my mom today?"

Mom was in front of me again, this time with an ankle-length blue chiffon. "Mother of the bride," I mouthed. Beverly threw up her hands and marched back to the dressing room.

"I did talk to her." Not a lie. "She seems

323

pretty happy with her blossoming social life."

"I can't believe I was trying to fix up the wrong couple."

"I can."

A grunt. "Oh, hey, what did you mean about the license plate on the vehicle following you? I couldn't understand the message you left. We have a couple of different cars on your tail."

"Is that present tense?" I looked outside Willie's window for the Escalade. How would I be able to identify any other car? Would there be a man in dark glasses sitting behind the wheel with a cup of coffee and a newspaper? "Does every citizen of Lincoln Point get this escort service, besides instant tire-changing?"

"Until we find out who slashed your tires. In a case like this we'd look at the camera footage and check the license plates of the cars in the lot, but everybody and his brother was at the ball, so that's useless."

"And no one showed up on camera with a machete?"

A big sigh. "I wish. Whoever did it either knows where the cameras are, or is just plain lucky. You owe us for those new tires, by the way. There'll be a bill in the mail."

"I should hope so. I still want to know

what the vanity plate refers to."

"I have no idea what you're talking about."

He had no idea? Then the Escalade was not a policeman's vanity-plate car. Back to the shivery feeling of being followed. Did the cop car see the Escalade? When a cop follows a person does he notice who else is following that person? These weren't questions for Skip at this time.

"Aunt Gerry? What was that plate again? Spell it for me."

"Never mind. I was confused for a minute."

"Aunt Gerry? What's going on?"

There was no call-waiting beep, but Skip didn't have to know that.

"Gotta go," I said.

Green was Beverly's best color, as it was for all the redheaded Porters. I gave thumbs-up to a rich green calf-length dress with long sleeves and a smattering of black embroidery on the bodice.

We left Lori Leigh's and picked up Maddie. I'd given her an advance on her week's spending money, which was holed up in some secret place in her room. On the last visit she'd kept her money at the bottom of a mug of pens and pencils, producing a considerable number of ink splotches on the face and beard of none other than Abraham Lincoln, whose portrait graced her fives.

Today while Maddie was demonstrating how her new soccer kneepads tied on, I scrutinized every parked car in the lot.

CHAPTER 21

An intriguing answering machine message from Chrissy Gallagher captured my attention when I got home around three o'clock on Sunday afternoon. I played it and then played it again.

"I have the item we talked about." Chrissy's voice sounded lower than her normal pitch, and muffled, as if she'd cupped her hand over the phone. "I hope we can get together to pool our resources. Give me a call."

The item? Carlos Guzman's notebook, I assumed. I felt the rush of anticipation, then caution took over. Did I really want to pursue an investigation with a reporter when (a) I might be the target of a stalker, (b) my tires might have been slashed as a warning, and (c) through (z) it was none of my business?

On the other hand, I wasn't positive about either (a) or (b). Maybe Skip didn't realize one of his cops was using his private S-something-CH Escalade. (I pushed right past the absurdity of an LPPD cop driving a Cadillac on a tailing mission.) As for (b), I made a note to check the "police blotter" section of the *Lincolnite* for the frequency of tire-slashing incidents, especially on evenings such as last night when nearly the whole town was focusing on the ball.

I didn't have to worry about entertaining Maddie for the rest of the day. She was getting changed to go with June to her gym, where they had an indoor pool, pickup sports for kids, and, counterproductively, a vending machine filled with junk food. My granddaughter's idea of heaven. June offered to give Maddie tennis lessons (I knew she'd bought her a racket for Christmas), which I applauded. It was time she took up something more ladylike than soccer.

Before I could decide whether to return Chrissy's call, my landline rang.

An exasperated Linda. "You're not picking up your cell," she said.

"The battery's probably dead, from talking to you all day." I put a smile in my voice, just in case Linda was in one of her sensitive moods. "What's new?"

"Gerry, you won't believe this. Mr. Mooney almost died." She paused to take a drink, probably her daily low-fat latte with whipped cream, causing a flurry of anxiety in my chest. "When I got to the lobby they were taking him to the care center."

"What happened?"

"It's kind of confused right now. Nadine is the one who called for help. She said she saw him passed out on the couch. It was like a miracle that a troupe of EMTs who were here for a tour happened to be a few feet away, on their way out the door."

"Did he have a heart attack?"

"I don't know. Apparently he just fell over. Knocked one of those miniature Christmas trees off the table. Well, they're not really miniature, just the small tabletop kind."

I took a seat at my kitchen table, stretching the phone cord to its limit. "Is he going to be all right?"

"They think so. His great-granddaughter is here. She's blaming herself because she was late and she thinks he got upset about that and that's what brought it on."

"Is that even likely?"

"No, not really. I told her it was a *good* thing she was late, because at least he had his attack here and could be attended to. What if they'd been on the road?"

Much as I'd wanted to hear something nefarious about Nadine Hawkes, I couldn't fault someone who'd saved the life of an old man who wanted to live long enough to give his great-granddaughter a handcrafted treasure.

Not that I didn't still have questions about Nadine's life as a bookkeeper.

"Aren't you coming to the gym with us?" Maddie asked, noticing my nonworkout attire.

"Not today. I have some errands to take care of before dinner."

She put her hands on her hips, or, technically, where her hips would be some day. "Are you still snooping around?"

I put my hands on my already formed hips and frowned as best I could, given her comic stance. "Where did you hear that?"

"I heard Uncle Skip tell June."

"Don't believe everything you hear. By the way — and this has nothing to do with the case — but I was wondering if it's possible for someone to go online and see who has a certain vanity plate?"

"You can track any license plate but you have to pay."

"Track? You mean trace back to its owner?"

"Uh-huh."

"Someone can just put in my license plate

number and find me?" I didn't know why I was startled since that's exactly what I wanted to do, but the easy access to so much information these days still astonished me.

"Uh-huh," Maddie said. "You don't have to pay to see if the word you want on your license plate is already taken, but if you want to look up the owner you have to pay. It's, like, about forty dollars. You get the name and address, the kind of car it is, all kinds of stuff." Her face brightened. "Do you want to sign up?"

"No, never mind."

"Yeah, it's a lot of money."

It wasn't the money, which, sadly, wasn't prohibitive enough to prevent your average thief or predator from gaining access. I just wasn't sure I wanted to be a registered license plate looker-upper. I'd never used my credit card online and I didn't want to start now, with a project like this. I'd have to find another way to figure out who was following me. If anyone.

"How do you know all this?" I asked Maddie.

"Dad wanted to get a plate that said surgery or something, so we looked it up. But then Mom said it was too show-offy and then Dad agreed so we didn't get one.

But I remembered how to do it."

"Good for you. You're a wonderful research assistant."

"Grandma, if you have a license plate you want to trace, I could just go up and down the streets and look and see who gets in the car. Jason said I could borrow one of his bikes any time. He has two that are too small for him."

I pictured my granddaughter trolling the hills and vales of Lincoln Point, like Harriet the Spy, with her little notebook, gathering intelligence on friends and neighbors, writing down license plates, and makes and models of cars.

"I'll let you know, sweetheart. We should call your parents this evening, okay? And you can tell them about the ball."

"Sure."

And I can ask how Richard is.

When June arrived to collect Maddie and her I-heart-soccer duffel bag, I took the opportunity to quiz her.

I began, "Maddie said Skip said . . . ," then rephrased. "So Skip thinks I'm snooping?"

She gave me her winning smile.

"Skip says you think someone is following you and you won't give him the plates. Is that right?"

I smiled back. "Ah, now he's got you working for him?"

"He's just concerned. He doesn't understand why you wouldn't tell him if you think a car other than a police vehicle is tailing you."

I wasn't sure myself. I knew I didn't want the LPPD questioning someone and finding out it was all a big misunderstanding or a coincidence. It might not even have been the same car behind me in every incident. I didn't always see the plates straight on, especially when I was trying to drive at the same time, and surely there was more than one blue Escalade in Lincoln Point. Also there'd been no S-something-CH in my rearview mirror all morning. Maybe STITCH or SWATCH or SNITCH had noticed the cop cars and called off his campaign. Maybe he went back East to celebrate the holidays in winter weather. Darned if I knew.

"What if I'm wrong? I'll feel pretty foolish," I said to June.

"Better safe than sorry," she said.

A wise young woman.

Maddie dragged her duffel bag to the foyer and kissed me good-bye. "Are you sure you don't need an assistant this afternoon, Grandma?"

"I'm sure."

"I always miss all the fun."

"What?" June said, in mock indignation. "We two are going to the most fun place in town."

"I wish I could go," I said.

Maddie grinned at June. "I was just teasing."

"Me, too," I said.

I plugged in my car phone charger and called Chrissy on the way to the Mary Todd. I was a real cell phone pro at this point.

"About the item?" I asked her, playing into her clandestine mood.

"Yes, that item has names and numbers."

"How did you get it?"

"You know I can't tell you that."

It didn't hurt to try.

We set up a meeting at the café inside Rosie's bookstore for around five. That gave me at least an hour at the Mary Todd to check on Mr. Mooney and perhaps pay Sofia Muniz a little visit. She was a free woman now, though Skip reminded me that could change. It was possible that her granddaughter might not be a free woman too much longer, however, depending on how the DA viewed Dolores's years of blackmailing Carlos Guzman.

I wondered if it mattered that she hadn't picked someone at random to blackmail, but felt sincerely that she was simply exacting justice.

Thanks to a friend on the inside, I didn't have to sign in or request pesky permissions to go up in the elevator to the now-familiar Mary Todd care center. I hadn't spent this much time in a care facility since the awful days of Ken's illness when we traipsed from one hospital, hospice, or clinic to another hoping for good news that never came.

Once again, I called up good memories — our faces covered with paint splotches as we tried to spruce up our drab first apartment; Ken's arrival at my bedside with furry pussy willows when Richard was born; his joy at surprising me with a "real" wedding ring, once we could afford it — and brought myself to the present.

Linda briefed me on Mr. Mooney's status, ending with, "They're saying it might have been just an allergic reaction. They'll probably do some kind of tox screen and compare it with his chart. In any case he's out of the woods."

"Would this be a reaction to something he took a while ago, or something just given to

335

him while he was sitting there?"

She shrugged. "Hard to say. Maybe he started a new medication. I haven't seen his chart."

"Or he was given the wrong medication?" I thought of the photo-matching method of distributing serious doses of medicine to the patients in the care center.

"I'd like to say that never happens, but no system is perfect, unfortunately. I did clear the way for you to have a few words with him, if you want" — she grinned — "while I take Jane to the office to fill out some forms."

"Yes, I want," I said.

Mr. Mooney looked older than ever, like a piece of cellophane tape that had dried up, turned yellow, and had no more sticking power.

"You look wonderful," I said to him, setting the flowers I'd picked up in the gift shop on a side table.

He frowned at me. "Miss Hawkes came."

"Yes, I heard she arrived just in time to get you some help." *Save your life* seemed a frightening phrase, given the way he looked.

"I shouldn't have been talking to Miss Muniz."

"You mean Sofia?"

"No, no." A frustrated slamming of his fist on the bedsheets. I doubted the cotton fabric even felt it. "Her granddaughter. She argued with me. I refused to do what she asked, but Miss Hawkes didn't believe me."

"What didn't she believe?"

"I told you — that I can keep a secret. Don't you understand, either? He gave me something to take. Something I saw in the pharmacy."

He? We were off again, it seemed. "Do you mean 'she' gave you something, Mr. Mooney? Ms. Hawkes?"

"He gave it to me because I saw him in the pharmacy."

Mr. Mooney's voice was weaker with each alleged answer. It seemed cruel to keep him talking, but it was to protect him, also, I told myself.

"When were you in the pharmacy?"

"I don't know. Maybe at Easter."

"But it was Ms. Hawkes who found you, today, right? And gave you medicine."

"Yes, she helped me. Then all the doctors came."

It seemed to me that the sequence of events got pretty scrambled in poor Mr. Mooney's brain. Then I remembered what I'd come for. One more question.

"What can you tell me about Dominik Ostrowsky, Mr. Mooney?"

Another fist-slamming gesture, weaker than the others, and accompanied by a smile. "Ha. That's me."

"You're Dominik?"

"Sometimes."

I heard a heavy sigh and a loud throat-clearing. I turned to see Ms. Hawkes in the doorway. She had her hands on her wide hips, looking even more comical than Maddie did with that stance.

She addressed me with a scolding tone. "How fortunate that Miss Mooney came to me about her great-grandfather's fees. And mentioned that he had a visitor. Apparently, Mrs. Porter, you have no regard for an old man's health."

"I'm beginning to think the same of you," I said. "Are you qualified to administer medicine?"

"I do not administer medicine, Mrs. Porter, not that it's any of your business. Visiting hours are over."

I couldn't help noticing how the little silhouette of Mary Todd Lincoln on Nadine's rectangular nameplate bounced up and down with her heaving chest as her remarks and attitude grew more and more intense.

I turned back to Mr. Mooney. "I'll be sure

my nurse friend, Mrs. Reed, looks in on you regularly," I said, in a loud voice, directed as much to Ms. Hawkes as to the patient. "She has direct contact with my nephew, Detective Skip Gowen, also, should you need anything."

I said this as if I had authority over both the Mary Todd nursing staff and the Lincoln Point Police Department.

My cell phone, still attached to its car charger, rang as I was on my way to meet Chrissy Gallagher at the bookstore café.

"Gerry, I need help."

Not Mr. Mooney or Dolores or Linda or Skip, or anyone connected to the Carlos Guzman murder case. Rather, it was Beverly. I had a feeling she was still obsessing over her new love life.

"What's wrong?"

"He wants to go to dinner tonight."

"Who?"

"Not funny, Gerry. The retirement party isn't until Friday, but Nick called to see if I'm free tonight."

Stop the world. Here I was struggling to piece together the Mr. Mooney story — an argument with Dolores Muniz? An allergic reaction? Medicine from Nadine Hawkes, yes or no? All this since I left him on the

339

couch in the lobby this morning? — and my otherwise mature, very intelligent sister-in-law was in the throes of a second adolescence.

"Does this mean you need another outfit?"

"No, but it's so soon. I thought I had the week."

"For what?"

"To get used to the idea."

"It's just dinner, right? Why the cold feet? You have to eat."

"Not at the most expensive restaurant in town."

"In town. That's the operative phrase," I said. "Lincoln Point. We're not talking about San Francisco."

"Goodson's doesn't even have prices on the menu," she reminded me.

"It's not like he has kids to feed. I'm sure he knows what he can afford."

"Am I nuts to worry?"

"That's Maddie's word, but yes, you are nuts."

"I'm sorry. Still love me?"

"You know it."

Passing Tucker's pharmacy on Springfield Boulevard, I got back to what I should be thinking about. Did Nadine give Mr. Mooney medicine? Yes, if I put any stock in his numerous digressions. Could that have caused his allergic reaction? Certainly. But Nadine wasn't one to lie outright, especially to me. I doubted I rated enough in her mind to deserve an answer of any kind. I had the feeling she just blurted out the truth to me before she could think about it. Maybe this was one case where Mr. Mooney was mixed up and it was actually Nadine who saved him.

If so, who administered the bad pill? If that was what happened. What if someone else had been there, besides the lifesaving EMTs?

Also nagging at my brain — why would Mr. Mooney think he was Dominik Ostrowsky, one of the charity cases?

I missed Beverly, with whom I could discuss matters like this. She'd been my sounding board and she'd turned into a single white female, seeking dating advice.

I hoped I'd get her back soon.

CHAPTER 22

I hardly recognized Chrissy, standing at the counter of the café in her regular twenty-first century clothes, which included a bare midriff, reasonable all year long in this part of the country. I wondered if this style of crop-top sweaters combined with low-slung pants was as popular these days during winters in the Bronx, where even a sliver of exposed flesh might result in a case of frostbite.

Chrissy had also changed from the tiny Victorian-style glasses with beaded frames she wore last night to regular-size, plain ones. The look of a serious reporter, except for the little butterfly tattoo above her navel.

I'd given up the nicer clothes I'd chosen for my morning meeting with Dolores. After last night's cumbersome and slightly uncomfortable caroler's outfit, it felt good to be in jeans and my oversize Irish knit.

Chrissy led me to the last table at the back

of the store, though the café area was hardly crowded — I said "hello" to a few unremarkable former students as we made our way.

She waited until I sat down to pull a packet of loose pages from her briefcase. Not the notebook, but I should have realized she wouldn't have been able to get an item out of the evidence room. It was amazing enough that she had contact with someone with access who was willing to copy it.

"I have just a few pages," she said, in a whispery voice, "but it's a start."

The text was in the middle of legal-size white paper, with some images crooked on the page. A rushed job, no doubt. I had visions of a tiny camera hidden in a wrist watch, clicking away, but these looked like good "old-fashioned" photocopies, where the center of a book can't be truly flattened on the machine and a wide band of black appears down the middle.

Carlos Guzman had kept a ledger of names and amounts, presumably dollars, in a simple multicolumn arrangement. The first column was labeled NAMES, followed by a slash mark and what I took to be a city designation, like LP for Lincoln Point, and PA for Palo Alto; the second was labeled IN; the third OUT. The fourth column didn't have a heading, but looked like it could be "reason for our illegal arrangement."

"I suppose I shouldn't ask how you got these?"

Chrissy frowned: not worth answering that question. "The names are sort of in code, but not very sophisticated. Like this one" — she pointed to an entry at the top of one of the pages.

NAMES/PA	IN	OUT
Farn-$	$5000	kback

"Farn–dollar sign must be Farnesworth. Remember him?" Chrissy asked.

I noted the "kback" designation in the last column. "Isn't he the contractor in Palo Alto who was imprisoned for fraudulent business practices?"

"Uh-huh, kickbacks. See, there's a line through his name. You can barely see it on the copy."

Apparently he stopped being a client once he was put away. It was a wonder he didn't turn Carlos in.

Chrissy covered the pages with her soft-sided briefcase when Rosie's weekend fill-in waiter, Randy, came by to take our order. We ordered coffee only, more to get rid of the talkative young man than because the brownies and maple bars weren't tempting. As soon as Randy left, Chrissy whipped the briefcase off the table and we continued scanning.

Another obvious line was for Dolores Muniz of Lincoln Point.

NAME/LP	IN	OUT	
DoLMuN		$8300/m	ID

Carlos was paying Dolores $8,300 per month. An odd number. I did a quick calculation. Rounded off, an extra hundred thousand dollars a year. Enough to support her family in style and to keep her from ID-ing Carlos.

In a way, I felt sorry for Dolores, who would now be called to task for her choices. She'd had other options for her grand-mother and herself, however. I wasn't an expert on California blackmail law, but I was sure there were stiff penalties. Would the DA be stricter or more lenient with someone who worked in city hall? Would it matter that the person she was blackmailing was a very unsavory sort who by all accounts had done great harm to her family? It remained to be seen.

"This is quite a list," I said, too over-whelmed to offer anything smarter or more insightful. "And this is only part of the notebook. He must have been doing business with everyone in three counties."

"I know." Chrissy ran her finger down the pages. "We have council members, store owners, people I recognize from the Civic Club. And geographically, we have San Jose, Santa Clara, Menlo Park, and, look, even L.A."

"Maybe that's for Los Altos," I said, trying to rein in Carlos's influence to the greater South Bay at least.

"Good point. And LG would be Los Gatos. Hmmm, maybe only two-word cities are overrun with crime. There's no C for Cupertino, and no M for Milpitas, where I thought most of the trouble started."

"Thanks for lightening this depressing moment," I said. "I'm almost afraid to look."

"I get it. Someone you trust might be on it."

That was it, exactly. But, so far, so good. No immediate family member or good friend. No Nadine Hawkes, either, I was sorry to see.

Another hiatus while Randy brought our steaming mugs of coffee. He made another attempt to engage us in conversation — something about how it was too bad it didn't rain more over the weekend since we really needed it — but it was all one-sided.

"What did you have in mind to do with this list?" I asked Chrissy once Randy had given up.

"I thought we could put our heads together and maybe make some sense of this and find out who killed the man. All these people had a reason to kill him, assuming this isn't his Christmas list. We could —"

Chrissy, who was facing the door, stopped. She swept the pages off the table and put on a practiced smile.

I turned to see what had that effect on her. My nephew's appearance was what did it.

"I heard that my number-one snoop is meeting with a reporter. So, I couldn't resist stopping in to say hi," Skip said, pulling up a chair.

"Aren't you off duty?" I asked him.

"The LPPD is never truly off duty."

"How did you know where I was? I guess I'm still being followed." (I was strangely relieved to think I was being watched over.)

"The LPPD doesn't divulge its policies and procedures to civilians." He turned to Chrissy. Having fun. "Or to reporters."

Chrissy, not swayed by Skip's charm, had a more substantive question. "Is it true that

Carlos Guzman went around digging up dirt on people and getting money from them?"

"I can confirm the spirit, if not the language of that summary. We went to a fast-food place listed in his notebook, for example, and all of a sudden half of their staff is on vacation. Carlos's murder sent up flags. You'd be amazed at how many businesses, small and large, use illegals."

"Wouldn't it be cheaper to hire legal workers and save the money Carlos was extorting?" I asked.

"I've seen this kind of practice," Chrissy said. "It's how many companies operate. I know several that choose to pay fines rather than clean up their toxic waste pits, for example. It's the same principle."

"You got it," Skip said. "I'm sure they had it down to a science, and Carlos came in under budget, cheaper than legitimate hiring practices."

Skip and Chrissy had more experience in the ways of the world than your average retired high school English teacher, I realized.

"So Carlos was your basic bad guy," Chrissy said. "Except the people he took money from all had something criminal, or at least scandalous, to hide." She'd magically produced a steno pad where, earlier, unauthorized photocopies had lain.

"Not that I'm sympathetic, but how frustrated he must have been, accumulating all that money and unable to use it openly," I said.

"He sent a lot of money to his son's family in Mexico, but he could never visit because he knew he'd never get back into the United States. INS has been looking for him for a long time. It would take us all into the next decade to investigate every one of the people on his list."

"And Carlos is not worth the trouble?"

"I'm not saying that. Anyway I'd think you'd be pleased. It means we're not pursuing a case against Sofia Muniz. Not right now, anyway. By the way, Chrissy, just to set the record straight, we didn't withhold information from the *Lincolnite*. Sofia Muniz was a person of interest for a time, but never arrested. And at this point there are way too many loose ends and too many possibles. The missing van driver for one."

Chrissy wrote furiously.

Skip played into the moment. "Plus" — Skip pointed to Chrissy's briefcase — "all the people on that list."

We both blushed.

"Gotta go," Skip said. "Everybody cool?"

"We're cool," we said.

I wanted to talk to Skip about Nadine and the finances of the Mary Todd Home, but not in front of Chrissy. I had my protocol. I'd corner him at dinner, which, since I'd be preparing the meal and feeding him, his mother (if she didn't go on her date with Nick), and his girlfriend at my home, I felt was my prerogative.

Chrissy pulled the pages out from her briefcase. "That was embarrassing," she said.

"Skip often brings that to a party," I said.

"He's cute. Is he . . . ?"

I thought of June, swimming with Maddie. "Yes, he is."

"Serious?" she asked.

How would I know? I shrugged my shoulders and gave her a helpless look. Here I was once again in the middle of my relatives' dating lives. "You'll have to ask him yourself," I said.

Chrissy was untroubled. "No problem. Back to these pages. We should go down the list and see who are the likely suspects. We can divide up the —"

I held up my hand. "Isn't that the job of the police?"

Chrissy's look of disappointment was the

same as if her favorite teacher had fallen from grace. "Don't you *care* who killed this man and why? I mean someone picked up a rock or a two-by-four or whatever it was and killed another human being."

Not a rock or piece of wood, but I got the idea. I may have been misjudging her, but I had the feeling Chrissy's good-citizen glasses were tinted with a Pulitzer prize plaque for herself and a gold medal for the *Lincolnite.* Here was the opportunity to expose nearly every prominent person in town.

"I'm not a trained investigator, Chrissy." I left it to her to admit whether or not she considered herself in that category. "What makes you think we can do better than the professionals?"

"It's not that I think I'm smarter than the police, but I do have investigative skills, and I can focus on this in a way that they can't. They're dealing with all the crime in town." She sounded as if Lincoln Point was near the top of the list of cities with the highest per capita crime rate. "You heard Skip. They have a whole notebook of people to look into for this case, plus keep the streets safe. All we have to do is put together some theories and follow through. What's there to lose?"

My own sense of safety, and that of my family for one. Neither was I willing to violate the privacy of the people on Carlos's list, a Pandora's box that surely would have far-reaching effects.

Chrissy tapped her steno pad. Waiting for an answer. *Are you in?* I read.

I stood to leave. "Investigating these people is just not my job, Chrissy."

She gave me a sideways look. "You're not going to work with another paper are you? *The Mountain View Voice? The Campbell Reporter?* Because if it's some kind of perk you're after, I might be able to arrange it."

Amusing as the idea was, it hit me the wrong way. I was annoyed that Chrissy knew that little about me.

"I have to bake holiday cookies," I said.

She folded the notebook pages and stuck them in my tote. Nervy. "In case you change your mind."

I turned to leave. "Merry Christmas, Chrissy."

CHAPTER 23

I headed down Springfield Boulevard toward home. As the number of shopping days till Christmas plummeted, the street became more and more busy and the quantity of sparkling decorations grew. I looked forward to visiting with my son and daughter-in-law soon and seeing firsthand that Richard was not suffering from a deadly disease.

I had to get moving on baking the cookies I'd used as an excuse to refuse Chrissy. I ran through the list of ingredients in my head, mentally checking off what I already had in my pantry (an outstanding feature of Lincoln Point's Eichler homes), but the list became inextricably entwined with elements of the crimes of the past few days. Maraschino cherries turned into the blood-splattered nightgown Sofia Muniz was wearing when they found her in her old neighborhood; licorice tubes became slashed tires; the rolls of dough I would twist into candy-cane shapes stiffened into a piece of rebar.

In spite of my "final" word to Chrissy, I had a nagging feeling that I already had all the pieces I needed to put together the puzzle that was Carlos Guzman's murder. Not that I would change my mind about working with the *Lincolnite* reporter. For all my feminist leanings — like wanting Maddie to be in a position of great influence someday — when it came right down to it, I didn't like pushy people, male or female.

But I hated loose ends even more, and right now there were many, sticking out everywhere, like the stray threads I wrestled with when I tried to fringe tiny swatches of velour to look like a beach towel. I wondered if I'd be able to sweep away my shiftless thoughts as easily.

It had been a long day, beginning with my meeting Dolores and extracting her confession and ending with my tussle with Chrissy. I was glad to arrive home, especially to the unexpected aroma of a pot roast dinner. Beverly had taken it upon herself to prepare our Sunday evening meal.

"What a treat, Beverly," I said. "But did I

miss something on the calendar for to-night?"

"No, no. It's a surprise. I know you had a tough time today."

Not a good enough reason for taking over my kitchen. My sister-in-law was behaving much too skittishly. "And?" I asked.

She patted down her beautiful hair and grinned. "I invited Nick. I hope that's okay."

"I thought you were going to Goodson's for dinner tonight."

"I couldn't do it. Too formal. I need to feel comfortable, like we're just hanging around with family. And, you know, my house . . . well, I'm not ready to have him over to my house. I mean cooking dinner for just the two of us? Not yet. It's okay, isn't it?"

"It's fine, Beverly." I savored the aroma of boiled carrots and potatoes and rubbed her shoulders. "Take a breath and calm down. You're a nervous wreck. You're making me realize how long it's been since I had to worry about these things." *And how glad I am I don't have to right now,* I added silently.

"It's not worry." She ran her hands down the sides of her apron (my apron). "Okay, it's worry. He'll be here about seven. Skip and Maddie are at June's making dessert. I'm glad we could have this chat first."

"Me, too."

Thanks to Maddie, who kept up a constant chatter about June's club and the "cool kids" she met there, the conversation around the dinner table wasn't as strained as I thought it might be. We resorted to such comments as "these carrots are perfect" and "wow, the meat melts in your mouth" only a few times.

Once Maddie left the table to help June dish out the dessert — fruit cobbler with homemade ice cream — I took advantage of having two cops, one on either side of me, eating from my holly-and-ivy china.

"Did you check out the finances at the Mary Todd?" I asked them. "Shall I repeat the suspicious names? Ethel Hudson, Juanita —"

"I got the names," Skip said. "I've had them for all of, like, three hours. What kind of miracles do you expect?"

"Skip doesn't want to give you too much credit, but the lead on the van driver has paid off," Nick said. He addressed Skip's frown. "It's going to hit the papers in the morning, anyway."

"I just don't want my aunt to hear it first."

If it weren't for his telltale smirk, which he tried to hide behind a buttermilk biscuit,

I would have thought Skip was serious. I turned my head to block him out, and asked Nick, "Did you find Gus Boudette?"

"On Thursday afternoon, about twelve hours after the murder, Gus Boudette flew first class to Biot, a little spot on the French Riviera."

Apparently I was among the last people to see Gus at the Mary Todd on Thursday morning, when he lied about being paged. "I've never heard of Biot."

"That was the idea. There's no guaranteed extradition to the United States, since Gus — Augustin, that is — has dual citizenship. He was born in France."

"And there's a lot of fine print on extradition treaties," Skip added. "We'd need much more cause than we have. We don't have that much against him, except that he knew where to pick up the Muniz woman."

"He does have a sealed record as a juvenile offender," Nick said. "But that's not relevant, and there's no motive that we can determine for him to have killed Guzman."

"He skipped town," I said. "Doesn't that matter?"

Nick shook his head. "Not if we didn't ask him to stay around. He left before we had a clue that we'd need to talk to him any more than we already did. He didn't violate any law, nor disobey us."

"Is he in Carlos's notebook?" I asked.

Skip looked at me with raised eyebrows. "Haven't you checked?"

I hoped my face didn't turn too red. "I don't have all the pages," I said in a near whisper.

My embarrassment drew a satisfied grin, happily interrupted by an announcement from Maddie. "Dessert is now being served in the atrium."

There was a mad scramble to move chairs and drinks to the part of my home that looked most like Christmas — unless you counted the bed on which Richard and Mary Lou were scheduled to sleep, now covered with gift boxes, rolls of wrapping paper, and spools of ribbon.

"Gus could have been working with someone else," I suggested, on the way to the dessert and coffee, as if I'd come up with a brilliant idea, a killer for hire, that no cop would have thought of.

"Then it's that someone else we need," Nick said.

How well I knew.

Maddie chose dessert time to report on a phone call she'd taken while she was home with Beverly.

"I forgot to tell you, Grandma. Mom and Dad called and they may not be here until Friday because of Dad's surgery," she said.

My arms went weak; I nearly dropped the heaping bowl of cobbler and ice cream on my lap. "Surgery?" I asked, barely getting the syllables out. "What kind of surgery?"

"You know this happens every year," Beverly said. "Lots of people use their Christmas to New Year's vacation for elective surgery." Of course. The holiday rush for nonemergency procedures. For Richard's patients, not for Richard himself.

My exhaled breath was loud enough to cause Beverly to ask, "Are you okay? You sound as though you thought Richard was having surgery," at which point everyone laughed and told "my son the doctor" jokes.

I laughed harder than anyone.

Tonight's project for the Bronx apartment was to add some Christmas spirit to it. We'd already erected a tree in the corner of the living/dining room and added beads and ribbons for ornaments.

Tonight we made a centerpiece for the dining room table; that is, the only table we had. We glued crafts-store lichen onto a mound of green florist's foam. For candles we poked red toothpicks from a package of multicolor party picks into the foam. I showed Maddie how adding a coat of clear nail polish to the toothpicks made the wood look waxy. We attached tiny bows and flowers and called it done.

"That was too easy," Maddie said.

Music to my ears. "We could make stockings."

"There's no fireplace. Where did you and Grandpa hang your stockings?"

My mind traveled back to our early Christmases in the Bronx. Not always snowy, but cold enough to keep the sidewalk Santas from perspiring as they did in the strip malls of Lincoln Point. "We hung the stockings on nails in the bookcase, and later on your dad's crib."

Maddie looked horrified. "You put nails in your bookcase?"

I realized Maddie was picturing our defacing the fine walnut bookcases Richard had built along two walls of the large Porter living room in Los Angeles. "Not to worry. Our bookcases were just cinder blocks and planks of wood. We could hardly ruin them."

We spent some time making a miniature bookcase with strips of wood and gray modeling clay "blocks." A dash of silver glitter gave the clay the sparkly, grainy look of cinder blocks. Maddie glued felt stockings decorated with sequins to the edges of the shelves.

"Did you glue things to your apartment bookcases, too?"

"Sometimes. We might have glued photos or a streamer for a birthday party."

"Just like with dollhouses?"

"Uh-huh."

"I could never put nails or glue on my bookcase. I wish I lived in the Bronx."

Some days I did, too.

After a day of shopping, swimming, tennis, and crafts (unchallenging though they were) Maddie was tired enough to suggest an early story from her teen (a bit premature?) magazine. I knew she could read at an impressively high level herself, but these were special moments and I was happy to hold on to them for as long as Maddie wanted.

It took only one column of text before I closed the magazine and tucked the baseball quilt under Maddie's chin.

Maddie liked to use a special nightlight — a ceramic figurine that had seen Richard off to sleep for many years. I turned it on. On top of the illuminated base, home plate rotated, as a wholesome-looking boy in a red cap swung over and over again at a nonexistent ball.

The futility of the game he was playing reminded me too much of my last couple of days. I turned him off and switched on a small bulb with a simple plastic shade.

My guests had cleaned up the kitchen for the most part. Skip and June had gone off soon after dinner, and Beverly and Nick drove separate cars to . . . I didn't know where. I expected Beverly to call with a report or a reaction to her relocated date. Maybe it was a good sign that she hadn't.

By ten thirty I was able to relax in my atrium in front of my twinkling life-size tree with a mug of hot cider and my thoughts.

On my long table near the foyer was my oversize tote/purse, in its usual spot until I cleaned it out and sorted the receipts and other scraps of the day. A tiny triangle of white stuck up from a side pocket — the pages of Carlos's notebook, stuffed in there by Chrissy. Just a couple of inches of paper, but they seemed out of place and almost frightening, as if they had blood on them, which, in a way, they did.

I wished they didn't also have a kind of magnetic force drawing me to pick them up.

I worried about Mr. Mooney. What if he

knew whatever it was Carlos Guzman had in his notebook, and Nadine had tried to harm him, not help him? He said she gave him medicine, which might have been a pill she knew Mr. Mooney was allergic to, or something generally toxic from the pharmacy.

So far there'd been a kernel of truth in everything the Mary Todd residents reported. The problem was, what was the kernel and what was the part that should be thrown away? A biblical expression concerning wheat and chaff came to mind, but I'd never studied the Bible enough to know if the analogy was apt here.

Nadine had no way of knowing that, given what we'd put together from Linda's snooping and the residents comments, her scheme was about to blow up in her face anyway. Neither could she know whether she was listed in Carlos's notebook. She might have figured that she'd be safe as long as Carlos and Mr. Mooney were out of the way.

On the other hand (there always was another side in this case), Mr. Mooney also said *he* gave him a pill. Did someone else happen upon him in the lobby? Maybe Gus had come back from vacation to clean up loose ends.

I knew I'd never forgive myself if anything

happened to Mr. Mooney and I could have prevented it. Maybe Sofia wasn't safe now, either, if the real killer thought she knew the truth. At the very least I should visit Sofia, who'd been a friend, now that she was not under guard.

I struggled for a few more minutes, holding on to my mug of hot cider more and more tightly, restraining my fingers lest they stray to the paper in my tote. Finally, I pulled the notebook pages from the pocket and opened them on my lap.

When my phone rang at that moment, I would have sworn it was Carlos Guzman calling to chide me from his grave. "Just as I expected," he'd say. "Your prurient interests have gotten the better of you."

"Did I wake you up?" Not Carlos, but Linda.

"No, I'm just winding down from the day." Hardly.

"We're still on for Jason in the morning, right?"

"Right." I tried to put a little oomph in my voice, as if that would be the highlight.

Now that I thought of working with Jason — it would be a nice, satisfying change from the puzzles of the Guzman case.

Chrissy had foisted three pages on me. I

wouldn't have been surprised if she'd held back a few, once she knew I was going to be neither her police insider nor her zealous partner.

The set contained about thirty entries, all in Carlos's large, loping handwriting. I'd been picturing his notebook as a "little black book," but looking closely at the copies, I saw that Carlos had used the standard, slightly larger than 8 1/2-by-11-inch spiral-bound variety. Thus, it took legal-size paper to accommodate the pages, with some margin for error. There were three dark circles down the side of the photocopies, the distances between them matching what you would expect from three-hole-punched paper. I imagined a shelf full of binders filled with these notebooks in Carlos's Nolin Creek Pines apartment.

I ran my finger down the lists on the pages, scanning quickly. To my relief, the number of LP designations was fewer than two or three per page. Other than spotting an occasional big man around town, I didn't recognize the names. I saw nothing that could be easily interpreted as pertaining to Gus or Nadine. Skip and Nick had more or less implied that there was no mention of Gus in the full notebook, or they would have had a reason to go after him more intensely.

On the third page, my finger stopped, then (almost) my heart. The entry read:

NAME/LP	IN	OUT	
STITCH	inf.	inf.	farm

There was my S-something-CH. At least, it could be. No money was changing hands here. Both Carlos and STITCH were putting out information (I guessed), the reason being "farm," whatever that meant.

I hated that the name was STITCH, as if the perpetrator of the crime (whatever it was) was a crafter. The ones I knew were incapable of anything other than cheating on the way they built room boxes — the equivalent of using a cake mix, but embellishing it, instead of starting from scratch.

I thought of the crafters who came to my house regularly on Wednesday evenings to do projects together. Besides Linda Reed and Gail Musgrave, there was Susan (Tennessee) Giles, old Mabel Quinlan (our Queen of Beads), and Betty (Tudor mansions) Fine, plus others who dropped in occasionally. Not a criminal bone among them.

The underworld of extortion was foreign

to me. I was beginning to understand only the top layer of its workings. Any one of Carlos's notebook residents could have turned him in — why didn't they? Trying to think like a criminal, I reasoned that Dolores and STITCH profited more from what Carlos could give them. The others, who were paying money into Carlos's IN column, must have had their own reasons for agreeing to the blackmail. I could only guess that in each case the one who had the most to lose paid the most.

In STITCH's case, it seemed likely that he and Carlos were sharing information by some mutual agreement. STITCH must also have something to lose, I reasoned, or he/she/it wouldn't have been following me around. Maybe he stood to lose the farm.

I said this to myself as if it were now all clear.

There were several ranches in town, and many more in the greater San Jose area, but Lincoln Point had only a "learning" farm at the edge of town where schoolchildren went to experience the daily life of a farm family. (Personally, I was happy having my farm products delivered to my local market.)

I looked out the narrow window next to my front door, into the darkness and a quiet, empty street. I hoped it stayed that way.

CHAPTER 24

While Maddie slept in, I got some materials ready for Jason, who was due to come for his tutoring session at nine thirty on Monday morning.

It was hard to concentrate on Steinbeck with STITCH running around my brain. I'd been so glib, telling Jason to make connections and then make more connections, and now I was stuck not being able to connect all the threads of the Muniz case.

Mr. Mooney's "he" who gave him pills or some kind of medication confused me, since I wanted to pin everything on Nadine. I envisioned her trying to poison Mr. Mooney but almost getting caught when the EMTs arrived unexpectedly, and then turning it around to look like she'd found him. All of which could still be the correct scenario.

Unless someone else had been in the lobby just before her.

I called Linda, catching her as she was

leaving her house for errands.

"You're not canceling, are you, Gerry? Jason just took off on his bike."

If there was a way to spin a negative interpretation of Santa Claus, Linda would find it. "No, I'm looking forward to seeing Jason."

"What, then? More Mary Todd research?"

She had me there. "If you don't mind."

"Okay, shoot."

"Does the home keep the daily sign-in sheets?"

"Yes, we have them going back to day one." Just what I hoped. "Who are you looking for, Gerry?"

"No one in particular." This much was true.

"We collect them by the week, so we've already filed last week's log away in the records room."

"Then that log would have ended with yesterday?"

"Right."

"Can you get a copy for me?"

"All three years' worth?"

Tempting, but I had to stay focused. "No, just last week's."

"Can you wait until tomorrow? I'm not working today and if I go in and putter around the records it will look suspicious."

"What good thinking, Linda. Tomorrow will be fine."

"That's it? No other questions? Don't you want to know how Mr. Mooney is?"

"I didn't want to nag." "Push my luck" was more like it.

"He had a guard outside his door last night. This place is getting to be Lincoln Point Jail North. He doesn't have anyone with him now though."

"Why did they remove the security?"

"They took Nadine in."

It was amazing what you could learn if you *didn't* ask.

While Jason and I worked out some ideas on how he might embellish his next paper with references to other works of Steinbeck and his contemporaries, Maddie seemed content to work on her own vacation assignments. She sat in the rocking chair and wrote laboriously in a spiral-bound notebook just like the one Carlos had used. I looked over every now and then, enjoying her contemplative mood, her serious pencil chewing, the way stray red strands fell across her forehead.

I projected ahead a few days to when her parents would be here, then past that to when they returned to L.A. I was missing them already, but that's how it was when family came and went as they did. I wished away the days till they arrived, and then wanted to stop time while they were here.

After about a half hour Maddie decided to abandon her history project and finish wrapping her presents for her parents.

"I'll be in my bedroom if you need me," she said. (Was that a wink?)

Just the opportunity I was waiting for. I took out my cell phone and handed it to Jason.

"Cool," he said. "You have a camera, a GPS, and text messaging."

Cool to Jason, maybe, but all I'd wanted was a way to make and receive phone calls. "Do you know how to reprogram these things to change the way it rings?" I asked him.

"Sure."

"Do I need to have a source of songs, like when you download music onto the iPod?"

Jason clicked away, his fingers flying as mine used to do on the typewriter. The computer keyboard didn't have the same feel to me, nor the same interesting sound, and I couldn't seem to get up to the same speed with the new keys.

"Not really," Jason said. "You've got a lot of tunes to choose from right here." He showed me a list of built-in melodies that were my options.

"I don't have time to review all these. We have to be quick, before Maddie comes back. This is our little secret, okay?" Jason smiled, his chubby cheeks filling out. "Can you just pick something for me?"

More clicks, and Jason handed it back, still grinning. I wondered if I should be worried about his choice.

"Thank you so much," I said.

"Anytime, Mrs. Porter."

With that out of the way, we got back to literature.

Jason's teacher had asked him to rewrite his *Of Mice and Men* paper, and he'd already given it some thought. "I'm going to do the theme of loneliness," he told me. "How all the characters in the novel are lonely in different ways."

I had a feeling that Jason knew a lot about loneliness, but he seemed to have turned a corner and was on the road to average teenage angst. I thought of the rough start he'd had. Both of his birth parents qualified as losers, in and out of jail, on and off drugs. His first few years with Linda and her second husband were rife with conflict that continued even after Linda and Chuck divorced. But this was a new Jason, working, studying, even warming up to vacation tutoring.

Sitting with him at my atrium table, I had great hope for his future. I was glad I'd decided to give this relationship a try (as if choosing anything else wouldn't have cost me my friendship with Linda).

"That's a terrific idea, Jason," I told him. "How do you plan to approach the essay?"

Jason pulled out a piece of paper, buried in the pages of his notebook — also the kind that Carlos Guzman had used. These must be standard issue now in schoolrooms. I brushed away the absurd image of Carlos going around to school- and office-supply stores, stealing notebooks.

"Here's my outline," he said, making my heart swell.

I looked over his plan, which was to give each character his or her own section, with an explanation of why the person might be lonely and how it was revealed in the novel through Steinbeck's choices of words and imagery.

"Cool," I said.

I wanted badly to go to the Mary Todd, to see both Sofia and Mr. Mooney. And whoever else might be around. But I had to cut my curiosity off somewhere, especially now that the police apparently had their culprit in the form of Financial Manager (or not) Nadine Hawkes.

I thought of inviting Beverly over for lunch, as a distraction. Surely her date with Nick was over by now. But maybe not.

I played it safe all around and decided to devote the afternoon to finally getting the house ready for Richard and Mary Lou and finishing up my Christmas cards.

"What will you charge for putting stamps on fifty cards?" I asked Maddie.

"Do I have to lick them?"

"No."

"Then it's free."

I insisted on a reward and we settled on pizza for dinner (her idea) and a supplement to the spending money her parents had given her (my idea). I'd wanted to do that anyway, indulgent though it was.

By two o'clock my secondary crafts room looked like a storage locker, with hardly room to open the door. The neatest room in the house was the guest room, now ready for Richard and Mary Lou, dust-free, with fresh sheets and two empty dresser drawers for their use. Maddie planned to buy flowers for the night table just before they arrived.

We sat with my cards, envelopes, and

stamps arranged on the dining-room table, the atrium table being unavailable due to a mound of odds and ends that had been in the guest room.

From somewhere we heard the unmistakable, majestic strains of the 1812 Overture. I traced the sound back to the kitchen counter where my cell phone battery was charging.

Maddie looked up, confused. I savored the moment, silently thanking Jason Reed for his technical prowess and his taste in music (or guessing mine). Maddie looked around, frowning, and then saw the green light of my cell phone.

We broke out in gales of laughter. "How did you figure it out?" she asked me.

"I'm smart."

I was dismayed by her doubtful expression. "Don't you think I'm smart?"

Clearly a pivotal decision for my granddaughter. Then the light — she made an attempt to snap her fingers, producing a soft rubbery sound. "Jason, right? When?"

"While you were wrapping your parents' presents."

"Nuts."

I was having such a good time with this coup, I almost forgot to answer the call.

■ ■ ■ ■

"Breaking news," Skip said.

"You took Nadine Hawkes in," I said.

"It's hard to beat your hotline."

"But that's all I know." Silence. "Please, Skip?"

"I do owe you."

"Oh, tell me more."

"First, I'm sure you'd want to know, Dolores made a deal just in time. She got the DA out of his daughter's wedding yesterday and told him what she knew about Hawkes's scheme. She was able to leverage that against her own case. Another half day and we would have had the grant people in tow and not needed her."

Maddie gestured to me that she was going to her room. I blew her a kiss, happy that I wouldn't have to watch my language while talking to Skip.

"I'm sure Dolores realized you'd be on it once the banks opened this morning."

"And that we were. She'd tried to get Mooney to testify to corroborate her story, but he wouldn't do it. I think he was afraid of Hawkes."

I agreed. I'd seen the frightened looks myself. I mentally put one more checkmark in Mr. Mooney's column. He did have an argument with Dolores, as he claimed — another kernel of truth from someone whose proclamations were more than likely discounted on a daily basis.

"How much can you tell me about Nadine's scheme?"

"You mean how right were you?"

"Sort of."

"We met representatives from that senior foundation today at the Mary Todd." The one day I didn't go there. As Maddie would say, *nuts.* "Not surprising, none of the three current grant residents could be found. Meanwhile, other reps of the foundation were at the banks they send checks to. Making a long story short, the clerks in all the banks ID'd a photo of Nadine Hawkes as either Ethel Hudson or Juanita Ramirez."

"And Mr. Mooney was Dominik Ostrowsky."

"Yeah. She was pretty clever — she recruited Mooney so she could collect on a male resident also. Who knows why?"

"Maybe to make it all look more legitimate?"

"Could be, since she was presenting these fake names to the foundation. One time on an unannounced visit by the grant people, she was able to at least produce the so-called Dominik Ostrowsky, if not the women."

I guessed when he wasn't afraid of letting the secret slip, Mr. Mooney had had a good time with the plot, calling himself Dominik's twin, and then Dominik himself. I wondered if what he thought was a joke had nearly cost him his life.

I was reminded of the fake mailman Beverly had uncovered in the course of her LPPD volunteer duties. I was astounded, not for the first time, at how many ways people came up with to cheat others out of their money.

"I think I owe you an apology or a thank-you or something," Skip said. "Dolores's confession really started things off."

"Let's not stop there. How is Nadine connected to Carlos's murder? Is she in his book?"

"Oh, that's right. You and Lois Lane don't have the whole book."

"What happened to the apologetic and grateful tone?"

"Okay, one more minute of this, then I have to go. Nadine Hawkes was not in Guzman's notebook, but that doesn't mean Guzman didn't know about her scheme. It certainly would be better for us if we had evidence that he knew, but we can work with what we have."

I gulped. "Did she try to kill Mr. Mooney?"

"There's every reason to believe that, although she's ranting that she didn't kill anyone. That she really did try to help the old man. She claims someone else must have given him the overdose."

"So it was an overdose of his own medication? What was it?"

"I think that's enough. Why don't I just copy you on my report?"

"That would be nice."

I heard his standard guffaw. "In your dreams. Gotta go."

"Wait, wait. One more thing. Was she working with Gus?"

"She claims she barely knew Gus or any of the van drivers. He was just a name on her payroll. Say good-bye, Aunt Gerry."

He hung up before I had a chance to ask if Nadine Hawkes could have visitors in jail.

CHAPTER 25

I couldn't believe I'd missed the excitement at the Mary Todd. After all the time I'd spent there, four days in a row, I felt I deserved to see some action. My goal now was to get there today, to see Sofia and Mr. Mooney. I mentally scratched Ethel Hudson and her two imaginary friends off my list.

Maddie came out of her room with a Christmas gift bag spilling over with red tissue. Since she had chosen to wrap this in her room, I took a wild guess. "For me?" I asked.

"Maybe."

I'd already devised a plan to trick my granddaughter into another trip to the Mary Todd.

"Remember that sink we started a couple of nights ago for Mrs. Muniz?" She nodded. "How would you like to finish it and deliver it to her today?"

Her face morphed into a doubtful expression as she processed the idea. "Shouldn't we wait until Christmas?"

"She's had a very tough time lately and this might cheer her up."

"What will we have for dinner?" the ten-year-old master negotiator asked.

"Pizza, of course."

She knew when she was being had, and so did I.

Maddie and I had worked on and off on the sink for Sofia. My original idea had been to build a whole old-style kitchen, such as Sofia might have had as a child, but now I was in a hurry. I needed the sink as an excuse for both Maddie and Dolores. I hadn't heard the details of Dolores's deal with the DA, but I imagined it included no jail time. I expected her to be hovering around her grandmother.

We'd already made the basic sink from white modeling clay and the faucets from brass jewelry findings. Adding a skirt, with a tiny fifties-style floral pattern, was the fun part. I showed Maddie how to make two rows of loose stitches and then pull on the ends to make gathers.

We tightened the skirt around the top of the sink, leaving an opening in front for access to the underside of the sink.

"Why do we need the skirt?" Maddie asked.

"To hide the pipes."

"This sink doesn't have any pipes."

"We're pretending."

"Oh, right. I keep forgetting." She gave me the cutest smile.

Poor Maddie. She must have tired of the employee lounge. She asked to be dropped at Rosie Norman's bookstore. It was quite a distance in the opposite direction, but I didn't dare refuse.

"This means you won't be with me when I give Mrs. Muniz her little sink."

"It's okay. You can give it to her."

A pang of guilt nearly threw me off balance as I entered my car. "You can pick out as many books as you want at Rosie's and I'll buy them for you," I said to her.

"I know," she said.

I cringed. Another home-grown lesson from Grandma — bribery as a form of contrition.

Since Linda was not working today I was worried that I'd have to resort to legitimate means to gain access to Sofia and Mr. Mooney. To my delight, however, I recognized the young woman reading a book in the lobby of the Mary Todd.

"Jane Mooney?" I asked, remembering the same lovely features and strawberry blond hair from a photograph her great-grandfather had showed me.

She looked up from, of all things, Steinbeck's *Travels with Charley.* "That's right," she said, in a lilting voice.

"I'm Geraldine Porter. I teach crafts here and —"

Jane jumped off the easy chair and took my hand. "Oh, I've been trying to get in touch with you." She pointed to the reception desk. "They won't give me your phone number." They don't like me very much, I almost admitted. "They said to wait until your class on Friday, but by then I'll be gone."

Jane's "gone" rhymed with "bone" and "phone," which I supposed made sense. "What a coincidence," I said. "Here I am, wanting to talk to you, too."

"Gramps has been asking for you. He's in therapy right now, so I decided to wait down here where it's so nice and cheery."

I pointed to her book. "Are you a Steinbeck fan?"

"Not yet, but I thought since I'm so close to his part of the country I should read at least one of his books."

Lincoln Point was more than an hour from the Salinas Valley, but compared to the trip from Kentucky, Jane was "close." We spent a pleasant few minutes talking about the Steinbeck museum, which Jane was planning to visit before returning home. I resolved to take Maddie there next time. I thought she might be impressed at seeing the truck that Steinbeck and his poodle, Charley, traveled in on their journey around the country. The idea of a museum might not thrill her at first, but she'd see that it would be more interesting than all the break rooms she'd spent this vacation in.

"Do you know if your great-grandfather had something in particular in mind when he asked to see me?"

She shook her head. "Just that he says you believed him about a lot of things that have been going on around here, when no one else would."

"I'm very glad to hear that." Jane didn't need to know about my poor record with Sandy Sechrest. I hoped Sandy enjoyed the flowers and the See's candy and that she and I could consider ourselves buddies.

"People think old folks don't know what they're talking about. They don't realize that most of them, such as my gramps, have had full and productive lives and are capable of a lot more."

Jane's rhythm almost forced an "amen" from my lips, but I checked it, lest she think I was ridiculing her. "I know your gramps is an amazing craftsman. Did he do that for a living?"

"No, he had a very responsible position as a manager with a shipping company for many years. He oversaw a ton of employees, negotiated contracts, and controlled a huge budget. And this was in the day when you did it all without an MBA, if you know what I mean. But he was always whittling things for all of us kids."

Jane's gaze shifted back through time, where her memories were apparently fond ones. I hoped Maddie's would be as pleasant, in spite of the frustrating hours she'd spent in Lincoln Point this vacation. "You're lucky to have each other," I said, meaning Maddie and me as well as Jane and Mr. Mooney.

"I wonder why that is." Why they were lucky? No, Jane was back on the earlier topic. "That no one takes them seriously once they reach a certain age?"

I'd given this some thought already, especially during the last few days, and especially since I'd proven myself guilty of the same prejudices. "I think once physical faculties start to go, younger people assume it's all over for that person. If you don't hear as well, people think you're dumber than you used to be, for example. Or if your bones start to creak, it's perceived as a mental failing as well."

"Wait until they get there themselves, I say," Jane mused.

Another "amen" formed on my lips. Jane had a much longer wait than I did. I decided it wasn't too soon for me to pitch in and try to change some attitudes. I could start by making sure I treated my Mary Todd students and all the older crafters I knew with the healthy respect they deserved.

Mr. Mooney sat in the living area of his one-bedroom apartment — the Fort Blakely floor plan, if I remembered correctly from Linda's tutorial. He was wrapped in a plaid blanket from the waist down, his walker nowhere in sight. I expected there would be a long recovery from the attack on his body and he wouldn't be the Wandering Irishman, cruising the hallways in the very near future.

"Mr. Mooney, I'm glad to see you looking so well." It seemed to me I'd been down this road with him before. "I've been eager to see how you were doing. I had a nice little talk with Jane just now."

Jane had remained in the lobby, having decided that her great-grandfather and I should have a private conversation. "I think he worries about me and he might not be so candid about whatever it is, if I'm there," she'd said.

"Truth be told, Jane's my favorite of the bunch, though we're not supposed to have them," Mr. Mooney said. (One advantage of having an only child who had an only child.) He picked up a paper cup with two very large yellow pills in it. "I'm waiting till later to take these suckers, so I can think and talk better."

"Do those pills make you sleepy?"

"Yup. And fuzzy, too, and that's when I can get confused. They're supposed to help my liver do its work, but they can make me crazy."

"Jane said there was something you wanted to talk to me about."

Mr. Mooney's nod was so animated, I was afraid his nose plug would disengage. "I heard Miss Hawkes was arrested. I know she was cheating some organization out of money, and, God forgive me, I helped her."

"You're not to blame if someone took advantage of you."

"Maybe not, but I feel bad all the same.

But I have to tell you, crooked and scary as that lady is, she wasn't the one what gave me the pill in the lobby. And the police won't listen."

"I think at first you said she was the one who gave you medicine."

Mr. Mooney slapped his knee in frustration, a gesture I'd come to enjoy. "I know that, but I told the police this morning that I was wrong. Can't a person make a simple mistake and try to correct it? It was a man there in the lobby. I'm tired of no one paying attention. Now you don't believe me, either."

"No, no, that's not true, Mr. Mooney. That's why I came here this morning. To find out what happened directly from you. I was confused when I saw you yesterday."

"Do you know they sent a Santa Claus here last week?"

Uh-oh. Had I lost him? "Santa came?"

"They had us all in the ballroom, seated in rows, like when someone comes to give a lecture. I like those, by the way. We had a black man come talk to us about the Tuskegee airmen from the war."

I knew when Mr. Mooney referred to "the war" he meant WWII, notwithstanding the unfortunate dozens there had been since then. "You were telling me about Santa."

"Santa came through the rows with his 'ho, ho, ho,' and foisted presents on all of us, asking if we'd been good boys and girls. Can you imagine?"

I groaned. "How offensive."

"Insulting, it was. Did you know that Gertie was a high school principal up in the Napa Valley? Her grandchildren brought her down here so they could watch over her."

Gertie was also the best knitter I'd ever met, still coming up with her own intricate patterns. "That was thoughtful of them."

"My point is that Santa was talking to us as if we were three years old. Gertie kept telling him, no, she didn't want the presents from that stupid bag on his back, but he kept trying to leave the gifts with her, talking more and more baby talk. Finally, she threw the box back at him. Got him on the noggin."

Good for her, I thought, and joined him in malicious laughter.

I was feeling guilty that Mr. Mooney had delayed his medication too long. "I should go soon," I told him, "but I want to be sure I have this straight. You're certain that it was a man who gave you the pill in the lobby yesterday?"

"Yup. And I'm pretty sure it was the guy who drives the van."

My heart sank. I didn't have the will to tell him that Gus Boudette had been lounging on a beach for the past few days, in a country with a name I'd forgotten. He wouldn't have been at the Mary Todd or anywhere near Lincoln Point yesterday unless he had a fervent wish to be arrested.

"Thanks, Mr. Mooney," I said. "You should take your pills now." I tucked in his blanket and patted him on the shoulder, as if he were a toddler.

Back to square one.

My visit with Mr. Mooney discouraged me, but I still had to deliver my little plastic tote with a sink attached to the bottom. If nothing else, it was time I paid my old student and friend, Sofia Muniz, a visit. I'd been glad to hear from Linda that Sofia was back in her luxury quarters, at least until further notice on her granddaughter's finances.

I knocked on her door and heard a soft "come in."

Sofia was sitting across the room in front of her wide living room window, a lovely pink bed jacket covering her broad shoulders and adding color to her cheeks.

"Dolores won't be here until after work," she said.

"I'm here to see you, Sofia," I said, surprised Dolores still had a job. I hesitated to ask if she'd been demoted, perhaps even ushered out of city hall. I imagined an ecstatic Steve Talley spearheading the move.

"Oh, Geraldine, of course. For a minute I thought I was back in . . . oh, never mind."

She held out her arms and we had a long embrace.

"Please sit down," she said, her smile as broad and pleasant as if she'd been taken to the care center for nothing more than a winter cold.

I found it understandable that Sofia had been confused for a moment, having spent a night in the trashy, littered parking lot of her old neighborhood and a couple in the care center, under guard. I was happy to have a few minutes alone with her, to offer some companionship.

I removed the sink from its carrier and handed it to her. I was sorry Maddie wasn't there to see Sofia's smile and the delight in her eyes as she turned it around and around. She ran her finger over the tiny silver finding from a broken necklace, shaped like a washer with jagged edges. I'd pushed it into the wet clay and, behold, I had a drain cap.

"So clever. Leave it to you to use something everyone else would throw away. It's wonderful, Geraldine. It takes me back to my happy, old kitchen." Sofia's eyes teared up as she fingered the cloth. "This is almost the exact pattern of a sink *falda* I had in the old country when Dolores was little."

I assumed *falda* was *skirt*. "I think there were only three fabric patterns in those days," I said, getting a broader smile from her.

Sofia's English was good, moderately accented. I figured she'd been in the United States about twenty years, since Dolores was pregnant with Ernestine. I was sure Dolores was responsible for the fact that she was fluent in the language of their adopted country. Like Lourdes Pino, however, she slipped back to a Spanish word or phrase at times.

She moved her head as if to inspect every corner of her smartly appointed suite, named for Ulysses S. Grant, Lincoln's general and two presidents after him. I followed her gaze. To the tabletop Christmas tree (Dolores had put one in every room), to the wall of family photographs (likewise), to the door to her bedroom where a lavish comforter covered the bed. "But you know, I'm starting to like it here, in spite of everything."

I longed to ask her about "everything," that is, what happened the night she was kidnapped and taken to her old neighborhood (my theory). I was afraid it might upset her, however. I was also afraid Dolores might walk in on us and not take too kindly to my interrogation, if not my very presence in her grandmother's quarters.

Sofia solved my problem. "You know, I've wanted to talk to you. I consider you my *amiga* and I hope you don't think I did anything bad to Carlos. As much as I hated that evil man, I could never commit such a sin."

"I didn't think so for a minute, Sofia."

"I know I was very confused that night. Something didn't agree with me."

"Something you ate?"

"Maybe, but I think I got the wrong medicine. There was a different person handing it out. There was a substitute that night, not the man from the *farmacia.* I think it was the man who came and took me to jail." She laughed. "Well, I know I said that, but now I realize it was just a different van, not jail. The medicine confused me."

I had the feeling this was not the same problem Mr. Mooney had had. Not a dose of a drug with a potentially lethal side effect. Instead, there was a good chance that Sofia was forced to take something to make her not dead, but delusional, in the perfect position to be framed for murder.

Given the two incidents, I guessed something was amiss in the *farmacia*.

A knock on the door, followed by a swift entrance, ended this train of thought. Dolores swept into the room, carrying two shopping bags of wrapped presents. She stopped short when she saw me.

For a moment I was afraid she'd swing the bags into me. But she dropped them and came over to the window where Sofia and I were sitting. She embraced her grandmother and — to my surprise — me.

"You might think I hate you, Geraldine, but you really did me a favor."

"Tell her about your new job, *querida*," Sofia said.

"You found a new job in less than a day?"

"It's not exactly employment. I won't be getting a salary. I still have to figure that one out. I'll be volunteering with the Senior to Senior Foundation." Dolores threw her head back and chuckled. "Obviously, they need help managing their program."

Though she didn't say it in front of her grandmother, I was sure this was part of her deal with the DA. And a clever one, at that. *Win-win,* I thought. I wondered if Catholics still went to confession — Dolores had the aura of the newly cleansed.

"Good for you," I said.

It was time to leave Sofia with her grand-daughter and get back to my own.

I hugged both women. "I hope you'll be in class this week," I said to Sofia. "You need to finish the Vatican."

"I'll be glad to be back." She took a deep breath. "Well, I guess it all worked out for the best. I can't say I'm sorry Carlos is dead, but" — she made the sign of the cross — "may he rest in peace."

Another statement that called for a silent "amen."

Maddie had taken full advantage of my vulnerable position, loading up with books from Rosie's children's shelves. She couldn't know how it thrilled me. Or maybe she did.

"Your parents will be packing up the car pretty soon," I said, with no ulterior motive.

"Uh-huh. Poor Mom, with Dad the way he is."

An EKG would have shown a blip in my heartbeat at that moment. I resisted turning around in the driver's seat to face Maddie full front. "What do you mean? What's wrong with your dad?"

"You know how he is. He's a backseat driver and he'll make the trip miserable for the first ten miles, telling my mom which lane to be in or to go faster, then my mom will stop the car at a gas station and tell him if he doesn't quit nagging, he has to drive the whole way himself, and then he'll be good for a few miles, and that's how it will be all the way to here."

I laughed, relieved. "I know how he is," I said.

I couldn't wait to know for sure.

Late Monday evening, my phone rang. How boring, I thought, just a few notes with no melody. I wondered if landline phones could be programmed to play music. It was Maddie's fault — I felt myself sinking down into the land of pop culture.

Beverly's caller ID appeared on my little box.

"Nick and I are officially dating," she said.

"Do I want to know any more than that?"

"Uh, no. Just that I'd like to invite him to Christmas dinner. I don't think he's ever met Richard."

"That will be nice."

"You're okay with this, right?"

"Beverly, what a question. Of course."

"Good, because it *is* your house."

I tried to make my laugh sound as genuine as Beverly's. It's a good thing we were separated by a few miles with no video available.

"What's new on the force? Any good stories?" I asked.

"Nothing much. Just my regular rounds." A brief sound for call-waiting. Hers. "I'd better take that," she said.

We signed off.

I missed Beverly. I missed her "force" stories and her thoughtful advice on things large and small. So many times in the past few days I would have called her and talked over what was happening. It hit me now with full force. I hadn't told her I was being followed or that my car was vandalized. She didn't know my concern for my friend, Sofia, or my newfound awareness of how seniors are regarded in our society.

I hadn't even shared my suspicions that Richard was ill.

Why not?

Because I didn't want to cast shadows on her current state of dating bliss? Or because I no longer trusted her to care?

It was a great loss in my life of late and I didn't know whose fault it was. I pulled the afghan around me and tried to shake off a feeling of abandonment.

CHAPTER 26

It was all wrapped up, like the piles of presents under my tree, each one sealed and tagged, and the latest package of Christmas cards, all the same size, ready to drop in the mail.

Dolores Muniz was guilty of blackmail. Nadine Hawkes had committed fraud, murder, and attempted murder. Gus Boudette was on a tropical island.

Too bad it wasn't as neat as it sounded. Like when I think I've finished a miniature scene and something is off. Maybe there's too much of one color, or the scale is inconsistent and the chair is too big with respect to the desk.

Once I did a subway scene and cut out a couple of inches of the *New York Times* to fold and lay on a seat. Every time I looked at it my attention was drawn to the print on the newspaper page. No matter how I tried to ignore the fact that the print was too big for the scale, I couldn't do it. I ended up discarding the newspaper, tearing up the orange paint on the seat in the process. Nowadays I'd just get Maddie to shrink and shrink and shrink (as she'd said) the print, as she did my wedding photo.

Several things were off in the Guzman/Hawkes case. Puttering around on Tuesday morning before Maddie was awake, I ignored the laundry piling up and the unopened mail from Saturday and Monday and settled myself in the atrium with a notebook and pen, a cup of chamomile, and an old afghan.

It was time for a one-on-one with myself, doodling included.

Why did Gus run off to a foreign country? Well, not so foreign if he's a citizen of France, but why would he disappear without even telling his roommates unless he's involved in the fraud or the murder or both?

I can't believe Nadine could drag Sofia into the van by herself. She's a heavy woman, but not large-framed like Sofia. Chances are she had an accomplice. Or Sofia was so drugged there was no resistance. But aren't people heavier when they're unconscious? I guess they can't be heavier but they can't help, either.

And why would Nadine choose Sofia to be her fall guy? Did Sofia figure out her scheme? Unlikely. Not even Mr. Mooney, who was part of the scheme, knew exactly what was going on.

Not one of the Mary Todd residents says it was a woman they saw that night; some say one man, some two men, but no one says a woman. Of course, Mr. Mooney changed his story again, now saying it was the van driver who gave him the medication in the lobby.

Why on earth is Nadine saying she doesn't know Gus Boudette? You'd think she'd want to spread the blame and point the finger at her accomplice or make a deal and give him up. This might not matter since we already know *where* he is, just not how to get him back. I'll have to ask Skip if we can get him back if Nadine tells us something incriminating about him.

I have too many questions and I haven't even covered who was tailing me and who slashed my tires. It's hard to picture the ponderous Nadine in her power suit, let alone that Victorian getup she had on for the ball, bending over to slash my tires.

The one person who can clear all this up is Nadine Hawkes herself. If I can get a few minutes with her, I can simply ask her these questions — did you have help? Was it Gus? Did you try to kill Mr. Mooney? Did you follow me? Slash my tires?

That would do it. I'll simply talk to Skip, aunt-to-nephew, about getting in to see Nadine in jail.

Back in the real world my phone was ringing — Linda, calling from work.

I'd almost forgotten her mission for the day, to give me the names on the visitors' log for last week. My initial interest had to do with who had been in the lobby when Mr. Mooney nearly died, but while I was at it, I wanted to look at the log for last Wednesday night also.

I realized the sign-in record gave only limited information. Dolores had visited her mother late on Wednesday without passing through the reception area. How many others slipped in through the garden on a nightly basis? So if only the people with nothing to hide signed in, what good were the logs? Better than nothing, I decided.

"I'm done, Gerry," Linda said.

"That was fast."

"You forget I start at seven. People don't realize what a commitment nursing is. You have to run your social life around the hours you work."

Didn't everyone? But I knew Linda felt more put-upon than your average worker, though no one had forced her to choose a profession that wasn't Monday to Friday, nine to five. Now that I thought of it, my teaching day had stretched well beyond that, also.

"What time do you want to come over and look at the log?" Linda asked me.

I felt skinny arms around my waist. "Morning, Grandma," Maddie said.

"You're up early, sweetheart."

"Huh?" Linda said.

"Maddie's up," I said to Linda. "And I think she has other plans for today. I promised to take her to a matinee of that Christmas movie."

"I have the pages right here," Linda teased.

I stretched the telephone cord out as far as I could and reached in the cabinet for a bowl for Maddie's cereal. Not that she couldn't get it herself, but I needed to feel like I was taking care of my granddaughter. "Can you read me the names?" I asked Linda.

"Are you kidding? There are a lot of them, Gerry."

"Do you see anyone interesting on the list?"

"What does that mean?" An exasperated voice.

"Does anyone stand out? Someone who shouldn't be there."

Maddie had poured out her cereal and milk. She came over and stood directly in front of me. "We can go to the home," she mouthed, supplementing her whisper with hand gestures. Her "go" was especially cute as she walked the index and middle fingers of her right hand across the palm of her left.

I covered the mouthpiece. "Really?" I whispered. "We'll still have plenty of time to make the one o'clock show."

She nodded in an exaggerated fashion, shaking her hair into her eyes and making a silly face. Unlike her father, Maddie always woke up in a good mood.

Lucky for me.

Maddie took her videos and a bag of cookies to the Mary Todd employee lounge. I could just imagine her "How I Spent My Christmas Vacation" essay. I wanted to stay with her this time, to make a small gesture toward togetherness, but Linda thought it was a bad idea to go over the papers in such a public place. I know she was reluctant to simply hand them over to me, even though they were copies. She didn't want to take a chance that they'd turn up somewhere and be traced back to her. I didn't blame her.

Linda took me instead to a small parlor in a new wing, an area that wasn't officially open yet. "There aren't any residents assigned to this part and sometimes we come here to really get away on break. But no one who's working right now knows about it."

Linda removed plastic covers from two easy chairs and we took seats next to each other. Since Linda didn't have a lap, the pages ended up in mine.

Linda had copied the lists from the past two weeks. These were simple charts, like Carlos Guzman's notebook, except in this case, NAME was for the signature of a visitor, not income from someone skirting the law. TIME IN, and PURPOSE OF VISIT were the next columns, then TIME OUT for the last column.

The record was incomplete at best, with many people signing in but not out or vice versa. Not all visitors specified a purpose or named a particular resident they were visiting.

I mentioned this sloppiness (unfortunate word choice) to Linda.

"Well, it's not the CIA, Gerry. We do a reasonable job of keeping track, but you can't expect perfection. It depends a lot on who's on the desk at the time, and what else she has to do."

Point taken. I ran my finger down the first column, tracing many visitors' names over to people I knew. Lizzie, Emma, Gertie, Mr. Mooney, Sandy Sechrest.

I picked out my own signature for class last Friday, and Jane Mooney's for visiting her great-grandfather. Skip hadn't signed in — detectives' privilege, I guessed.

"Gail Musgrave is here a lot," I said to Linda.

"She has an aunt in the care center."

"How come I didn't know that?" I said half aloud. I considered Gail a friend. She was part of my crafters group and I'd helped with her campaign when she ran for her seat on the city council.

Linda heard my question. "I'm not saying this is true of Gail, but lots of people like to keep it private, especially if the relative is in the care center."

"As if it's something to be ashamed of?"

Linda nodded, giving me a knowing glance. "I've been a nurse for how many years, Gerry? A lot. And I can tell you it's all part of us not wanting to get old and incapacitated, so we don't acknowledge that others close to us do. Not only that, some of the residents in the care center don't accept their situation. For example, they won't wear wristbands with info on their medications, doses, times, and so on. That's why we have that flaky system where the new people have to use a flip chart with photos when they deliver meds."

I was struck by Linda's observations and insight. I knew she was a very intelligent woman, but she wasn't given to philosophizing very often. I filed her gem of wisdom — made more serious by our stark surroundings — away for further contemplation.

We moved to Sunday's sheet. Jane Mooney was on the list, as was a visitor for Lizzie. I wondered if she and Emma shared visitors the way they shared everything else. Gail Musgrave had signed in at eleven.

"She usually comes after church," Linda said. "I see her car in the parking lot often. I can pick it out because she has a vanity plate."

Uh-oh. A crafter and someone whose political views I shared tailing me? "What does her plate say?" I asked, pulling my sweater around me. I really needed to pay more attention to license plates. As it was, I hardly knew what kinds of cars my friends drove.

"It's GRAVE 241. Can you believe there are two hundred and forty other California drivers who want GRAVE on their license plates?"

Not even close to S-something-CH. But how sure was I of those letters? I'd never gotten a good, clean look.

"You know, I still don't know exactly what you're looking for, Gerry," Linda said, accusing. I felt she deserved to know at least as much as I did. That is, not much.

"I'm looking for suspicious visitors," I said, in a mock dramatic tone. Linda rolled her eyes. "I'm just trying to see who was here on Sunday morning, who might have given Mr. Mooney whatever he's allergic to, other than Nadine Hawkes. Do we know what it was exactly, by the way?"

"Nuh-uh. Once he got better, it didn't matter."

"What?"

"It would be very, very expensive to run the kind of test you'd need to determine what was in his system that shouldn't be. And he's fine, so . . . case closed."

I was learning more than I cared to about health-care philosophy.

Linda picked up the Sunday sign-in sheet again, now on a plastic-covered table in front of us. "There's one more name that should be here. I guess he didn't sign in, but I distinctly remember that Steve Talley was here."

"Don't tell me he has an uncle in residence?" I was sure Dolores would have ferreted out that piece of information.

"No relative here that I know of. He comes around now and then to do the licensing audits although he has a staff to do that. I remember on Sunday, I was in the pharmacy and he came in with his new brochures for the Nolin Creek Pines restoration plan. I think he left some in every single department." Linda looked at her watch. "It's past my break time. I don't think there's anything else here, Gerry."

I gave the sheets one more quick shuffle.

"You're right. It was a long shot."

"I have to go back to work, and lucky you, you get to go to a movie," Linda said.

I couldn't tell if she was serious or not.

To my chagrin, the longest line at the theater was the one for our show. It was family time at the multiplex two towns over. I reminded myself that this was what grandmothers were supposed to do — take their grandchildren to a kid-friendly holiday matinee, not shuffle them from one television set or babysitter to another while they poked around doing what should be left to the police.

I'd hoped for a nap during the movie, but the sound volume was very high and the audience laughter quite loud. Maddie fell easily into kid mode, laughing when the other kids did and kicking her feet in front of her at the "exciting" times, such as when a snake came out of the grass and scared one of Santa's elves.

The popcorn, however, was excellent, so I focused on the crunchy, salty pleasure with only a few scattered thoughts on the problem of Mr. Mooney's mysterious anti-nurse.

June came by to take Maddie for another tennis lesson before dinner. "It's very slow at work these days," she explained. "Every day we go out to a long holiday lunch with the different groups we belong to, and then head home afterward."

I silently gave thanks for June, her flexible tech-editing job, her gym, and its indoor tennis courts.

During those few quiet movie moments, I'd come to the decision that I had to see Nadine Hawkes. She was the only one who could answer a whole list of questions.

As soon as Maddie and June were out the door, I called Skip and got quickly to the point.

"I need to talk to Nadine Hawkes," I said.

"I'm sorry. Who is this again?"

I chose to ignore his disrespectful attitude. "Remember when you told me that murder was such an awful thing, so important in a person's life, unless he's a hit man" — I chuckled, with no reaction from Skip — "that the killer is going to tell someone about it? And the cop's job is to find that person whom the killer told?"

"I love when you throw my words back at me. But let's put the emphasis on *cop's job.*"

"I know. That's what you're trained for, but what can it hurt to have someone else make an effort?"

"Someone such as you?"

"Is there some legal reason I can't see her?"

"In other words, can you go behind me or over my head and get in anyway?"

"I guess that's what I'm asking, yes."

A long pause. Making me squirm. I pictured him — his feet up on his desk, leafing through a magazine while I waited. He came back on the line. "Okay, ten minutes, with a cop present."

I could hardly believe it. "Thanks."

"*If* Hawkes agrees."

"Okay. I'll hold while you find out."

"Aunt Gerry! Do you enjoy hassling me like this?"

"I'm on a tight schedule. June has Maddie at the gym, but they're coming back for dinner."

"June's something else, isn't she?"

"She is. And she adores you."

"June or Maddie?"

"Both. Please, Skip. I just need you to —"

"Okay, okay. You had me at *adores*."

"What?"

"Never mind. You're hopeless when it comes to popular culture. Come to the police station in twenty minutes."

I hung up the phone, picked it up again immediately, and ordered a large pizza with extra cheese and no "funny stuff" (Maddie's term for olives, mushrooms, or other items from the list of toppings) for dinner. I hoped this would make it up to Maddie for not taking her on a trip to jail.

Skip led me down a narrow staircase to the area that served as Lincoln Point's jail in the basement of the police department building. I'd never been here, and it was as bad as I imagined. Indescribable odors emanated from the exposed brick walls. I held my breath nearly all the way along a dark, damp corridor.

We finally arrived at a windowless room with a table and two chairs. No Christmas decorations here. A sign read, VISITING ROOM, NO SMOKING. Curious, since the entire police department building was a no-smoking facility. From the condition of the sign, as well as the outdated message, I suspected it had been here for ages.

"Is that disgusting hallway the only way to the visitors' room?" I asked.

"We use the journey as a deterrent," Skip said.

"It works. You should schedule school field trips here on a regular basis."

Skip gestured for me to take one of the chairs, but I hesitated. "You can sit," he said. "This room's cleaner than it looks."

Whatever that meant. "Are you going to stay here with me while I talk to Nadine?"

He nodded. I breathed a sigh of relief. The place was creepier than the bins of dismembered doll parts in crafts stores.

It was certainly one of the strangest settings I'd ever been in for an interview. Skip stood in the corner, arms across his chest, like a bodyguard. It occurred to me that his presence and his stance were deliberate, to give me a sense of security in the frightening venue. I was very grateful.

Nadine sat across from me, frowning (who wouldn't), in a boxy, gray dress that, ironi-

413

cally, was more flattering to her chunky figure than the outfits I'd seen her in. She wore no makeup, but her short hair looked the same as it always did.

I started with a pathetic "How are you?"

She licked her lips, most likely missing their special blend of moistening gloss.

"Look, Mrs. Porter, the only reason I agreed to see you is that you're nosy. In fact, you're so nosy that maybe you have information for me." She jerked her head in Skip's direction, off to the side. "And maybe you can talk some sense into him."

From down the hall I heard assorted thumping and smashing sounds, but it might have been my imagination, stirred by the dark, clammy venue.

Where to start? With myself I decided.

"Have you been following me around town, by any chance?"

I noted Skip's reaction — he rolled his eyes, shook his head, and stuck his hands in his pockets. I realized I'd never admitted to him that I felt someone was following me.

"Don't be ridiculous."

"I don't suppose you slashed my tires the night of the ball?" I could guess what Skip might be thinking — what a lame interviewer!

Nadine's response to the tire question

resembled Skip's, limited only by the fact that her hands were cuffed in front of her. "Why don't you just ask me straight out if I murdered anyone?"

She leaned across the table, her handcuffs notwithstanding. When they clanked on the table, I jumped back. "Did you? Murder anyone?"

"No, I did not. Yes, I cheated the foundation. They're rich and they try to rationalize their wealth by trickling some money down to the poor folk. What kind of system is this when we have to depend on the generosity of the rich for the most basic things? I wasn't ripping off anyone except people who have too much money."

I found it interesting that both Nadine and Dolores had managed to justify their crimes to themselves and ultimately to the police. They almost made you want to call them heroes, to say, "Thanks, Dolores, for taking money from the monster Carlos Guzman. Thanks, Nadine, for taking money from the affluent people who make up the Senior to Senior Foundation."

Skip went back to his muscleman stance. I was feeling cramped and captive in the dingy room, despite the fact that I could leave anytime I wanted. I started to sympathize with Nadine, who would spend this night and maybe many more down the hall.

But blackmail and fraud were one thing; murder was something else. I tried to play hardball. "I know you couldn't have kidnapped and framed Sofia Muniz by yourself. Was Gus Boudette your accomplice?"

"I have no idea who that guy is except a number on the payroll sheet. Why would I protect him if we really did this awful thing together?" My question, exactly. "Besides, if I wanted to kill someone I wouldn't travel to that crappy old neighborhood and hit them over the head with a brick." Not a brick. Rebar. I almost corrected her, but there was no point. Nadine's eyes started to tear, her arrogance dissipating. "Mrs. Porter, can you find a way to make the police listen to me?"

I looked at Skip. He could tell I'd fallen for Nadine's story.

"Are you ready to go?" he asked.

I was.

CHAPTER 27

Skip walked with me, up the stairs, toward the building's exit. I had to give him credit for not pulling "I told you so" out of his hat. I'd gotten nothing from Nadine Hawkes except the uneasy feeling that she was innocent of murder, facing charges for a much harsher crime than she'd committed.

I ran through Nadine's words in my head. She'd suggested that Carlos had been hit with a brick. I remembered that ace-reporter Chrissy Gallagher had used the phrase "hit by a rock or a two-by-four." But someone else I'd talked to recently had named the correct weapon: a piece of rebar.

Who was that? It wouldn't come to me.

"Did you release the information that the murder weapon at Nolin Creek Pines was a section of rusty rebar?" I asked Skip.

"No, we held that back. Why do you want to know?"

I realized that this was a futile effort on

my part, that even if I did figure out who'd said "rusty rebar" even though the police had held it back, it was hardly proof of murder. Rebar, rocks, bricks, and two-by-fours were standard debris in the parking lots of the Nolin Creek Pines neighborhood, and anyone might inadvertently mention the correct one to describe the murder weapon.

Still, I wished I could remember.

"Aunt Gerry? Why are you asking about the rebar?"

"No reason."

Skip grunted. "No reason. Right." He stopped at the door to the building, gave me a perfunctory kiss on my cheek, then turned and walked back toward his office.

It wasn't often that Skip and I parted with such unpleasantness. I couldn't blame him for his frustration with me. I was unhappy with myself, withholding information from him from the beginning. He shouldn't have had to learn in front of his prisoner that I suspected someone of following me.

Moreover, why hadn't I congratulated my nephew on solving the crime instead of essentially accusing him of arresting the wrong person? I'd have to correct that at the next possible opportunity.

As soon as I hit the cold, fresh air, I took

a long, deep breath, and vowed never to get so much as a traffic ticket, lest I have to spend another five minutes in the basement of the police department.

I needed to rid my senses of the sights, sounds, and smells of Lincoln Point's dank lockup. I came up with a mental picture of Maddie and June at home making ornaments, perhaps some upbeat tune like "Frosty the Snowman" playing through the house, and the aroma of a large extra-cheese pizza wafting across the rooms from my oven to greet me.

To fix the new scene even more firmly in my mind, I dug my phone out of my purse and dialed home as I walked to my car. I'd parked all the way around the civic center circle, on the library end of the complex. At the time I arrived, the areas on the police station side were full. Now, at nearly seven o'clock, the lots were empty and I wended my way along the shadowy curved road.

Walking and dialing. Another cell phone skill under my belt.

June answered on the second ring. Maddie must have been indisposed, or she'd never have allowed anyone to beat her to a beckoning phone.

"How was your time in jail?" June asked.

I gave her a very brief report on my excursion to the dark side.

"Imagine Skip's working there every day," she said. "Maybe not in the jail, but in awful conditions, dealing with the worst side of people. It would completely depress me."

When Skip first entered the police academy, I used to think about that a lot, worrying constantly about his psyche as well as his safety. Now I took it all for granted, picturing him always in his clean (if not neat), safe cubicle. I'd even been adding to his tough job. Never again.

"Thanks for reminding me what he does for us every day," I said to June.

"Guess who's back from the powder room and wants to talk to you?"

Maddie took the phone, out of breath. "Where are you, Grandma? And tell me the truth."

By now I was facing the grim reality of Lincoln Point life after dark as a few apparently homeless people pushed their carts and carried their bundles across the lawn that surrounded the complex of buildings.

They seemed harmless enough, but I was glad Maddie wasn't with me.

"I had an errand downtown, sweetheart," I said. "And that's the truth. I hope you saved me some pizza. I'm starving."

"We're keeping it warm," she said. "And June brought over her special tea for you to try. She's teaching me how to brew it."

"I can hardly wait."

I passed two old men in ragged clothing. They appeared to be heading for a spot under one of the many sets of stairs that led to the library balcony. I seldom wandered in this part of town at night, except for events like the Mary Todd gala. Where were these people then? And why was our town not able to support them?

Not for the first time, I resolved to become more active in city politics.

I had a fleeting thought of Dolores and wondered if she'd ever be allowed to resume her political career. I could think of more than one case where a government official had left office in disgrace, only to return and be reelected a few years later.

"Uncle Nick is coming to Christmas dinner," Maddie said, and for a minute I thought she'd said St. Nick.

When the true identity of Uncle Nick Marcus dawned on me, I knew that Beverly was beyond serious, heading for the critical holidays-with-the-family stage.

"Uncle Nick. Well, he's certainly welcome."

"We're making an ornament for him. It's a foam cop."

"That's wonderful," I said.

I hung up with a promise to Maddie that I would head straight home. No more errands.

I came to the last stretch. It was hard to see my Ion, a bulging shadow among many others. I wished I'd parked under a light. But Skip is probably still in his office, just two buildings behind me, I reminded myself. Never mind that each building was about a city block wide.

To my right was Springfield Boulevard. Here and there were twinkling lights offering a bit of cheer from a store window, but most of the shops were closed and dark. No problem. In a few minutes, I'd be driving along the boulevard, heading north to home and warm pizza.

Crash.

I stopped short after a thunderous sound sliced the cool, still air. About thirty feet ahead of me, an enormous object had fallen to the ground. It was a calm evening, with nothing more than a slight breeze, so, like a good Californian, my first thought was — it's an earthquake! But nothing else was moving or swinging. No other outward signs of disturbance. Maybe an earthquake in another hemisphere? Nothing to worry about here.

I kept walking toward my car and saw that the object was a large tree branch, or perhaps an uprooted shrub, like the western redbud, blocking Civic Drive. To get to my car, I'd have to leave the path and circle around onto the grass, where it was much darker than on the road. I'd have to circumvent the tree branch, or whatever it was — I could see that it was much too large for me to climb over — and then come back to the road a few yards from my car. How the branch got there was a mystery to be solved later.

I slowed my pace, and fingered my cell phone, now in the pocket of my sweater. Should I call for help? How silly was that idea? What would I say? Rescue me from a tree branch?

I forged ahead onto the grass just past the library, trying to make out a couple of blurry shapes waiting for me on the other side of the dismembered foliage. In fact, I could now discern the image of another car, on the opposite side of the road from my car. Too dark to tell, but it might even be Skip's. I took comfort in that.

Safely past the branch — which, to my

relief, didn't assume the form of an alien and envelop me in its many arms — I started across the road toward my car.

Until a set of taillights came into view just ahead of me, on the shoulder.

The car door opened about the same time that I saw the license plate. STITCH.

Or was my mind playing tricks? If so, it was a double trick. The vehicle looked too much like an Escalade to ignore the situation.

Before I could evaluate all this new data, Steve Talley stepped out of the car.

"Geraldine, what a coincidence," he said. He stood by his vehicle, hands on his hips. He was dressed in suit and tie, ready for a photo shoot, his thick, dark hair recently patted down. I caught a whiff of aftershave freshly applied. Not the way you'd dress for an assault. But in the light of the open door, his eyes told a different story.

My knees felt as though they were made of pipe cleaners. *Don't panic. There may be many, many Escalade STITCHes in Lincoln Point.*

What were the chances that this was not the same STITCH? Or that this was truly a random meeting? Zero and zero, I realized.

"Steve." It came as a whisper.

He pointed to the interior of his car. "I

have that cute little scene here," he said.

I blinked. "A scene?"

"Yes, the one I bought at the auction. It appears to be broken and I wonder if you can take a look?"

I took a tentative step, backing away, but Steve was through with subtlety. He moved quickly toward me, grabbed my upper arm and pushed me against his car, my face toward the window.

I saw what was once my lovely Victorian Christmas scene on the backseat, now looking more like a crime scene than a cozy holiday parlor. The beautiful spruce was on its side, ornaments scattered everywhere. Nothing was upright. Not the chair, ottoman, lamp, or coffee table. It was odd to see the books still glued in place on the shelves of the toppled bookcase, as if the works of Shakespeare were defying gravity.

"Do you think you can fix it?" he asked, his voice low and harsh, almost unrecognizable. The look on his face was nothing I'd seen before, angry and ominous.

I forced myself to frame a question, as if I were the teacher again and Steve a temporarily unruly student.

"What's this about, Steve?" *Do I want to hear this?*

"I think you know, Geraldine. I bought

this piece of junk just in case I needed it to get to you. I was pretty sure you were on to me. I hoped I was wrong."

"Is that why you followed me?"

"Until I noticed you had an armed escort and I had to pull out. Quite a slip, using my Escalade at first. You see, I'm not a career criminal and I make mistakes."

"And you resorted to slashing my tires?" Maybe I could still be that special person that a murderer confessed to, to get it off his chest. Looking at Steve's expression, his wide, frightening eyes, I feared his confession would be the last thing I heard.

"I tried to discourage you, but you're worse than the cops. They recognized that a miserable piece of trash like Carlos Guzman wasn't worth the trouble of an investigation. As soon as you started poking around the Mary Todd, and then at Gus's place, and now . . . visiting Nadine in jail. That was the last straw. I knew I had to protect myself."

"Did you have to protect yourself from a weak old man as well?"

"It wasn't my fault that Mooney saw me in the pharmacy."

My mind, which I thought was frozen, went from pharmacy to *farmacia* and then to the line in Carlos Guzman's notebook:

NAME	IN	OUT	
STITCH/LP	inf.	inf.	farm.

Steve "Stitch" Talley was addicted to whatever Gus could get him from the Mary Todd pharmacy and Carlos knew it, giving him an edge over what Steve had on him.

"That must have been some arrangement with Carlos, sharing information to further your mutual goals. But I guess he overstepped his bounds." I didn't have a clue where this bravado was coming from, except that I felt I had nothing to lose.

"That's about enough, Geraldine." He reached into his pocket and my greatest fear was realized. He pulled out a gun.

"We're going for a ride," he said. "In your car." He pushed me roughly toward my Ion, across the road.

For a few seconds, probably to preserve my sanity, my fear was overcome by my outrage that someone had bought my beloved handiwork with such an ignoble purpose in mind. That he called it a piece of junk was beyond forgiveness.

CHAPTER 28

If anyone had seen Steve and me enter my car, that person might have assumed I was simply driving Steve home after a meeting. Steve walked the few yards nonchalantly behind me, not touching me. He didn't need to. I felt as severe a pain in my back as if he'd been poking me.

Steve was silent, while I rattled on. "Be reasonable, Steve. We can go to the police. We don't have to tell them about this little slip at all. I know you're just panicked. Think about your children."

I didn't hold much hope that sentiment would tug at his heartstrings, since he'd already used his young daughter as a contingency plan in case he had to get to me.

We entered my car. "Where are you taking me? My family knows I'm here."

"They also know how nosy you are, and when they find you next to a Dumpster in that same crappy neighborhood, they'll think you were still snooping around and they'll assume you're another innocent victim of the slums. The newspapers will praise your courage. 'Respected retired teacher, blah blah blah.' "

I wished he didn't make sense. It was a clever plan, accomplishing two goals — getting rid of me and making another point about the neighborhood his proposal was designed to clean up.

"You don't have to do this," I said, grasping at phrases that sounded weak even to me.

"I regret that I do. I hoped that with Nadine's arrest the case was now closed in your mind and we could go our separate ways in peace. Watching you this evening, I knew that was not going to happen. I'm not a murderer. Carlos was an accident. We had a nice information exchange business going, but he got greedy. He was being squeezed by Senorita Muniz and now he wanted money from me, otherwise he'd ruin any chance I had to keep my job, let alone get the promotion and recognition I deserve. I just wanted to shut him up, but one thing led to another."

"You can go to the police." My worst idea yet.

"Drive, Geraldine. Head out the back

road to New Salem."

The buildings of the complex were dark, but I thought surely somewhere in its bowels there was a late-night crew, perhaps someone guarding Nadine Hawkes, whose crime now seemed minor.

"Steve . . ." I began. But I had nothing more to say.

Captive in my own car, I drove out of the complex. Steve sat in the backseat, in Maddie's place, which enraged me. I thought of accelerating to ninety or one hundred or whatever my Ion could do and crashing us into a tree. Or turning around quickly and barreling through the fenced-off area that housed the police cars. I thought of simply pulling over, refusing to drive. None of the options seemed guaranteed to spare my life. It would be only a minor inconvenience to Steve if he had to shoot me in my car and run away before anyone arrived.

All I could do was play out Steve's plan and hope for intervention or a brilliant move on my part before he carried out the final step.

If the situation weren't so tense, I would have laughed when the 1812 Overture rang out from the pocket of my sweater. Before

Steve realized what was happening, I had the phone in my hand and open. My personal best response time.

Steve put the gun against my head. I thought of shouting out to the caller, or better yet, saying Steve's name. He pushed the gun harder into my skull and I knew I couldn't get an SOS out. It might not matter anyway, even if my caller later figured out what had happened. I wouldn't have been surprised if Steve had a chartered plane at the ready to take him to join Gus Boudette on the French Riviera.

Mostly, I was trying to stay alive as long as I could.

"Make it good," Steve whispered.

"Hello?"

"Hi, Gerry," Beverly said. "I've been wanting to chat and there's no answer at your house."

I remembered that June and Maddie were going to make an ice cream run to Sadie's. At least they were safe.

I couldn't blow this one opportunity to get help. My lips were so dry I could hardly speak. I cleared my throat. "I, uh, I'm with Nick Marcus. Remember? I told you we had a date."

A pause while Beverly processed what I said. Then a laugh. "Okay, what's up? Are you teasing me for spending so much time with him? I've been with Nick all afternoon. He's just leaving my driveway."

I kept my voice as steady as I could. I cleared my throat again. "We're at Sadie's now, waiting for ice cream."

Whether it was due to her sisterly intuition or her civilian volunteer training, Beverly snapped into action. "Gerry, listen to me. Hang up, but make sure you leave the phone on and we'll use your GPS. I'm getting help right now on my other line."

"I'd better go. Our sundaes are here."

I placed the phone back in my pocket. Then I made a wrong turn. *Stall, stall.*

"Don't mess with me, Geraldine."

"I don't know exactly where you want me to go."

Steve was leaning on the headrest in front of him. There were lights in many of the windows in the neighborhood buildings. I knew he'd have me drive to the most remote part of the lot. "I guess it doesn't matter now that we're in smelling distance of the projects. Take a left here."

I turned down the street I recognized as Lourdes Pino's.

At Steve's prodding, I got out of my car and walked toward a stairway. I tried to read the number on the building, but it was fuzzy. I was frustrated because I thought it was important that I know the number, otherwise I'd be lost.

Steve wandered a few feet in either direction, his demeanor alert, listening, I supposed, for an impediment to his plan. I closed my eyes, waiting. When I opened them after what could have been a few seconds or a few hours, I saw that Steve was still pacing. At every little sound, even a twig snapping under his own feet, he'd stop and listen, and point his gun in the direction of the sound.

My heart hammered in my chest. What was he waiting for? Was he hoping I'd die of fright before he had to kill me?

He might get his wish.

I heard a crash. A sound too dull for a gunshot, but what else could it have been? A shot through my heart? I shut my eyes. But I felt no pain.

A rescue!

I saw Steve Talley sprawled on the ground and Kyle Pino standing over him with a two-by-four. I thought I must be in a fantasy world where all the incorrect murder weapons were taking shape.

Steve staggered up and grabbed Kyle's ankle as Kyle swung again. The gun had slid across the asphalt away from the stairway. I ran toward the gun. I saw Steve pick up a pipe or something similar. Kyle jumped on him. Or maybe it was vice versa.

Finally, I heard sirens.

I picked up the gun as three Lincoln Point PD cruisers turned into the lot.

I saw Skip get out of one of them and wondered if he'd had his dinner yet.

CHAPTER 29

After a mandatory checkup at Lincoln Point Hospital, I held court in my atrium. At least, that's how it felt with visitors filling the area.

Linda ministered to me as if she were on duty, propping pillows behind me and checking the labels on the orange containers of pills that graced my little table. Though I hoped the ER staff hadn't prescribed anything I could become addicted to, I did enjoy the calmness that had swept over me since my last dose.

But even in a less-than-full-alert state, I was eager to hear the resolution of the case that had taken so much of my energy. Skip explained the deal Steve had with Gus, who had an unauthorized key to the pharmacy.

"When Steve needed help after accidentally killing Carlos, Gus was the logical one to call to help set up the frame. Apparently Gus was easy to buy off," Skip said.

"The promise of spending the rest of his

life on the Mediterranean was all it took," said Beverly, who kept a steady pace of wiping my brow unnecessarily. "Maddie is with June," she told me, leaning close to my ear. "We didn't think she needed to hear all these details."

"Thanks, Beverly," I said. I owed her gratitude for more than taking care of Maddie. "You saved my life, you know."

"Me and Kyle and the Lincoln Point PD," Beverly said.

"Nothing like having back-to-back nine-one-one calls," I said.

Beverly's eyes were teary. "I can't believe how selfish I've been this past week. Maybe if I'd listened to you and we talked as usual, none of this would have happened.

"No way, Mom," Skip said.

I patted her hand in agreement.

"Anyway, I'll never do that again, Gerry."

Linda had her own pieces of the puzzle and she was eager to add them. "Remember when Mr. Mooney said the van driver gave him medicine in the lobby, when it was really Steve Talley who gave it to him? Well, I figured out he must have seen Steve and Gus together in the pharmacy, probably more than once, and that's why he was mixed up."

I loved how Linda looked after her patients

on so many levels. I didn't even mind being one of them now.

I thought of all the little events that brought us to this point. Maddie's help finding the fence image on the Internet, Linda's using her resources to dig out facts here and there, Beverly's picking up on my signal for help, Kyle Pino's coming through at the end, in a way defending his neighborhood.

"I got lucky," he'd said during a brief visit earlier in the day. "I was looking out the window when you pulled up. And it didn't look right down there, you know? So I called nine-one-one."

"Lucky for me you're a responsible young man," I'd said. "You didn't have to risk your own life."

"The police don't always come right away in my neighborhood."

"That's going to change," Skip had said.

Skip assured us that with Steve now sitting in the basement of the police department building, the city council would scrap the Talley plan for Nolin Creek Pines and open the discussion to a neighborhood committee interested in true restoration.

In hindsight I was overwhelmed by the amount of information and advice we'd received from Sandy Sechrest, Mr. Mooney,

Emma, Lizzie, Sofia, and the other residents of the Mary Todd Home. I hoped in the future they might be taken more seriously when they offered their observations or the benefit of their life's experiences.

Skip was the last to leave my house. My nephew had outdone himself to protect me through the week, and, without a lot of fanfare, had looked into everything I'd brought to him.

"I thought we'd lost you," he said now, holding my hand as tightly as when he was a small boy and we crossed a street together.

CHAPTER 30

On Christmas morning, all Porters were present and accounted for. We'd decided to open our family gifts early and have June Chinn and Nick Marcus join us later. I looked forward to having them share Christmas dinner, the menu for which went on and on: pork loin roast with cranberry stuffing, potato puree, Waldorf salad, and many potluck surprises. Plus, of course, a long list of desserts.

Richard and Mary Lou had arrived only last night due to unforeseen emergencies at his hospital. We'd agreed ahead of time to spare them the details of the Carlos Guzman case. Even without that to talk about, the three of us had stayed up half the night chatting, rebonding.

The only mention of the case while we were all gathered came from Skip.

"Reporters," he said, tossing a newspaper in my recycling basket. "Chrissy Gallagher sounds like she closed the case herself by inspiring a Lincoln Point citizen to action." He turned to me. "That would be you, I suppose."

"Time for presents," Beverly shouted. "Only happy talk, please."

We'd made a rule some time ago that whatever else we gave each other, there would always be something handmade. Big or small, even if only the gift card, as long as there was something personally crafted.

Skip complained the most about this tradition, but always came up with something unique. This year, June had talked him into an afternoon at our do-it-yourself ceramics store and he'd created clever switch plates for each of us.

"I can't believe you did this," Beverly said, showing off hers, which looked vaguely like an LPPD volunteer patch.

"I can't either," Skip said. "You can see why June and I won't be dating anymore." We all looked horrified, and Skip slapped his knee. "Gotcha."

Maddie had made me an upholstered couch using sponges and fabric from one of her "baby dresses" as she called them — a tight floral print that I must have given her before I realized she'd have a personality of her own.

440

This rule was easiest for Mary Lou, the professional artist, of course. This year she outdid herself, taking advantage of their spacious minivan to transport a painting.

"Direct from L.A. to LP," she'd said when she handed me the large package. I expected a landscape, which Mary Lou did very well, or a garden, á la the French Impressionists. Instead, I gazed with delight on a painting of Ken and me, copied from one of the last holiday photographs of the two of us before he was forced to bed.

Memories poured over me as strongly as if Ken were in the room with us, in the home he loved so much.

"I thought a long time about doing this," Mary Lou said. "It's just from a photograph, so it's not as nice as . . . well, I hope you like it."

I let the tears make their way down my cheeks. No wonder Maddie could hardly contain herself all week about the presents coming from L.A. "Nothing could please me more."

"Maybe this will," Richard said.

My son stood up and reached into the pocket of his jeans (he'd instituted "casual dress for holidays" many years ago). He pulled out a business-size envelope, folded in half, a bit crumpled, and handed it to me.

"I told him he should wrap it," Mary Lou said, with a little cluck.

A gift certificate, I guessed, probably a generous one to my favorite crafts store. But — why was Maddie still looking ready to burst? I'd already seen the painting. Maybe this was a plane ticket for my next visit to L.A.?

I shook the envelope, as if that would give me a hint. When it came to presents, I had infinitely more patience than any of my relatives. Everyone jeered.

"Come *on,*" from Skip.

"Hurry up, Gerry. You're *so* going to love this," from Beverly, on the edge of her seat. (How come everyone knew but me?)

"Grandma! Please!" from Maddie.

I opened the envelope and found another envelope. I looked more closely. The Stanford Medical Center logo. My heart fell. But this was a present. It couldn't be bad news. It seemed to be a letter to Richard.

No, a copy of a letter *from* Richard.

I heard, "Read it. Read it," from everyone. I read aloud.

To: Dr. Michael Olson
From: Dr. Richard Porter

442

It gives me great pleasure to accept your offer to join the Stanford University Medical Center staff.

My family and I plan to relocate to the Palo Alto area soon after the new year, so I should be able to assume my duties by . . .

The letter went on, but I couldn't.

Palo Alto, not ten miles from Lincoln Point.

Maddie skipped around the room. Mary Lou beamed; Richard looked more like his father than ever. Beverly and Skip had smiles that could have stretched up and down the state of California.

I started to form the words about how this secret had caused me so much grief. But why take away from this moment? It was really a message to me — to communicate more directly, not to make assumptions, to think more positively.

"Did you guess, Grandma?"

"I had no idea."

"It was so-o-o-o-o hard for me to keep it secret."

Maddie accepted enthusiastic praise from all for her outstanding restraint.

By the time June and Nick joined us, we were all in a very jolly mood.

I cherished the promise of many more such times.

MINIATURE TIPS FOR A LIVING ROOM

- To make a quick easy chair: cut two three-inch-by-five-inch sponges in half. Arrange two halves perpendicular to each other, like the seat and back of the chair. Cut one of the other halves in half again, making two quarter-sponge-size pieces. Arrange these smaller pieces on either side of the "seat" to act as chair arms. Glue all the pieces together. Spray paint a color of your choice. Add rounded buttons for feet.
- For a slightly fancier look, wrap (as you would a present) each piece in leatherette or a fabric of your choice before gluing.
- Add a footstool: paint or cover the spare one-half sponge to match, and add buttons as above for feet.
- Partitions and room dividers can be made in several ways. The easiest way is to photograph a scene that you like, such as

an ocean or skyline or wooded area, in a horizontal aspect. If you use a digital camera and home printing, print to size; otherwise order an enlargement that suits the scale you're working with. Score the photograph and fold in thirds or fourths. Stand in place. If it's not sturdy enough, use two copies glued back to back.

MINIATURE TIPS FOR GARDENS

- For trees and shrubbery, in an atrium or outdoors, use florist's foam, cut to size and shape. Twigs and trimmings from your life-size yard become tree trunks and branches. You can also use steel wool and scouring pads, spray-painted to look like hedges and bushes.
- Flowers crafted from modeling clay are very effective, but it can be tedious to achieve the detail necessary for a lifelike appearance. Consider using a flower-shaped punch and colored paper, or an arrangement of sequins (petals), or dabs of paint for tiny blooms.
- Ground cover can be made of beans, seeds, sand, dried leaves and herbs, or any material that can be crumbled and spread on the "ground" of your miniature setting. For gravel pathways, cut pieces of black or mottled sandpaper to size and lay

down among the shrubbery.

- Add an ornament or two to your garden, using game pieces, such as a rook or knight from a chess set. A coil of green garden wire becomes a hose when a "nozzle" of silver paint (sculpted for texture) is dabbed on one end.

MINIATURE TIPS FOR LUGGAGE

- Use various sizes of plastic pillboxes to make luggage pieces. Round pillboxes make excellent hatboxes. Rectangular pillboxes can be briefcases or hard-backed luggage.
- Glue on small leather pieces (available in crafts stores, or from your own worn gloves and purses) to cover the box. Cut a tiny strip to act as handle, and glue to one side. Dabs of gold paint look like rivets on either side of the handle.
- Glue on pieces of fabric instead of leather, to make more colorful luggage, or a child's set.
- To make rolling luggage, glue fabric onto a rectangular pillbox, as above, except for one side, where you will insert a large paper clip, painted black, between the fabric and the box. The rounded top and a portion of the side of the clip serve as the pull-out handle of the rolling luggage.

Small black beads glued onto the opposite side of the box act as wheels.

MINIATURE TIPS FOR JEWELRY

- Jewelry pieces to place on a miniature dresser or in a "shop window" are easy to create. Purchase beads and findings at a crafts store, or (my way) take apart a scatter pin or other life-size costume jewelry, such as an inexpensive bracelet or necklace, and use the parts as raw materials for miniature settings. Knotted gold chains that can't be undone for regular use can be cut up for miniature jewelry.
- Ring. Wrap thin bead wire around a toothpick, twice. Slip off the toothpick and trim ends. Glue a colored bead anywhere on the circle.
- Necklace. Choose an ornate but narrow metallic trim, such as might be used to decorate a life-size uniform. Cut a two-inch piece and glue end-to-end to make a necklace. Or use regular thickness thread to string tiny beads together in various sizes for necklaces and bracelets.
- Evening purse. Use a box-shaped filigree necklace fastener, about half-inch size. Attach a thin chain to two spots on the narrow side, for a dressy strap.

ABOUT THE AUTHOR

Margaret Grace is the pen name of Camille Minichino. She is a lifelong miniaturist and is currently at work on the next Miniature Mystery. As Camille Minichino, she is the author of eight other mystery novels as well as short stories and articles. She lives in northern California and can be reached at www.minichino.com and www.dollhousemysteries.com.

The employees of Thorndike Press hope you have enjoyed this Large Print book. All our Thorndike, Wheeler, and Kennebec Large Print titles are designed for easy reading, and all our books are made to last. Other Thorndike Press Large Print books are available at your library, through selected bookstores, or directly from us.

For information about titles, please call:
(800) 223-1244

or visit our Web site at:
http://gale.cengage.com/thorndike

To share your comments, please write:
Publisher
Thorndike Press
295 Kennedy Memorial Drive
Waterville, ME 04901